Messenger in a Battle

book three of the Messenger Trilogy

by Joel Pierson

iUniverse, Inc.
New York   Bloomington

iUniverse books may be ordered through booksellers or by contacting:

iUniverse
1663 Liberty Drive
Bloomington, IN 47403
www.iuniverse.com
1-800-Authors (1-800-288-4677)

ISBN: 978-1-4502-2605-9 (pbk)
ISBN: 978-1-4502-2606-6 (ebk)

Printed in the United States of America

iUniverse rev. date:5/4/10

Acknowledgments

As ever, I owe boundless gratitude to my writing group, Jamie, Melissa, Holly, Christy, and Andrew, who have seen the trilogy through to the end. Thanks also to Juliet, who shared her ideas and told me when mine needed work. All of you had a hand in making this book what it is.

Thanks once again to Kate for keeping all those lawyer terms proper.

And thanks, of course, to Dana, my biggest fan, for believing in me, in talking deer, and in my desire to share these stories with the world.

About the Author

Joel Pierson is the author of numerous award-winning plays for audio and stage, including French Quarter, The Children's Zoo, The Vigil, Cow Tipping, and Mourning Lori. He also co-authored the novelization of French Quarter. How he has time to write is anyone's guess, as he spends his days as editorial manager at the world's largest print-on-demand publishing company. Additionally, he is artistic director of Mind's Ear Audio Productions, the producers of several popular audio theatre titles and the official audio guided tour of Arlington National Cemetery. If that weren't enough, he also writes for the newspaper and a local lifestyles magazine in his hometown of Bloomington, Indiana. He stays grounded and relatively sane with the help of his wife (and frequent co-author) Dana, and his ridiculously loving dogs.

The Messenger Trilogy

Don't Kill the Messenger
The Messenger Adrift
Messenger in a Battle

Upon the shores of the great peninsula shall the battle commence.
Hamesh shall encamp under the banner of the wolf,
though it be stained with blood.
Though few in number, still shall they defend mightily
the stronghold of their people.
Far from home are they, with no land, no fortress to protect them.
Wood and steel, net and trap alone speak for
them in this hour of dark need.

—Found in a cave outside of Jerusalem, 1763
Author unknown

PROLOGUE

LIBERTYVILLE, ILLINOIS

FRIDAY MORNING

CASSIE REFLECTS ON HER QUEST

It began like any other school day, but I know it isn't. Today is the day, the one I've been waiting for. At home, I linger in the bathroom for a few extra minutes so I don't have to encounter my grandmother before she leaves for work. I don't want to take a chance of betraying my intentions with a stray facial expression. I get one chance to do this, and today is it.

Once I hear her leave, I relax again. I won't leave for school until after lunch period. Yes, I'll be marked absent for my morning classes, but if everything goes as planned, they'll never hear from me again.

Going to the kitchen, I take the time to have a proper breakfast, beyond the usual bowl of cereal or pair of Pop-Tarts that passes for a morning meal. Today, I want eggs and sausage links. After all, I know I'll be skipping lunch, and who knows where I'll be at dinnertime. So I scramble the eggs just the way I like them—soft and fluffy. When my grandmother makes them, she cooks them into flat, rubbery things that are barely edible. The sausage I heat in a small frying pan, also not too crispy. Two pieces of sourdough bread become toast, a perfect vehicle for butter and some strawberry-and-champagne jelly I picked up at Whole Foods.

In the quiet and solitude of the kitchen, I enjoy the hell out of it all. As I eat, I try not to let the words *last meal* enter my mind, though I know that if things go wrong this afternoon, that could very well be what this is. *Well, if this is my last meal, at least it won't be Cocoa Puffs.*

After breakfast, I turn on the TV to pass the time, but the inane programs coupled with my restless thoughts lead me to switch it off after a single pass through the channels. *How do people watch this shit all day?*

I return to my room and go into the walk-in closet again, to visit my creation. That word makes me feel like Dr. Frankenstein. My creation isn't a monster either. Just big, dangerous, and misunderstood. And beautiful. Fifteen pounds of plastic explosives. Made by me, thank you very much for that B-minus in chemistry, Mr. Charpentiere. Bet you'll be rethinking that when you inspect the crumbling remains of Leonard High School in a few hours.

Of course, I don't get to sign my work. I must remain anonymous as I disappear in the confusion. Now, I know some people would say that blowing up a school to create a diversion so I can run away from home is extreme, and maybe it is. But this isn't just any running away. What I have to do is so important, no one can know that I'm alive, not even my family. And besides, those bastards at my school deserve this. If I wanted to hurt them or even kill them with this, I could, but that's not what this is about. I'm not psychotic. That's why the timing is so important. This afternoon, when the horde of brainless little miscreants is in the football stadium for their pep assembly, my creation will fulfill its purpose. And in the confusion and destruction, I can slip away unnoticed.

Yes, I could probably just cut class and slip away, but the explosion is more to me than a diversion. It's a statement about getting too comfortable as you make others uncomfortable. It's about the power one person can have. I could just as easily come to school with a gun and start killing my tormentors, but despite everything, I don't want them to die. I want them to have an epiphany—to realize how close they will come to dying today, so they can appreciate life more. Not just their own lives, but everyone's. I'll give them a few days to think I was killed in the explosion. And then, if I choose to re-appear, maybe they'll appreciate me a little more.

I'll need to make a show of arriving at midday, so I'm not marked absent for the whole day. But that will give me time to get there, set everything up, and keep my arrival fresh on the minds of the office staff.

Going through it all in my mind, I know how extreme this sounds, and it is. A year ago, I would never even think of doing something like this. But my world is upside down. I've worked out fifty different plans for doing what I have to do, and none of them would work—except this. My father means the world to me, and this is the only way I can get to him to save him. I expect I'll have time for regrets when all of this is over.

I bring the block of explosives out of my closet and place it on the desk in my room, to see it by the light of day. At the moment, the only way it could hurt me is if it falls off the desk and lands on my foot. The material is completely inert without the detonator, which is tucked safely into a drawer. At fifteen pounds, the block is heavy, but it will fit into a backpack. I'll have to walk to school with it. I can't risk taking the bus while carrying it. So it'll be an interesting mile and a half, but it's the safest way to go. I can't risk anything going wrong.

I stare at this wondrous creation of mine and I discover that ten minutes have gone by without my even realizing it. I'm letting myself get too deep into my thoughts—into the what-ifs and the possible futures. I have to follow the plan and not get bogged down in what might be.

In the bottom drawer of my desk is an old shoebox. I dig it out and produce the contents. The detonator is army surplus. It didn't work when I bought it, but it's perfectly fine now, in conjunction with the remote control I adapted from a radio-control car. I check the batteries in the remote by switching it on. Four LED lights on the receiver light up. They're actually kind of pretty. More importantly, they work, and the receiver works from 150 feet away. Plenty of room to get to safety.

As the hours of the morning pass in solitude, I can feel my heart beating faster. *Should I really do this?* Of course, the answer is no. How could anyone in their right mind answer *yes* to that question? *Can I do it?* I find that the answer to that question is a much easier *yes.* It's a building, filled with people who think nothing of mocking me, harassing me, tormenting me every day. And that building is their hive. What do you do when faced with a dangerous hive? Smoke the bees out and then set it on fire. This I can do. This I must do. And then, when their perfect little lives are disrupted, and they're standing around the wreckage, some of them celebrating, others crying, others thanking God or whoever that everyone was safely outside, I run for it. Three-quarters of a mile to the Illinois Central Railroad tracks leading north and south. At 1:32, a freight train will pass through Libertyville, slowing down for the railroad crossings. I'll find a boxcar, climb inside, and make my way to Florida. And I'll get the evidence that will free my father.

Far too quickly, 12:30 arrives, and it is time for me to start my walk to school. I place the explosive in the main compartment of the oversized backpack, the detonator in a smaller pocket, and the remote in a third pocket, keeping them apart so there'll be no unexpected surprises on the way to school. With everything in place, I zip up the backpack and slide it onto my back. The weight is surprising. I realize that in all my testing and planning, I have never yet carried the full load on my back. It takes a minute or two to get used to, but before long, I can stand it without even appearing overloaded.

It is a beautiful autumn day, and I let myself be glad for that detail. Though Hollywood might portray the day with dark clouds and distant rumbles of thunder, to me there is nothing sinister about my plans. The destruction of Leonard High School is a means to an end for me, and if that makes me a bad person, then I'm a bad person. I'm focused on the greater good.

As I walk down each block, I try not to tell myself I'm seeing it for the last time. Thoughts like that are counterproductive. This isn't a suicide mission, not in the least. But as I finally see the school building in the distance, my pulse quickens yet again, knowing that in just a few minutes, I alone will be responsible for its destruction.

At 1:00, I enter the building and make my way to the main office. The students will be going to their fifth-period classes in just a couple of minutes, and from there, they'll be led out to the stadium at 1:15. That doesn't leave me much time. I approach the front desk.

"What do you need, Cassie?" Miss Canaday asks. We've met before. *Heartless old bitch.*

"I'm checking in after a morning absence, so I need an attendance slip," I answer.

She hands me the piece of paper, and the interrogation continues. "Why were you out this morning? You weren't cutting class, were you?"

She wants a reason? I'll give her one she'll remember. I deliberately raise my voice just enough that the five or six other people in there can hear as well. "I'm having girl troubles today, and things were kind of a mess down there this morning." Out of the corner of my eye, I see one or two of the male students laughing at this announcement. *Fine, let 'em laugh.* "So I figured I'd better stay home until I could get things under control, so I didn't walk around this place looking like I'd been stabbed or something."

My response has the desired effect. She blanches a little and doesn't pursue it further. But the answer is just awkward enough that everyone who hears it will remember it in half an hour, when I turn up missing. Just to put the frosting on the cake, I offer one parting shot. "Must be nice not to have to worry about that anymore, huh, Miss Canaday?"

One of the boys present actually whispers, "Daaaaaaamn." *Have I actually impressed him with my rudeness? If only that mattered to me.*

The attendance slip completed, I quietly leave the building one more time, just long enough to duck into an unused corner of the schoolyard and attach the detonator to the explosives. This time, when I go back in, it'll be time to plant the device.

The detonator has electrically conductive prongs on it, so attaching it is as simple as sticking it into the cube of C4. Should anything go wrong, detaching it is as simple as pulling it out. *Safety explosives. God bless America.* I glance quickly at my watch—1:08. Time to do this.

I re-enter the building, and in among the sea of faces is one I don't recognize—a man, maybe six feet tall, wearing some kind of lab coat and carrying a clipboard. He appears to be looking for someone. He scans the faces of the students, and then he sees mine. There is instant recognition on his face, though I know I've never seen him before. I try to maintain my composure as he makes his way over to me. *Could he be a cop? Not dressed like that. And besides, not a single soul knows what I'm about to do. I didn't do the stupid teenager thing and write about it in my blog—which I don't even have—or videotape some stupid manifesto for YouTube. Maybe he wants to talk to me about something completely innocent. If so, I'll play along, get past it, and then do what I have to do.*

I am entirely focused on keeping a calm demeanor as the strange man with the lab coat and clipboard approaches me and asks, "Excuse me, are you Cassie Haiduk?"

And that is how I met Tristan Shays, a man armed with something even more powerful than a block of explosives: the knowledge of what I was about to do. I'm still not clear on exactly how he knew. I guess he gets warnings and he goes and helps people. Apparently, someone or something felt that I was worth warning.

He did it, too—stopped me from blowing up the school. And not only that, but he and his partner Rebecca agreed to take me all the way to Florida to help get my father released from prison. Dad was convicted of something he didn't do, and I'm the only one who can prove it.

My name is Cassandra Haiduk. It's a Romanian name meaning "outlaw," and that's what I am. I'm on the run now with Tristan and

Rebecca, and there's an Amber Alert spreading across the country for my safe return. But I don't want to return. Not to my school, not to my grandmother, not to my life. I'm going to Pensacola, Florida, and I'm going to save my father from a fate he doesn't deserve. And even though I've just met these two people today, I already trust them more than I've ever trusted anyone before.

Chapter 1

It's a fine kettle of fish we're in. That's what my grandfather would have said about our current predicament if he were here. "This is a fine kettle of fish we're in, Tristan." I can almost hear his voice. A very colorful phrase, to be sure, and one that they used in the 1930s because no one had yet come up with the equally colorful phrase, "Well, this really sucks ass." Make no mistake—fish or no fish, our current situation truly sucks ass. Despite my proven track record as altruist and all-around decent human being, I am wanted for kidnapping.

I'm scared. Macho bullshit bravado aside, self-entertaining internal monologue be damned, I'm scared. Because once again, I'm risking my life, my safety, and my freedom to protect someone I don't even know. Someone I met a few hours ago. Someone who—truth be told—would probably irritate the hell out of me if I met her on the street. This girl, this teenage child for whom a little knowledge is definitely a dangerous thing. Cassie Haiduk. She wanted to blow up her school, with only the slightest regard for the 1,800 souls within it, and now, instead of turning her in so she can get the help she almost certainly needs, I'm driving her across the country to help get her father out of prison.

Is it because she's female, is that it? Am I so pathetic and desperate for a woman's attention and approval that I put common sense aside and play the hero when I know damn well that's not what I am? Would

1

I be making this epic and foolish journey if it were Casper Haiduk in the back seat? I don't know. Knowing me, probably. After two years of being destiny's errand bitch, I don't even know if I remember how to politely decline.

I'm over-thinking it, as usual. Now that we're on the road again, there's a lingering silence in the car, and it's giving me far too much time to think about everything. I think Rebecca's angry at me ... *again*. I know she was displeased when I agreed to take the assignment I got at the park in Urbana, Illinois. And because of it, we're detouring to New Orleans, to warn a police detective that her life is in danger.

I know the risk we're taking. I'm smart enough to figure out that seeking out law-enforcement officials is not the smartest thing to do when one is wanted by other law-enforcement officials. But I have a plan to keep us safe.

When Cassie breaks the silence fifteen minutes later, her voice actually startles me. "Would someone please say something?"

Glancing at the clock on the dashboard, I realize that we left Urbana almost an hour ago, and in that time, no one has spoken. "I'm sorry, Cassie," I say. "Rebecca and I spend a lot of hours traveling in the car together, and sometimes we can go for long stretches without talking."

"Yeah, that's fine," she replies, "but it's a little tense in here, with you two pissed at each other."

"We're not pissed at each other," I reassure her.

"Yes we are," Rebecca retorts with no uncertainty in her voice.

I turn to look at her, annoyed at her contradiction. "Do we *have* to do this now?"

"Why not? It's a long way to New Orleans, after all."

"Well, as long as you're not pissed at each other or anything," Cassie says, slumping back into her seat.

"I can't believe you're mad at me for taking this assignment," I say.

"It's too big a chance we're taking, traipsing right into a police station in a major city when there's this Amber Alert out."

"Okay, for the record, I'll be the only one traipsing. The two of you will stay safely in the car, out of sight. I'll deliver my message, get the usual confused reaction, explain what I can, and be on my way. Like I do time and time and time again."

"And when she asks your name?"

"I'll make something up. Wouldn't be the first time for either of us, right, *Persephone?*"

"Persephone?" Cassie repeats.

"Long story," Rebecca answers. "Don't interrupt the grownups."

"I think I liked it better when you two weren't talking."

"Why are we doing this?" I ask Rebecca. "Squabbling like this? You wanted to travel with me, to watch me work, carrying out these assignments. Well, this is one of them. Now I feel like ... like you're blaming me for agreeing to complete it. Is it because it's dangerous? You followed me to Wyandotte, to Cedarsburg. Those were dangerous. You came with me to find Ha Tesha, not even knowing what to expect. Why now? Why this sudden change of heart?"

She sits in silence for many long seconds, long enough for me to believe that she won't answer, that she'll just let the question hang and the conversation die. Finally, after almost a minute, she quietly says, "Maybe I made a mistake."

I wait for her to explain, but she doesn't, so I'm forced to prod. "A mistake? What do you mean, in getting angry?"

"In coming with you," she says.

The words hurt more than I thought they could, because that wasn't the answer I thought she'd give. "You really mean that?"

"I don't know. I don't want to mean it. I don't want to believe that I've left my home and my job and my friends to pursue a relationship that lasted two weeks."

"Then don't," I reply. "Think of all we've been through, everything we've shared. Yeah, some of it's been difficult and scary and awful, but not all of it. When I met you, I didn't know you. As I got to know you, I started to feel like we were meant to be together. When all my assignments started revolving around you, that just confirmed it."

"All your assignments revolved around Rebecca?" Cassie's voice from the back seat interrupts my train of thought and reminds me that we've been having a very personal discussion in front of a near stranger. "Even mine?"

Oh, shit. How can I answer that without telling her about Rebecca's father? "We've … had problems with Consolidated Offshore before. When you told us that they were responsible for what happened to your father, it fit into the big picture. It's one reason we agreed to help you." I hesitate for a moment. "Cassie, at the risk of being rude, could I ask you to put on your iPod for a few minutes? Rebecca and I need to talk privately, and I don't want to pull over to do that."

"Yeah, it's fine," she answers. "Just … you know … work this out. We still have a long way to go together." With that, she puts on her headphones and drowns us out.

Out of the mouths of babes. Or, you know, precocious, potentially psychotic adolescents. But it's a good icebreaker; I'll give her that. Never one to miss an opportunity, I tell Rebecca, "She's right, you know. We do have a long way to go together. I promised you early on that if you ever wanted out, all you had to do was ask. That's still true. But I'll tell you this: I will be very very sad if you go, and I will miss you terribly. Because I'm going to Florida after our little detour, and I'm taking on Consolidated with every weapon I have, whatever that might be. I'd be very proud to do that with you by my side. Or in front of me if it gets dangerous."

She tries not to smile at my dumb joke, but I catch a hint of one. "So what's it like in New Orleans?" she asks quietly.

"It's nice, actually," I reply. "It's like Key West, only more intoxicated and more naked."

"I like intoxication and nakedness," she says shyly.

"Then what are we waiting for?" I ask with a smile. "Truce?" I ask, just as I did the night we met, after the first time I had upset her.

"Truce," she answers, just as she did that night.

I look back at Cassie, who has her headphones on and her eyes closed in the back seat. "Look at her back there," I say to Rebecca, "resting so peacefully, like the little evil genius we never had."

"I'm between songs and I can hear you," Cassie declares without opening her eyes. "And you guys still suck at talking privately."

I have to laugh at that. The women in my life are too damn smart for their own good.

After a few miles, I see a road sign: JCT I-57. Giving the matter a moment's thought, I maneuver the Sebring into the turn lane for the on-ramp. Seeing this, Rebecca asks, "What are you doing?"

"Getting onto the interstate," I reply.

"But what about the Amber Alert?" she asks. "They'll be looking for us on the interstates, won't they?"

"It's a question of time. If we take the interstates, we're about eleven hours from New Orleans. If we don't, it could be twice that. Every little town between here and there slows us down to a crawl. So we'll play the percentages. In the rural areas, we'll take the interstates, make up some time. Closer to metropolitan areas, where they're most likely to be looking for us, we'll duck onto state roads or county roads and avoid all the traffic anyway. Fair enough?"

"I guess," she answers as we merge onto I-57 southbound. "As long as you think it's safe."

"You think I'd let something happen to my favorite person in the whole world?" I ask. "By which I mean me, of course."

This time she laughs. "You're such a douche sometimes."

"Cleansing and refreshing, you mean?"

"Right."

The tension successfully broken, we continue south in better spirits. After a few more minutes, I am surprised to hear the words, "Cat's eye."

I turn to Rebecca. "What?"

She looks confused. "What, what?"

"You just said something to me, and I'm not sure what it was."

"Not a peep," she says.

"I could have sworn I heard you say 'cat's eye.' It was definitely your voice."

"Sorry to disappoint you, but any feline anatomy lessons you're hearing are a product of your own imagination."

I let it go for now, chalking it up to the long, tiring day. Neither of my traveling companions said anything, so I must have imagined it. A check of the dashboard clock tells me that it's almost 10:00 at night. Cassie is dozing in the back seat, and Rebecca has a weary expression on her face. As for the driver, he's not at his sharpest either. We still have a long way to go before we reach New Orleans, and a good night's sleep will make a world of difference.

We are just a few miles from Effingham, Illinois, where Interstate 57 crosses Interstate 70. That much traffic means plenty of available hotel rooms. "I think I'll find us a room for the night," I inform Rebecca.

"That sounds good," she says. "You thinking Hilton or Wyndham?"

I shake my head. "Not tonight. Tonight, I'm thinking fleabag."

"Excuse me?" she replies. "Tristan Shays chooses one-star accommodations for the night? What prompted this?"

"Circumstances. We're still wanted, so the possibility exists that the police would be looking for us. I don't want to use credit cards, and I don't want the three of us checking in together. What we need is discretion and low-impact, and to get that, we need cheapo, unfortunately."

She spies a roadside sign. "How about that one? The Canfield Inn, Effingham. Thirty-eight dollars for a single."

"That'll work."

I follow the signs to the off-ramp and make two turns until I see the Canfield Inn ahead. It looks exactly like I imagined it would. About a dozen cars are parked in their lot, in front of dingy room doors that look like they haven't been repainted since the 1960s. The "vacancy" sign is lit—no surprise. Fluorescent light illuminates the office, off in a corner of the two-story building. I head for the decrepit overhang out front and park the car. This wakes Cassie.

"What's up?" she asks wearily. "Where are we?"

"Getting a motel room," I answer. "You two stay here. Cassie, please lie down in the back seat until we get to our room."

I exit the car and head to the office. It looks like a place where law-enforcement reality shows visit frequently. Two vending machines offer off-brand beverages and snacks of questionable vintage. The place reeks of cigarettes and despair. A stain on the floor might be blood; it's hard to tell. Behind thick glass is my host for the evening. He can't be more than twenty-five years old. "Room for the night?" he asks.

It's time to get into character. "Hi, how ya doing? Yeah, I'd like a room for the night, please."

"One room, one night?" he asks.

"Yeah, but here's the thing. I'm here with a woman. Y'know, a woman who kinda isn't my wife." He smiles a little and nods knowingly. "So if we could do this in cash and skip the part where you ask for identification, I'd really appreciate it." I punctuate the sentence with a twenty-dollar bill slipped through the pass-through to him.

"John Smith it is," he says. "It's $42.50 with tax. I'm guessing you want a king bed?"

That would be the logical assumption, but not such a good idea with a fifteen-year-old girl along. "Actually," I answer with a little laugh, "two queens would be better. She's a little … clingy … and she wants to cuddle all night afterwards. Me, I need a little more room to get some sleep. Y'know what I mean?"

"Yeah, my girlfriend's the same way. I can get you two queens."

"And if you can get me something on the first floor, around the back of the place, away from other people, I'd be grateful." I slide the cash to him.

"You got it, Mr. Smith." He hands me a room key. "Room 148. Check-out is at eleven. Have a good night."

Three cheers for the enduring privacy of the sleazy motel. As long as there isn't a video camera hidden away in the room, we should be quite undisturbed all night. I take the room key back to the car and start us up again. Room 148 is indeed around back, and there is not another car on this side of the building. I park in front of the door, and Rebecca and I get our overnight bags out. Cassie is without luggage.

"You mind sleeping in your clothes tonight?" I ask her.

"I guess not. What about a toothbrush?"

"There's a gas station next door with a convenience store. I'll go over there and get you one. Tomorrow, we can get you some more supplies."

"Thanks."

I brace myself a bit as we enter the room. The interior décor lives up—or perhaps I should say *down*—to the exterior décor. Cassie's initial question gives voice to my own thoughts. "What's that smell?"

"Try not to think about it," I suggest.

There are, indeed, two queen beds. Drag queen beds would be a better description, as they sport the tackiest bedspreads I've ever encountered. A few ancient paintings are on the walls, signed by artists who probably deserve to starve. Across from the beds, a twenty-year-old television sits sadly on a dresser, more likely to emit B.O. than HBO. A quick check of the bathroom confirms that only the most perfunctory amenities are present. There is water. It runs. It goes into appropriate holes when the user is finished with it. Beyond that, the Canfield Inn makes no promises.

The place is clean, in the strictest sense of the word. There are no bugs or rodents, and a cleaning person has visited the room at some point since the last guest left. I shudder to think what a black light would reveal, but since ignorance is bliss, I'm going to let myself believe the place is clean enough to sleep in. I'm beginning to think that sleeping in our clothes isn't a bad idea for all three of us.

"This place is gross," Cassie says for the entire group.

"It's cheap and it's private," I reply. "Two good things tonight."

"So are you two, like, poor?" she asks.

"Just frugal," I answer.

"Where's my room?"

I point to the second bed. "You're lookin' at it."

"I have to share a room with you? God, even my grandmother gave me my own room."

"Yes, and she gave us a nationwide manhunt, so you can thank her for both of those things the next time you speak to her. I'm going to go get that toothbrush. Does anybody need anything else?"

"I'd like a Sprite," Rebecca says.

"Maybe some Funyuns if they have them," Cassie adds.

"You like Funyuns?" I ask, suddenly very tickled at the prospect.

"Yeah."

I give Rebecca a look that simply says *ha,* and she discreetly sticks her tongue out at me. "I like them too," I offer. I grab the room key, and as I'm about to leave, a thought occurs to me. Taking forty dollars out of my wallet, I leave the wallet itself in the room. That way, if I'm stopped by a cop for an identity check, I can say I left it at home. "You two stay here," I instruct. "Lock the door behind me. I'll be back as soon as I can."

The night air feels quite cool as I walk down the block to the convenience store on the corner. The place is brightly lit and quite well cared for, two qualities lacking in my current accommodations. A single cashier watches the register at this hour, as five other customers join me in browsing the aisles.

My luck holds out, and I find a toothbrush and some toothpaste. Stepping back to the cold case, I grab a twenty-ounce Sprite for Rebecca and a liter of bottled water for me. I can feel fatigue pushing against me as I make my way to snack foods and pick up a bag of Funyuns large enough to share.

Three of the other shoppers manage to beat me to the register, so I find myself at the back of a short line. Fortunately, nobody's doing the weekly grocery shopping, so it won't take long, unless of course somebody wants fifty lottery tickets. I'm actually feeling like I can get back to the motel and get some rest soon—until *he* walks in.

Looking like he came directly from Hollywood Central Casting, the store's latest arrival is young, maybe nineteen or twenty, Caucasian, not overly tall or strong. As he enters, he looks dangerously nervous. Even without Rebecca's ability to read his thoughts, I can tell by looking at him what brought him here. Discreetly, I set my purchases down on the counter, keeping my hands free in case I need them.

I don't have to wait long. Within seconds, he produces a handgun from his waistband—a .22 or a .38, I'm not sure which—not big, but big enough. "All right, everybody be cool!" he says in an extremely shaky voice, prompting the five other shoppers to display varying degrees of panic. Only the cashier and I manage to maintain our calm—he, most likely, because he's been in this situation before; I, just because it figures this would happen.

I see the cashier discreetly reaching for something under the counter. It could be a gun; it could be an alarm button. Neither would be good for the robber—or for me, for that matter. Fortunately, our all-American boy sees this too and quickly warns the cashier, "Get your hands up! Don't be reaching for nothing until I tell you to!"

The cashier obliges, absent any good options. As the other customers try to make themselves invisible by ducking, crawling, crying, or praying, the robber approaches the cashier. "Give me what's in the register. All of it."

The clerk obliges, opening the register and bringing out the paper money, which the robber snatches out of his hand and stuffs into his pocket. In my tired mind, I want to see him bring out a white canvas bag with a big black dollar sign on the side, but I realize that would just be silly and impractical. This *should* be the end of it, but then dumbass gets greedy and fucks things up.

Turning to the customers in line, the thief orders, "I want your wallets, cell phones, jewelry! Anything you got, give it to me."

The woman at the head of the line is already terrified, and hearing this, she begins to sob loudly. "Please, please, not my wedding ring. I can't, I ..."

Compassion is not high on the list of the intruder's turn-ons, and he looks like he's running short on patience. So to reinforce his point, he cocks the gun and aims it at her, saying in a low, guttural voice, "I don't have time for this shit."

And then it happens. I know for a fact that prior to this exact moment, I am content to keep my mouth shut, give him what he wants, and let him get the hell out of there. But when he turns that weapon on someone who just wanted to get a pastry and a cappuccino, something courageous and immensely, profoundly stupid in me awakens and declares, *this far; no further.*

With my hands in the air (though I really do care) I step between the robber and the robbed. "Okay, okay, wait—wait," I say in my most conciliatory voice. "It doesn't have to go down like this."

He's clearly not expecting this. "Man, who the fuck are you?"

"Just a guy who wanted some chips and a soda."

"You want to live long enough to get that stuff, you'll get out of my way."

"We're cool, we're cool," I hear myself saying, though I know I've never uttered those words before. "I just ... I don't want to see anybody get hurt, and I don't think you do either."

I am painfully aware that my school of diplomacy omits the crucial planning stage, opting instead to leap boldly forward to the talking-out-of-my-ass stage. Clever boy that he is, he picks up on this. "You don't want anybody to get hurt? Then you best tell these people to get their shit out and give it to me."

With my hands still raised, I turn to the others and loudly instruct, "Do what he says, please. Give him what he wants. Things can be replaced; people can't." Like I'm suddenly the mayor of Gas-Stationville, giving decrees to my adoring public.

Crying Woman parts with her wallet, her phone, and—despite the anguish she's conveying—her jewelry. The other two ahead of me in line do likewise—with considerably less anguish—as do the two who are standing by the fountain-drink dispenser. The robber must be wearing clown pants, because he's managed to find pockets for all the swag. Finally, he stands in front of me, the gun pointed squarely at my chest. "Your turn, Mr. Chips-and-Soda. Give."

Slowly and deliberately, I reach into my pocket and pull out the forty dollars in cash, handing it to him. He looks at the money like I've just taken a crap in his palm. "Forty bucks? You're holdin' out on me. I want your wallet."

"Didn't bring it. I walked here."

"Cell phone, then. Car keys. Everything. Those are nice shoes. I know you've got money."

"Like I said, chips and a soda. I didn't count on needing more."

He's clearly not buying it. "Turn out your pockets," he orders.

I put my hands down long enough to oblige. My heart sinks as the motel room key drops to the floor with a disturbing clank. "What's this?" he asks, looking newly interested. He picks up the key and examines it. "Hotel key. Maybe I'll stop over there, see what else you got in your room."

"No," I say quietly but assertively. "Not gonna happen. You got my money. You got these people's stuff. You win. Walk away. Because I'll tell you this: you're not ready for what's in that room. Whatever you think you'll find in there, it's not. There's nothing but a world of hurt in that hotel room if you try to go there. Walk away, man."

For too many seconds, he and I stare at each other in silence. It is a bluff, but it's all I have. Maybe, God willing, if I believe it, he'll believe it. I try to keep a calm, vaguely dangerous expression as he makes up his mind. Finally, he throws the key back at my chest. "Fine," he says, "fuck you. Keep it."

Without another word, he turns and exits the store. As he passes the graduated tape at the entrance, I notice that he is five feet seven. Not that it matters to me.

I can finally breathe a sigh of relief as I pick up the room key and put it back in my pocket. I'm relieved to see that the room number is not printed on the key fob. Neither, I notice with equal relief, is the name of the motel. I've caught a break.

Everyone around me looks extremely upset. "Is everyone okay?" I ask the group.

The second man in line turns to face me. I'm confused to see hostility on his face. "Are we okay? You stupid son of a bitch!"

"Excuse me?"

"What'd you have to go and do that for? 'Give him what he wants.' What were you trying to be, some kind of hero or something?"

His anger is moving the woman in front of him to stronger tears and moving me to my dark place. "Well, excuse the shit out of me!" I retort. "I just thought it might be nice if this lady didn't get killed over a ring!"

The man won't let up. "He was bluffing, you asshole. He wasn't going to kill anybody. He just wanted to intimidate us into giving him our valuables, and thanks to you, he got everything."

"And just what do you think we should have done?" I ask.

"Overpowered him. Like they did on United 93."

I can't believe what I'm hearing. "Yeah, and you remember how well *that* ended up. In case you hadn't noticed, he had a gun, and he was ready to use it if he didn't get what he wanted."

"How do you know?" the man asked. "Are you working with him?"

"What?"

The question is too absurd to contemplate, but it motivates others to join him. "Yeah," the other man in line says, "how would you know he was going to use it?"

The woman at the drink station pipes up, "It's pretty convenient that you're the only one here with no valuables to lose."

To my astonishment, the woman at the head of the line—the one I put behind me as I faced the loaded gun—adds, "And just as he came in, you put your groceries down, like you know what he was going to do. Why would you do that unless you knew?"

This stirs the small crowd into a rhubarb of anti-Tristan sentiment that is thoroughly and completely pissing me off. "I saw the look on his face and the gun in his hand. Okay, maybe he would've killed her and maybe he wouldn't. Were you ready to take that risk? Were *you?*"

"No," Crying Woman says, "but why would you do that? Interfere with strangers in a dangerous situation when you knew that doing it could make things worse?"

Her question hits me like a speeding train. Without realizing it, she has just voiced the central theme of my existential dread for the past two years. Why would I interfere with the lives of strangers in a dangerous situation? Doing so could make things worse. I know that; I've seen that. And yet I do it, time and time again. It's why I'm going to New Orleans, and by extension, why I'm in this gas station tonight. And suddenly, my anger and my defensiveness deflate, and I'm left without an answer to the question.

"Yeah," I say quietly, "why *would* someone want to do that?"

My lack of fight catches them off guard and buys me a moment's silence. I walk over to the counter and pick up my purchases. "I'm taking these," I tell the cashier. "I need to go now."

He waves me on, and I make my way to the exit. Behind me, I hear a chorus of voices asking questions: *You're just going to let him go? What about the cops? What if he's an accomplice?*

The cashier raises his voice at this point. "Hey! Everybody just relax. Let him go." As they start up their protests again, he adds, "I've been robbed six times in this place, and this is the first time anybody had the guts to try to help. Buddy, you can go."

"Thank you," I say quietly. "I'm at the Quality Inn if they need me. My name's Bill Ferguson."

With that I exit the store. I won't answer the other customers' questions. The biggest question on my mind right now is the one I can't answer.

Chapter 2

I make my way back to the motel room and open the door with the key, juggling the unpurchased purchases with my other hand. Rebecca and Cassie stand anxiously as I enter. "Oh, thank God!" Rebecca says. "We were worried. You were gone so long."

Silently, I place the objects on the dresser and walk over to the bathroom. Leaving the door open, I turn on the light and splash water on my face.

"What is it? What's wrong?" Rebecca asks from outside the bathroom. I'm still not ready to answer. I guess I don't have to, because within seconds, she adds, "Oh my God, are you all right? Are you hurt?"

"I'm not hurt," I say quietly.

"Is he gone?" she asks, fear evident in her voice.

"Yeah," I answer plainly.

It's more than I'm ready to deal with right now, so I step outside and stand in front of the room, clutching my hair with both hands. Rebecca follows me outside, closing the door behind her. "Talk to me, Tristan. You're scaring me."

"Why am I doing this?" I ask her.

"Doing ... what?"

"This. All of this. Why am I driving to Louisiana to help someone I've never met? Why am I clearing out homes before they collapse and going to places that a tornado is about to devastate? Why am I

15

risking my freedom and yours to drive some kid across the country, just because she says she needs to help her father? It's crazy. It's utter bullshit and it's crazy."

"But you help people," she says quietly.

"Strangers. People who mean nothing to me. And half the time, they resent me for doing it."

"I don't mean nothing to you. And I never resented you for doing what you did."

"Look where it's got you," I reply. "On the run. Out of work. You left your home and your friends, to put yourself in danger on a daily basis. And now we're on our way to stand up to an incredibly dangerous man who, oh yeah, happens to be your father. When you look at everything that's happened to us in the past two weeks, why would you possibly want to be here now?"

She looks at me for many long, painful seconds, fighting back tears, until finally the words slip quietly from her mouth. "Because I love you."

My heart is still for a moment. *Did I hear her correctly?* "What did you say?"

Louder this time, and with some tears to accompany the words: "Because I love you. Because you're my compass, and without you near me, I don't know which way is up. Before I met you, I felt like I was wasting my life. I was too scared to finish college, too scared to get a real career, too scared to live anywhere near my parents." She pauses as the tears take over for a second; she fights them back and continues. "All I knew how to do was take my clothes off for men who didn't love me, who didn't even like me. And with every dollar I took from them, I mortgaged a little piece of my soul."

"Rebecca, I ..."

"But you gave me back my dignity. You let me be a person again, someone who could be strong and smart and powerful, and I needed that. I forgot that I could be that person. And yeah, we've seen some weird shit since we've been together, but we can't stop now. What you do is so important. So important. You change people's lives. My life."

Before I can answer, she puts her arms around me and kisses me. It is the first time in days that we've kissed like this, and it feels like powerful medicine flowing into me, restoring me when I was at the brink. I don't know how long the kiss continues, but I know that I never want it to end. When at last she pulls away, I can feel her tears on my face, taste them in my mouth. I want to say the exact right thing, but the only thing that comes to mind is, "You think we could give the kid ten bucks to go to the movies?"

She laughs at this, and I join her, aware that my own tears have arrived. "I'm so tired," I confess.

"Me too. Me too."

"We don't have to go to New Orleans if you don't want to," I tell her.

"What?" she responds, surprise evident in her voice. "What about the danger this person is in?"

"I can call her, leave an anonymous tip. That way, we don't even have to set foot in New Orleans, and we can head right to Florida."

"Tristan, that's very thoughtful of you, but we both know how much more weight your messages carry when you deliver them in person. This is someone's life at stake. We should go there and deliver the message. It's the right thing to do. We'll be careful."

I run my fingers through her hair, feeling how much softer it is than mine. "Let's get some sleep, what do you say?"

Despite the level of anxiety running through the three of us, we all manage to get a good night's sleep. By 7:00 in the morning, we are packed up, cleared out, and checked out, heading back on the road south to Louisiana. Though a sit-down breakfast sounds good, restaurants will be very crowded on a Saturday morning, so we must settle for drive-thru fast food. And so, as a farewell to Effingham, I'm forced to have effing ham, effing cheese, and an effing egg on an effing biscuit.

Mercifully, the traffic is lighter today than it was yesterday, so I venture off the interstate at a convenient point, opting for two-lane roads southbound for a few hours. If we can keep our average speed at fifty-five or sixty, we won't lose too much time. If things slow down too much, we can take our chances on the interstate at midday, when the cops are less likely to be patrolling.

Illinois gives way to Missouri without incident, then briefly into Arkansas, followed by Tennessee, just long enough to see Memphis before we cross into Mississippi. "Look over there," I point out to my passengers as we cross through Memphis. "There's Graceland."

When Cassie responds with, "There's *what?*" Rebecca and I both offer an audible groan. Finally, Rebecca gets the opportunity to feel old for once.

We get back on the interstate in Mississippi, fairly well convinced that the fervor of the manhunt has died down a bit. Hourly radio news broadcasts don't even mention us now, which I take as a good sign.

"Cassie," Rebecca says, turning to face her in the back seat, "you said you have evidence in the safe-deposit box in Florida that will exonerate your father. Can you tell me what it is?"

She hesitates only briefly before answering; the time for mistrust is past. "It's different things that my father collected while he was working for Consolidated Offshore. There's letters, e-mails, invoices. And there's recorded conversations between Consolidated's directors and the Chinese oil company."

"Why was he collecting these things? Did he know they were planning to do something illegal?"

"I think he suspected. He'd been with them for three years, and over the last six months he was there, he saw and heard things that worried him. So he started collecting evidence and storing it away, especially when there were implied threats made against him."

"Threats?" I ask.

"At first, they were said almost in passing. People would tell him not to ask too many questions or not to dig too deep into things that didn't concern him. But soon, he started getting negative performance reviews. Then he got called in front of management, and they would threaten his job and stop just short of threatening his family. That's when he sent me to Libertyville to live with my grandmother."

"Where's your mother?" Rebecca asks.

"I don't know. She left eight years ago, and none of us have heard from her since. I don't even miss her." Cassie pauses a moment before asking, "If we can get this evidence to the right people, will they just let him out of prison then and there?"

"It's usually not that simple," Rebecca replies. "We'll have to petition for what's called a miscarriage of justice to quash a wrongful verdict, and those aren't always easy to get. It involves proving that some element of the case was flawed—the jury, the judge, the prosecutor, or the defense counsel. That can take time and a lot of effort. But if the evidence is as damning as you say it is, that should help."

"I hope it is," she answers. "I mean, I believe my father completely, and I know he would never sell secrets or anything like that. I just hope what he has on them is enough to free him."

"We'll do everything we ..." Rebecca stops in mid-sentence and looks at me. "Okay, that was weird."

"What?" I ask.

"I just heard your voice in my head. What was the thing last night that you thought you heard me say?"

"What, you mean cat's eye?"

"Yeah, that's it. That's what I heard you say just now. Cat's eye. Were you thinking it?"

"No. I haven't thought about it since last night."

"What's going on, Tristan? Why are these words in our heads? What's cat's eye, anyway?"

"I don't know," I reply. "I wish we had Internet access. We could look it up."

Cassie turns on her cell phone and hands it to Rebecca. "I've got 3G. Go ahead."

Rebecca looks up cat's eye on a search engine. "It's a movie. It's a kind of pavement marker. There's a Japanese cartoon with that name. It's a kind of marble. It's a brand of sunglasses. None of this stuff is helping."

"Can I see that phone, please?" I ask. She hands it to me.

I pull the car to the side of the road and turn on the hazard lights. Once traffic clears, I get out of the car and find what I'm looking for: a heavy rock that I can pick up. I place Cassie's phone on the ground, and in one swift motion, I obliterate it with the rock.

This action, to no one's surprise, elicits an equal and opposite reaction in Cassandra, who opens her door and sprints over to me, exclaiming, "What the hell? I love that phone!"

"You know who else loves it?" I ask. "The FBI. Every cell phone has a GPS locator in it. The minute you turned the phone on, the authorities can trace the signal. I'll get you a new phone when this is over. For now, we can't take the chance."

She pouts a bit, but she seems to understand the importance of what I'm saying. We both get back into the car, and I put us back on the road.

After a few seconds of uncomfortable silence, Rebecca breaks the tension. "So ... cat's eye."

"There must be something to it," I surmise. "We've both heard it now, each in the other's voice. We just have to keep our eyes open for anything that sounds suspicious."

"Well, *that* narrows it down," she says, sounding defeated.

"Something tells me when we need to know it, we'll know it."

The miles pass uneventfully as we head south through Mississippi. The highway is surrounded by stately old trees, growing out of a rich red clay soil. Traffic is very light all day long, and we are able to cross into Louisiana in the late afternoon. Unless things take a turn, we should arrive in New Orleans around 6:30 in the evening.

The lull in the conversation has given me ample opportunity to contemplate this assignment. As is often the case, I don't know everything about what will transpire, just enough to warn the victim, who can then make her own decision about whether to avoid the situation. The details are particularly disturbing this time. This policewoman's life is definitely in danger if she isn't warned, because of a dangerous criminal she's been tracking. But by warning her, am I sentencing this criminal to die? And if so, am I okay with that? He was clearly going to kill her. Once upon a time, I was content to believe that things happen for a reason. Sometimes people die, and there's nothing anyone can do about it. Except me, apparently. When I started getting the assignments, I did a lot of soul-searching. Am I upsetting the natural course of events? Am I correcting mistakes in fate? Am I a second chance for people who are on a karmic waiting list? When the assignments didn't stop, I tried very hard to stop thinking about it.

Tonight, I won't push. I'll deliver my message and allow the detective to decide for herself if it's true. And I won't let myself feel any guilt if she decides to ignore it.

We cross the long bridge over Lake Pontchartrain, the very waters that overflowed into the city during Hurricane Katrina, laying waste to thousands of homes, taking some lives, ruining others. Where was the messenger then to come and warn this city of its impending peril? Why would the 11,000 people of Cedarsburg, Kansas be given a chance of salvation, while hundreds of thousands in New Orleans were left to their fate? Religious fundamentalists at the time tried to say that Katrina was God's punishment of New Orleans for its sinful ways. That kind of talk sickened me. New Orleans's sins may have been public and purchasable, but they were no more wicked than the sins of Cedarsburg or anywhere else, for that matter.

"Welcome to New Orleans," I say to my passengers as we finally enter the city limits. I've been driving for eleven hours today, and I'm feeling it. I know I should be sharing the driving with Rebecca, but ever since she learned that she had to be twenty-five to be on the rental car contract, she's been gun-shy about being behind the wheel.

"So where exactly are we headed?" she asks.

"District Eight headquarters, in the heart of the French Quarter," I reply. "And, lucky us, we get to be here on a Saturday night. I think you'll understand if I ask you to stay in the car and keep it locked."

"Uh, yeah."

Traffic picks up as we get into the city, particularly as we cross the Central Business District and enter the French Quarter. Though I still have a few hours to warn this person, I just want to be there and be done with it, so we can get back to where we should be. A little dinner would be good; New Orleans has some fine restaurants. Maybe a hotel—a proper hotel—outside of the city tonight. Business first; no time to think of anything else now.

Following the directions in my head, I turn onto Conti Street and follow it to Royal. Eighth District headquarters is right at the corner, in the heart of the Quarter. One would think it would inspire better behavior from the neighborhood's visitors. All it really means is that the miscreants have a shorter distance to travel when they get caught.

Given the location, I dread the parking prospects, but I am pleasantly surprised to see a couple of spots reserved for police department visitors only. I pull into one of them and shut off the Sebring. "This is it," I tell the others.

"Be careful," Rebecca replies. "Be as quick as you can, okay?"

"I will. You two do what you can to draw as little attention to yourselves as possible. I'll leave you the car keys. If I'm not back in …

let's say twenty minutes, take the car and go somewhere else. I'll try to find you by phone."

"Good luck," Cassie offers.

"Thanks. I might need it."

Fighting back the anxiety I feel, I walk up the steps to the front door of the building. Through the glass doors, I can see that the squad room is busy. Saturday night means lots of work for this group, I suspect. The person I'm looking for might not even be in. But that's not true; I know she's in, because this is where I was told to go. With a deep breath, I open the door and go inside.

There is a central desk with a sergeant behind it, a middle-aged man who is currently entering information into his computer. He looks up as I approach. "Can I help you?" he asks.

"Um, yes. May I speak to Captain Bronwyn Kelsey, please?"

"Do you have an appointment, sir?"

"No. No I don't. But if she's available, it's important that I speak to her. I have some information that's relevant to an ongoing criminal investigation, and I'd like to share it with her. Please."

He looks at me, probably deciding that I'm not dangerous (at least I hope so), and then picks up his phone and dials an extension. "Cap, there's a man out here says he wants to talk to you.… Says he has info on an investigation.… Don't know; he didn't say.… Okay, thanks." He hangs up and tells me, "Wait here, please."

I maintain my composure, hoping that the delay isn't a bad sign, that someone hasn't recognized me and they're coming to lock me up. In less than a minute, a woman emerges from a back office. From the details of the assignment, I know that this is Bronwyn Kelsey. She appears to be in her mid-forties, with a hint of world-weariness to her otherwise powerful features. She is what I would call a handsome woman, but in a complimentary way.

She approaches me at the desk. "I'm Captain Kelsey, Mister …?"

"Thompson. Paul Thompson. Thank you for seeing me."

"Let's go back to my office."

She leads me through the squad room to a corner office with frosted glass walls atop ancient wood paneling. On the door is a nameplate that reads Capt. Bronwyn Kelsey. After I enter, she closes the door behind me and offers me a seat in front of her desk. "Can I get you some water or coffee or something?" she asks.

"No, thank you."

"Sergeant Jacobs tells me you have information for me about an investigation. Is that correct?"

"Yes, ma'am."

"Well, Mr. Thompson, NOPD is always grateful for tips. If you're interested in reward money, though, you'll want to go through Crimestoppers."

"No, it's nothing like that. It's more ..." *Time for the speech.* "Captain, you may find this hard to believe, but I promise you it's true. I sometimes receive visions about people who are in trouble or in danger, and when I'm able to, I go to these people and warn them about the danger. Yesterday, I saw you in one of my visions, and in that vision, just before 11:00 tonight, a man you've been pursuing is going to catch you by surprise and kill you. I'm very sorry."

To my surprise, she takes this news very calmly and rationally. "I see. These visions that you get—I'm assuming that because you make the effort to warn these people, the events you foresee can be changed, is that correct?"

"Yes, it is. You believe me, then?"

"Mr. Thompson, I've been a police officer in New Orleans for ten years. You see a lot of strange things living in this city. I don't know you, so I don't know of any reason why you would want to hurt me. You sound calm and rational, so I don't think you're suffering from any delusions. So I have to go based on the belief that for whatever reason, you can see things that haven't happened yet, and you've come here to warn me."

"Yes," I reply, quite relieved. "Thank you for believing me. I've driven about fifteen hours to give you this message." *Oh, shit, why did I tell her that?*

"Fifteen hours?" she repeats with surprise in her voice. "That's a huge trip. Why didn't you phone me?"

"I've found that for the most important messages, people are most inclined to believe me in person. Besides, for better or worse, this is what I've chosen to do with my life."

"What else can you tell me?" she asks. "What did you see in your vision?"

"Usually it's a combination of images and facts that are sent to me. I knew it was you; you were identified by name, and I was told where to find you. I know it's a man who will try to kill you, but I don't know his name. All I know is that he's someone you've been looking for, probably for quite some time, but he doesn't know who you are."

She looks fascinated at this. "Do you know where this is supposed to happen?"

"I received some images in my mind, but they were very dark and it was hard to see. I saw grass and some trees, and what looked like statuary. But the weird part is, I got the feeling I was indoors. And then there was a name."

"A name?"

"It may have been the name of the place, but I don't speak French, so I don't know what the words mean: Champ des Douleurs."

For the first time since I've met her, Bronwyn Kelsey looks upset by what I have said. "Oh my God," she says quietly.

"What? Does that name mean something to you? What do the words mean?"

"They mean Field of Sorrows. I think I know who was in your vision. It's him. It's Kalfu."

"Kalfu?"

Snapping out of her momentary distraction, she looks squarely at me. "Mr. Thompson, what I'm going to tell you is confidential police business and can't be shared with anyone else. Do you understand?"

"Yes," I reply, curious why she'd be telling me.

"For the past two months, the New Orleans Police have been searching for a serial rapist and killer. Every lead has come up dry. He's eluded us at every turn. Detectives at Third District started calling him Kalfu, a name of a powerful spirit out of local folklore. It sounds like this is him. But if he doesn't know who I am, why would he want to kill me?"

"From what I've seen, you'll be called out to this place, this Field of Sorrows, for a report of suspicious activity, and that's where he'll be."

"Suspicious activity? Why call a police captain from another district out on a suspicious activity call? Someone must suspect this is an active lead."

"All I know is what I saw in my vision."

"At that time of night, it must be where he hides out. Maybe where he lives. I'll be damned. All this time looking for him …"

"What is the place?" I ask.

"An experiment from the days before Katrina. An experiment that worked for a while, until people left the city en masse. Now it's still open, but it's fallen into such disuse, almost no one goes there."

"Now that you know, I'm hoping you won't go out there tonight."

"I wish it was that simple," she replies. "This is an incredible opportunity. I know where and when he'll be. This man has raped and killed eleven high school girls that we know of. Three others are missing. If I can go there and apprehend him, I could save so many lives and bring closure to the grieving families."

"Just please be careful. Bring plenty of backup with you."

"I wish I could, Paul. This guy is smart. If we storm the place, he'll run and we'll never see him. But if I go in there by myself and I surprise him …"

"He could still very well kill you," I answer.

"Yeah," she says solemnly. "He could. I don't suppose your gifts extend to reading people's thoughts, do they?"

"No, I'm afraid not," I say. I am perfectly content to leave it at that, not offering her anything else, but then I see the picture on her desk. A five-by-seven in a wooden frame, it shows the smiling face of a little girl looking right at the camera.

She sees me looking at the picture and holds it up for me. "That's my daughter. She'll be six in three weeks. I'm raising her by myself, which isn't easy with my job, but I have friends who help out."

"She's lovely," I say, trying not to choke up at the thought of this child growing up without a mother. "What's her name?"

"Miranda," she says.

And with that single name, any resolve I had left dissolves utterly, leaving no doubt that I will help this stranger, this Bronwyn Kelsey, to catch this horrible man, using any resource at my disposal. All because this woman's child happens to have the same first name as someone I couldn't save.

"Captain, I know this will sound strange, but my friend—my … girlfriend—does have the gift of reading people's thoughts. She's still learning to use it, but I suspect that she would be able to help you track this man."

"Paul, that's … I don't even have words for how incredible that is, but I could never ask civilians to put their lives at risk in such a dangerous situation. Thank you, but I just couldn't."

"Remember when I told you it's what I do? I meant it. Three days ago, a tornado tore through Cedarsburg, Kansas. My friend and I were there, because I was warned about it ahead of time and told to get as many people to safety as I could."

At these words, she stares at me in amazement. "I saw that on CNN. A huge tornado destroyed most of the town, but almost everyone got out safely because they had advance warning. That was you?"

"Yes. We risked our lives to save theirs. Miranda can't grow up without her mother. We'll help you catch him, both of us. But to do that, there's something we need in return. A favor that I need you to do for us."

"If it's within my power to do, I'll do it," she says.

And so Bronwyn Kelsey sits patiently, listening as I tell her the story of Cassie Haiduk and the drive to Florida, and the Amber Alert. I leave out the part about the plot to blow up the school; it was thwarted, so there's no need to cast suspicion over Cassie. The detective takes this all in, listening carefully to the remarkable circumstances of the last two days. When I finish, she pauses to take a breath, then pulls a piece of paper off her bulletin board. At the top are the words "Amber Alert." A chill runs up my spine.

"It came in yesterday," Bronwyn says. "Given how far we are from Chicago, I haven't expended any manpower toward it. Just kind of a 'keep your eyes open' situation. I may be able to help you, but you have to understand what a chance I'm taking. You're wanted for kidnapping, and all I have to go on is your word that it isn't true."

"Captain, if it were true, believe me, the last place I'd be right now is a police station, telling you all about it. I'll let you meet Rebecca and Cassie. Cassie can tell you for herself that we mean her no harm."

"Paul ..."

I interrupt her. "That's not my real name. I'm Tristan. Tristan Shays. I usually give people a different name when I warn them, so they don't track me down later. But I figure it's important that you trust me, so there it is. Would you like me to bring them in?"

"No, not here. I don't want someone out there seeing the three of you together and figuring it out. There's a place where we can go and talk about this, just a few blocks from here."

"What about the Amber Alert?"

"I don't have the power to cancel it. That happens when the child is found or the person who requested it notifies authorities that it's no longer needed. But ... and I can't believe I'm actually saying this ... I have friends at the Gary, Indiana P.D. I can offer a bit of misdirection for a day or two, to keep local authorities off your tail as you head to Florida."

"Thank you," I reply with a relieved sigh. "Won't you get in trouble for doing that, though?"

"I could, yes. Most of the time, I try to do things strictly by the book. But twenty years in police work have taught me that sometimes you have to put the book aside. I think this is one of those times."

"I'm grateful to you," I tell her.

"My help is contingent on you promising to return her home when all of this is over."

"Of course. I promise. I want to see her reunited with her family too."

"Where are Rebecca and Cassie?"

"Outside in the car."

She rises and I follow. "Let's go get them. We can walk to our destination."

We leave her office and cross back through the squad room. She stops at the front desk. "Sergeant, I'm checking out for the night, following up on a lead. If I'm needed, you can page me. But if I don't respond, it's because I'll be in pursuit of a suspect. I also need you to get me some inter-district backup standing by in case I need them."

"Yes, ma'am. Where will you be? What district?"

"Algiers," she answers.

"Yes, ma'am. I'll get word to them. Good night, Captain. Be careful."

"Will do."

She escorts me outside, and I lead the way to the Sebring. I see Rebecca through the window, and she looks panicked to see me return accompanied. I tap the side of my head, encouraging her to read my thoughts, which tell her, *It's all right; it's safe. Come on out of the car.*

My message gets through, because moments later, Rebecca unlocks the doors and encourages Cassie to join her on the sidewalk. "This is Captain Bronwyn Kelsey of the New Orleans Police Department," I tell them. "I'd like to introduce Rebecca and Cassie."

"Nice to meet you both," Bronwyn says. "Cassie, I have to ask you an important question now, and I want you to know that you're absolutely safe, no matter what you answer. Are you here with these two people entirely by choice, of your own free will?"

"Yes," she answers without hesitation. Then she turns to me. "Tristan, what—"

"It's all right," I answer. "I've told Captain Kelsey about our situation. About how you're taking time off of school to go help your father. She knows about the Amber Alert, and she's going to help us."

"Tristan …" Rebecca begins.

"It's okay. We all trust each other. She's going to help us … and we're going to help her."

"Go ahead and lock the car," Bronwyn instructs. "We're going someplace close so we can talk. It's about three blocks down Royal Street. Follow me."

She leads the way down one of the quieter streets of the French Quarter. The bars of Bourbon Street are a few blocks away, and the sound of jazz and zydeco music comes from the distance, getting louder in spots where buildings aren't blocking it. Along Royal Street are boutiques and art galleries and antique shops. Most are closed at this hour. On the 600 block of Royal, she pauses in front of a store bearing the name The Age of Gaia on an old-fashioned sign. In the window are various new-age items—candles, powders, crystals. A sign says "closed," but the lights are still on, and I can see a woman inside, straightening up. Bronwyn knocks on the door and the woman looks up. Recognizing her, she comes to the front door and unlocks it.

"Bronwyn," the woman says, "I didn't expect to see you tonight. Is everything all right?"

"Iris, I'm sorry to bother you, but I needed a private place to talk with these people. May we come in and talk in your store?"

"Of course. You look like it's important."

"It is. I may be able to capture Kalfu tonight."

The shopkeeper lets out an audible gasp. "Oh my gods, really? Please, come in."

We enter, and the door is locked behind us. Bronwyn makes the introductions. "This is Iris Aiello. She owns this store. Iris, this is Tristan, Rebecca, and Cassie. They've got information that might just help me catch him."

"That's wonderful," Iris says. "I'll leave you alone so you can talk."

"No, don't. What they have to say is right up your alley."

Iris gathers chairs for everyone, and we sit in a circle in the middle of the store. Bronwyn tells the group what she knows. "Tonight, Tristan came to me with information he saw in a vision. A man I've been pursuing for two months is going to kill me." Iris puts her hands to her mouth at this. "Or at least he would have, without this information. Based on what Tristan tells me, it's Kalfu."

"Kalfu?" Rebecca asks.

Bronwyn starts, "It's …"

"The supreme evil spirit in the voodoo religion," Cassie finishes. When the rest of us look at her with surprise, she says, "What? I read a lot."

"It's a name some of the local police gave him," Bronwyn explains, "because we don't know who he is. He's a very very dangerous man. One I want off the streets desperately. Until now, I haven't had a clue where to find him. Now I know where he'll be, and I'm going after him. Tristan saw the place where he'll be tonight, and I think it's a place he's been hiding out."

"Where is it?" Iris asks.

"He's at Champ des Douleurs."

"Oh, Bronwyn, no. You can't go there. There's so much dangerous energy there."

Rebecca interjects, "What is this place?"

"It's a cemetery," Bronwyn replies. "On the other side of the river, in the neighborhood called Algiers. It's in a rough area. The cemeteries of New Orleans are tourist attractions, but they're also notorious for crime. So about fifteen years ago, the city took an enormous warehouse in Algiers and created an indoor cemetery. We can't do in-ground burials in this city. Most people are interred in mausoleums. Champ des Douleurs was engineered by a film crew to look like a park, with realistic artificial trees and grass. The warehouse had some areas with storage vaults under the floor, so people could choose mausoleums or under-floor burial for their loved ones. And in the beginning, it looked beautiful."

"What happened?" Cassie asks.

"Neglect. Burial there was very expensive, and people couldn't afford it. After a few years, the owners went bankrupt, and the company that took over let things go. They stayed open, but things like security guards and cameras fell by the wayside. Pretty soon, Champ des Douleurs was as dangerous as any cemetery in New Orleans. After Katrina, so many people left New Orleans, and the place was mostly ignored. Because people are buried there, they have to keep it open regular hours or have all the bodies moved out. But that was too expensive. So there it sits, unique, brilliant in its design, and terrifying to almost everybody."

"And this man," Rebecca says, "this … Kalfu is there?"

"If Tristan is right, yes."

It's time for me to ask. "Rebecca, Bronwyn believes that she can capture this man if you and I go in there with her. She thinks you'll be able to know what he's thinking, and that will help her stay one step ahead of him."

She blanches visibly at the suggestion. "Go in after him?"

"Yes. If you'd be willing. We'd have the advantage. He's not expecting us. He thinks the police have no idea where he is or who he is. And until tonight, he was right."

"What did this guy do?" Cassie inquires.

Quietly and matter-of-factly, Bronwyn answers, "He's raped and murdered eleven girls between the ages of fourteen and seventeen. There are three others who are missing; we're hoping they're still alive."

"And it'll just be us against him?" Rebecca asks.

"I'll be armed. And I've arranged to have backup available on a moment's notice."

"Can't we have the backup there when we arrive?" I ask.

She shakes her head. "This guy's a rabbit. If he senses trouble, he'll run and hide, and we may lose our chance to catch him. So we have to do this covertly. At least until there's no chance for him to escape."

Rebecca thinks about it for a short while. "My being there will really make a difference?"

"It could be the difference between catching him and letting him kill again," Bronwyn answers.

"Okay, I'm in."

"Thank you," the detective says. "Iris, would you please keep Cassie here with you until we …"

"No," Cassie interrupts.

"What do you mean, *no?*" I ask her.

"I mean I'm going with you."

"Absolutely not."

"Tristan's right," Bronwyn says. "It's dangerous enough bringing civilians with me on this. To include a minor who's in this man's exact target group—"

"Is exactly the point of my being there," Cassie says. "This asshole is raping and killing girls my age. If you want to catch him by surprise, you need to distract him. And the best way to distract him … is with bait."

"Cassie," Rebecca says, "that is the most selfless thing I've ever heard. But it's also very risky. This man could do unspeakable things to you. You don't have to do this."

"Yes I do, Rebecca. I've had a lot of time to think while we drove down here. I was prepared to do something pretty unspeakable myself yesterday."

"What's she referring to?" Bronwyn asks.

"Nothing," I chime in. "Tell ya later."

Cassie continues. "I've got some things to atone for, and if I can help you catch him, I think I'll be a lot closer to doing so. How about it, Captain Kelsey? I'm right, aren't I? I'm your best chance of catching him."

Bronwyn quietly admits, "This goes against every fiber of my better judgment and every police procedure in place. But she's right. If Cassie can distract this man, I can apprehend him."

"Then what are we waiting for?" Cassie says. "Let's nail this son of a bitch to the wall."

Chapter 3

"I need to stop back at the station," Bronwyn says. "I want us to be in radio contact with each other, and I have some headsets that will work. We should take my car to the cemetery." She pauses a moment and then says, "It's not too late to change your minds. No one will think less of you if you don't want to be a part of this."

"We're in," Rebecca says. "Usually when Tristan gets an assignment, it's because our being there can make a difference. This guy sounds like trouble, and the four of us working together have a better chance of taking him down."

"Thank you," she replies. "Iris, thank you for letting us talk here."

"Of course," Iris answers. "Just please be careful."

"We will. I'll let you know tomorrow what happens."

We walk the three blocks back to the police station with Captain Kelsey and wait outside while she goes in to get the headsets. A few minutes later, she emerges with what looks like four small Bluetooth earbuds and hands us each one. "They're discreet," she explains, "and if someone sees them, they look like telephone equipment."

She leads us to her personal vehicle, a late-model Ford Taurus parked behind the building, and opens it up for us. I take shotgun—the seat, not the weapon—while the ladies pile into the back seat. A turn of the key and we are on our way, hopefully not to a horrible death.

"Is there a plan?" I ask as she navigates through the streets of the French Quarter.

"When we get there," Bronwyn says, "I want us to split up. Tristan, you and I will pose as a couple, coming to visit a loved one. Rebecca, you and Cassie will be another pair on a similar purpose. You can be sisters or friends, whatever you like. We'll hang back along the perimeter of the building, leaving the two women to their own devices. Rebecca, I want you to use your abilities to try to find this man and get close to where he's hiding in the building. Tristan and I will be far enough away that we can see you but we won't dissuade Kalfu from making a move on Cassie."

"And if he does?" Rebecca asks.

"I'll be on him in seconds."

"That still gives him plenty of time to hurt or even kill Cassie," I remind her.

"Remember what this man does," Bronwyn says. "He's a rapist and a killer."

"That's so comforting."

"No, Tristan, that's not what I mean. He doesn't just want to kill these girls. He wants to keep them, use them for his own purposes, and then kill them. He'll see Cassie as a prize."

"I'd really love to change the subject," Cassie offers at this point, in a tone armed with sarcasm to mask the fear she must be feeling.

"I'm sorry," Bronwyn says. "I know this is frightening, but our best chance of success is if we're all on the same page, working together."

During our conversation, we have made our way to the banks of the Mississippi River, and we are currently in line to board a motor ferry to the other side. The boat arrives, we pay our dollar, drive into the lower level, and all exit the car to go topside for the short trip across the river. There are few other passengers on the boat at this hour, so we can talk privately as we stand at the rail, looking at the lights of the city.

"Do you think you can take him alive?" Rebecca asks Bronwyn.

"I'm going to try. Primarily because I want to know if those three other girls are still alive somewhere. But also because I prefer not to use deadly force. I shouldn't have that much power; no officer should. If he gives me no choice, I'll use it. But I want this night to end with an arrest, and let the courts determine his fate."

The conversation is sobering, and no one knows quite what to say. Bronwyn breaks the silence with a moment of practicality. "The three of you, please go to different corners of the boat and let's test the headsets."

Rebecca and I go aft, she to port, I to starboard, while Cassie crosses to the fore starboard side. "Testing," Bronwyn says. "Can you hear me?"

"I can," I answer.

"Me too," Cassie says in my ear.

"I hear you fine," Rebecca says.

"Okay, good. Let's head back to the car. We're almost across the river."

We meet back at the car and get in, closing the doors behind us. With no window view in the lower level, it's difficult to tell just where we are, but a thump tells me we've arrived at the opposite shore. And as if on cue, the twelve other cars aboard with us all start up. As the auto gangplank lowers, we make our way off the ferry and onto the streets of a neighborhood known as Algiers. Dusk has given way to night, and the streetlights alone light our way to Champ des Douleurs. I look over at Cassie, trying to get a sense of how she must be feeling as we approach, but her face is inscrutable. I offer a half smile of reassurance, quite sure of how *unsure* I truly look. All I can do is hope that my continuing need to do the right thing doesn't get everyone around me killed.

Bronwyn takes us down street after street, through neighborhoods lacking any hint of affluence. This area appears to have been spared the worst of Katrina's wrath. Nowhere are the familiar post-hurricane sights of houses ruined by water and mold, later marked with spray paint as rescuers searched for the living and the dead. There are many houses for sale, and others that appear to be simply abandoned.

After a few minutes, a large building looms ahead. As we draw near, I begin to realize how very large it is. From the outside, it looks like what it once was—a warehouse, spanning at least a city block on each side. We make our way around to the back, where a huge parking lot sits empty.

"There's nobody here," Cassie says.

"I wish you were right," Bronwyn answers. "Most likely, there's one person here."

"Are they even open?" Rebecca asks.

"Until 10 PM. Then someone comes by to lock up."

This amazes me. "So until that time, there's no attendant, no office workers, no security guards?"

"During the day, maintenance teams keep things clean and orderly," she says, parking the car close but not too close to the entrance. "At night, typically nobody from the staff is here."

We get out of the car and stop in front of a large sign that reads:

> Welcome to Champ des Douleurs Cemetery, New Orleans, Louisiana. This is a place of sacred rest. Please speak in quiet tones and show respect to those who are sheltered here in eternity. For the convenience and comfort of other guests, please observe the following rules. No smoking, no food or drink, no radios, no pets. Please supervise your children and be respectful of all flowers, decorations, and grave markers. For information about funerals and interment, please consult the pamphlet below. Lock your car and please keep all valuables safely stowed away.

I wish the sign also said "No raping or killing of visitors," but no such luck.

"Let's get in pairs and get in character," Bronwyn says. "We don't get any rehearsal."

We take a few more steps toward the entrance when suddenly Rebecca loses her balance and begins to pitch forward. Fortunately, I am there to catch her, but even when her balance returns, she seems too weak to stand.

"What is it?" I ask. "What's wrong?"

"I was just overcome with the most terrible feeling of … I don't even know how to describe it. Darkness, maybe. Evil. I know that sounds hokey, but I don't know any other word for it. The closer we got to the building, the stronger it got."

Bronwyn looks around. "He's here. I'm sure of it now. Let's go in."

As the door opens, I brace myself for a bad smell; I'm not sure why, but I expect one. What I inhale is not nearly as bad as I'd feared. It is musty and a bit stale, but not rank with death. But what truly surprises me is the beauty. Champ des Douleurs looks like a cemetery, like a stately old parklike cemetery you would find in any city in America. The film crew that designed it did astonishing work. Rather than stadium-grade artificial turf, the ground is covered with a soft green layer that looks and feels—at least through shoes—like grass. Artificial trees of a dozen varieties are spread throughout the building, along with faux shrubs and flower beds. Mixed into this landscape are the inhabitants, some in small mausoleums, others interred under the floor, their resting places marked with headstones. Statues dot the cemetery as well, some of children, others of Jesus. An angel weeps over a grave, her wings held low with sorrow.

In its prime, the place must have been magnificent, a resting place for those of privilege, whose loved ones wanted only the best for them. But now, time and disuse are taking their toll, and decay is creeping in. There are chips in headstones and statues, rust on the iron works of some of the mausoleums, damage to trees and flowers.

The part that is most disturbing is the light. I can see that the goal was simulated natural light, combined with actual sunlight coming in from high windows. But many of the lighting instruments have dimmed or failed, and the cemetery has about half the light it needs, which gives someone plenty of shadows where he can hide.

It is time to split up. Rebecca takes a deep breath to steel herself, and she and Cassie walk away from us, away from the entrance, deeper into the rows of graves. Bronwyn and I stop at the grave of someone named Gerard Moncrief. I don't know who he was, and at the moment, I don't care. All I know is that his monument is large enough that we can watch the others and still remain partially hidden.

Rebecca and Cassie continue forward, a hundred feet from me, then two hundred, then three hundred. "That's far enough," Bronwyn instructs quietly. "Find a grave, and pretend to be visiting it."

The women stop at a headstone near a row of mausoleums and stand over it.

"Rebecca, can you tell if he's near?" Bronwyn asks.

Her voice returns in our headsets. "I feel something. It's so awful. It has to be him." After a few seconds, she adds, "Oh my God, he sees us. I know he sees us. What do I do?"

"Stay calm. Just stay calm. Remain in character. Now, I want you to wander away from Cassie. Maybe ten or twenty feet. Cassie, I want you to let her do that. Don't follow her."

"You want us to split up?" Rebecca asks, clearly disturbed at the prospect. "I've seen enough horror movies. I know how that ends."

"I want him to make a move on Cassie, and I don't think he'll do that if the two of you are together. My guess is he'll leave you alone and go toward Cassie."

"And then you'll get him, right?" Cassie asks, concern in her voice.

"Yes. Right away."

"Okay," Rebecca says in a whisper. "Walking away."

Everything happens in a flash. Rebecca gets no more than twenty feet away from Cassie when, in a blur of motion, a dark-clad figure emerges near Rebecca and grabs her from behind. On my headset, I hear Rebecca start to shout out, but it is almost instantly muffled, and then there is silence. Instinctively I rise, a gasp escaping my lips, but Bronwyn acts quickly, holding me back in our hiding place and signaling for me not to speak. She quickly mutes my headset as well as her own.

"We have to help her," I whisper.

"Not yet. I've lost sight of him. We have to wait until he moves for Cassie."

"But Rebecca—he might have hurt her."

"No, I don't think so."

"What if he cut her throat?"

"We would've heard that on the headsets. I know the sound it makes. My guess is he chloroformed her and put her somewhere. I promise you we'll find her. For now, let's concentrate on finding *him*."

I look back at Cassie, who remains at the grave, either unaware of Rebecca's disappearance or so deep in character that she isn't betraying a thing in her facial expression. With Rebecca's headset now potentially in the hands of our quarry, we can't talk to Cassie any further; for the moment, she's on her own.

Out of the corner of my eye, I see the dark-clad figure return. Rebecca is nowhere in sight. I don't see any blood on him, so I have to hold out hope that he hasn't harmed her in any way. Bronwyn sees him too; she tracks him as he returns to the area where Cassie is standing. I finally get a good look at him. He's tall, probably six-four, with shoulder-length dark brown hair and pale skin. From this distance, I can't tell if his appearance is natural or made up to inspire fear in his victims. But it makes him look like a ghoul or grave robber, and it certainly inspires fear in me.

"It's time," Bronwyn whispers to me, drawing her revolver. "Stay back where it's safe."

She emerges from our vantage point when the man is just a few steps away from Cassie, who has not yet seen him. Weapon held high in front of her, Bronwyn announces, "New Orleans Police! You're under arrest. Step away from the girl."

I follow a few steps behind her, in case I am needed.

At the sound of Bronwyn's voice, the killer produces a large knife and grabs Cassie, who emits a cry of surprise. He stands behind her, in a cowardly but completely expected reaction to his threatened capture.

"Kalfu!" Bronwyn calls to him, stopping less than ten feet in front of him. "It's over. Knife versus gun. You know you can't win this."

At last, he speaks. I expect something dissonant and otherworldly to emerge, but his voice is a rich baritone, almost soothing, were it not for the words. "You know what they call me, so you know what I am."

"I know what you *think* you are," she replies boldly. "You may be doing the devil's work, but I assure you, if these bullets hit you, you'll die like a human. It doesn't have to end that way, though. Let the girl go. Tell me where the three missing ones are, and I'll talk to the D.A. about cutting you a deal. Maybe no death penalty. Life without parole."

"Don't dangle your deals in front of me," he scoffs. "Deals are made by someone who's won. You haven't won. You're in *my* house. And I saw you from the moment you entered. You're still alive because I let you live."

"One call, and twenty cops are all over this building. Your house or not, you're either leaving it in handcuffs or a bag. Where are the missing girls?"

He smiles a sickening grin and says, "They're already here. I'm done with them. So much for your deal."

"Shit," Bronwyn mutters.

Kalfu runs his fingers through Cassie's hair. "There's always this one. She's not as pretty as I like, but she'll do."

"Fuck you," Cassie retorts, shaking her head to get his hand off of her.

"Mouthy," he observes. "I like it. They're usually so timid. I think I'll enjoy this one."

"There's no way out of this," Bronwyn tells him. "Don't make me kill you tonight. Let this girl go, and tell me where the bodies of the other three are, and I *will* speak to the district attorney about clemency."

"You just don't give up, do you? Haven't you figured out yet that you can't hurt me?"

To my complete surprise, it is Cassie who responds. "Yeah? Well maybe I can." And with that, she holds out her left hand and sprays her captor in the face with a small canister she was concealing. It is not a direct hit, but enough of it reaches his eyes that he releases her and takes two staggering steps backward. Cassie uses the opportunity to run from there, standing behind Bronwyn and me.

Kalfu's eyes are now bright red from the spray as he looks at the new, less hopeful scenario. I'm silently praying that he will give up peacefully, absent any good options, but Cassie's attack has inspired rage in him. "Little whore!" he roars, his words echoing through the cavernous space. As he takes a charging step forward, I brace myself and cover Cassie as best I can with my body.

The loudest sound I have ever heard fills my head as two explosive shots emerge from Captain Bronwyn Kelsey's firearm. I look up just in time to see the shots strike Kalfu in the chest. He drops the knife and stumbles backward a few steps. Ahead of him, Bronwyn stands resolute, ready to fire again if necessary. I'm sincerely hoping she doesn't. Seconds pass as this hated figure struggles to cling to life.

Finally, he trips over a low grave marker behind him, striking his head on another next to it as he hits the ground.

Instantly, Bronwyn takes out her phone and presses two buttons. "Officer needs assistance. Suspect down. This is Captain Bronwyn Kelsey. I'm at Champ des Douleurs Cemetery in Algiers. Code six. Please send backup and ambulance."

She puts the phone away. "They're on their way. Cassie, are you all right?"

"Yeah, thanks to this," she says, holding up a canister of pepper spray.

"You did great," Bronwyn tells her.

"We have to find Rebecca," I interject.

"You two go look for her," the detective says. "I'll check on the suspect."

As Bronwyn goes over to the killer's motionless form, I scan the surroundings, hoping to find Rebecca. I call loudly to her. "Rebecca!"

Cassie joins in. "Rebecca! Where are you? We got him!"

"Rebecca!"

I hear her voice, faintly but very close, and I realize that she is speaking in my headset. I turn off the mute and speak to her through it. "Honey, I'm here. Do you know where you are?"

"I'm not sure," she says faintly. "I'm inside something. It's dark, and it smells awful in here."

"Keep talking," I tell her. "Try to figure out where you are."

As I walk through row after row, she tries to get a sense of where she is. "It's small, and the walls feel like brick or stone." Then it hits her. "Oh, God, I'm in a mausoleum, aren't I?"

"Stay calm."

"Shit, it *is* a mausoleum. I gotta get out of here."

"I'm trying to find you. Now, chances are he didn't have time to lock you in, so I want you to try to make your way to the door and see if you can get it open."

"Okay," she says. "I'm getting up." I hear her shuffling around for a few seconds. "I think I found the door." She pushes against it and then reports, "I can't open it. It's either locked or stuck."

"Is it made of metal?" I ask.

"Yes."

41

"Pound on it as hard as you can."

I hear the pounding, first through the headset, then resounding through the building. I turn and head quickly in that direction. "I hear you. Keep pounding."

After a few more seconds, I find the mausoleum where she is being kept. The killer has leaned a heavy headstone against the door to keep Rebecca inside.

"This is it, this is it," I tell Cassie. "Help me move this." She and I strain together to move the bulky object. The fact that Kalfu was able to move it by himself tells me how strong he is. The stone falls to the side, and I open the latch to the mausoleum door.

The door swings out, letting the muted light into the mausoleum. Rebecca dashes out and into my arms, and the smell that follows her out is unbearable. The chloroform must have subdued her sense of smell temporarily, otherwise she would not have been able to stand it. *She wasn't alone in there.*

"Thank you so much," she says, not even looking behind her. I'm glad she doesn't, because I don't want her to see what she's just come out of. I take her headset from her.

Cassie obviously smells the same thing I do, and she cranes her head to look inside. "Don't," I caution her quietly. "You don't want to look in there."

As Rebecca sits on a nearby bench, I take a few steps away and softly tell Bronwyn via headset, "We need you over here. I found the three missing girls."

"Stay where you are," she instructs. "Backup is on the way. They'll take care of it. I need to stay with our suspect."

"Is he alive?" I ask, fearing an affirmative answer.

"He's still breathing, but just barely. He's been unconscious the whole time. I don't think he's going to last much longer."

"So it's over?" I ask.

"Yeah. It's over. Is everybody there all right?"

"Plenty shaken up," I answer. "But not hurt."

Within five minutes, the sirens approach. Police backup units storm the building with weapons drawn, but Bronwyn orders them to stand down; the scene is secure. She directs a half dozen of them over to the mausoleum where Kalfu's final three unfortunate victims lie, in a state too horrible to describe.

Flanked by Rebecca and Cassie, I make my way back over to Bronwyn Kelsey, who is standing at the site of the shooting. She is busy with two plainclothes officers as we approach. A uniformed officer stands watch over the suspect until the paramedics can arrive. I steer clear of the supine form, but Rebecca ventures too close. She lets out a gasp of surprise as Kalfu's hand shoots out and grabs her firmly by the ankle. The motion is unnaturally swift, so much so that no one who witnesses it knows what to do. The most disturbing part of all is that the suspect himself remains unconscious, fighting for his last few breaths. Yet his grip is relentless, and Rebecca cannot get free.

I start to move toward them, but Bronwyn holds me back. I manage to get the words "Somebody do something!" out, but before anyone can move to help, Rebecca speaks. But not exactly. Her mouth moves and words come out, but they are clearly not hers. Her expression is miles away, and the voice that comes out of her is deep, distant.

"Hamesh, born of Hosea," it says.

"I'm here," I reply. I can feel all eyes on me as I calmly engage in this dialogue.

"You go to battle. Why do you tarry here?"

"To save this woman's life," I reply, gesturing toward Bronwyn.

"She is far more capable than you. Look to your own life."

"Who are you?" I ask. "I demand to know who's speaking to me. Tell me your name."

Rebecca's mouth curls into a grotesque parody of a smile. "Legion."

"Cut the biblical shit and tell me who you are!"

"We are many. We know what awaits you in your quest."

"Really? What awaits us, then? Enlighten me."

"The death of you all."

It's what I was afraid I'd hear, but I can't show that fear. Not without knowing what I'm dealing with. "I'm not afraid to die for this cause," I declare.

"No, not for yourself. I know what you fear. Her thoughts are mine now. You fear *their* deaths. The woman and the child. The brutalities that await you, which you cannot stop. You fear cat's eye."

"What do you know about that?" I ask the voice. "What does it mean?"

"It is in here with us, and it will destroy you. The sins of the father, revisited upon the child. He waits. He knows you are coming."

Cassie looks upset at these words, so I try to change the subject. "Why did you use this man to rape and kill children?"

"For the same reason you got into a car to come to this place," the voice retorts calmly. "It was a convenient vehicle to take you where you needed to go. I assure you, he enjoyed it. Come closer. Let us touch you. You can experience it for yourself."

"Yeah, I'll pass on that, thanks. I think it's time you let Rebecca go too."

"Soon," it replies.

"Your little vehicle there is almost out of gas, and I'm not going to lose any sleep over it either. Now let her go, and let us get on our way."

"You can turn back. You've done your heroic deed. Go home and don't interfere. Events will proceed as they should, with or without you. Go home and live, or go to battle and face certain death."

And with those words, Kalfu's grip loosens on Rebecca's ankle. Her eyes flutter and she begins to fall forward. Cassie and I hurriedly support her, easing her to a nearby bench. On the ground, the conduit lets out an agonal groan and a final breath before falling silent. Though I couldn't show it during the confrontation, my heart is racing with fear. I sit on the bench with Rebecca's head supported in my lap as she lies next to me, trying to regain her strength. Cassie hurries over to Bronwyn, who just stares at the killer's body in what appears to be quiet awe.

After many seconds, the officer standing over the body finally blurts out, "Would somebody please tell me what the hell is going on?"

No one leaps up to offer an explanation, probably because no one present could possibly explain it. "It's over," Bronwyn says to the officer and to anyone else who needs to know that. "A very dangerous man is off the streets, and that's what we need to focus on. Gentlemen, gather round, please."

The Algiers District officers huddle in front of Bronwyn. "There's a lot left to do here tonight, and then there's the reports to write. When you write them, stick to the parts you can detail and delineate and explain. When I write my own reports, I'll do the same. Lieutenant Fisk?"

An older plainclothes officer replies, "Yes, Captain?"

"I'm putting you in charge of this part of the process. Close the cemetery to the public and get forensics in here with an evidence team. Collect as much information as you can. I want positive ID on the suspect. The public's going to want a name to put with this news; they won't accept a John Doe."

"Understood."

"I have some civilians here who have had a very long day. I need to get them out of here and into someplace safe. I'll get in touch with you in the morning to coordinate efforts."

"Yes, Captain."

She approaches me on the bench. "How's Rebecca doing?"

"She's pretty out of it," I reply. "But given what just happened, I think that's probably a good thing."

"Do you want her to go to the hospital?"

It is Rebecca who answers. "No, I'm fine. I'm just a little dizzy."

"Welcome back," I say gently. "Are you sure you're all right?"

"I will be. Whoever ... *what*ever that was, it didn't hurt me."

"Do you remember what happened?"

"Every bit of it," she says. "I could feel it sharing my mind and my body. I heard every word it said, and I can remember it like it was my own, but I didn't control any of it."

"I'm just so relieved you're all right," I tell her, stroking her hair.

"Tristan, what *was* that? What just happened here?"

Bronwyn attempts an explanation. "This city has a reputation for alternative religion and spirituality. The cemeteries are sometimes hotbeds of paranormal activity. I'm not a big believer in that sort of thing. I prefer to trust what I can see and hear. But it's hard to deny what I just heard and saw. The best I can figure, something—some spirit—that lives in this place got a hold of our suspect and channeled its thoughts through him."

"Is that what you're going to put in your report?" I ask.

"I doubt it. Division doesn't like to read supernatural stuff. Besides, I think they'll be far more interested in the fact that we took down a serial rapist and killer."

Rebecca sits up on her own. "Are you all right to stand?" I ask.

"Yeah, if I can lean on you a little."

"What are friends for?" I ask with a smile.

Together we make our way out of Champ des Douleurs Cemetery and back to Bronwyn's car. No one speaks as we return to the ferry dock and await the next scheduled river crossing. Once aboard, we get out of the car and head to the upper deck. Bronwyn stays with Cassie to offer comfort after her ordeal. Similarly, I stay close to Rebecca, making sure she's all right.

"You mad at me?" I ask gently.

"No. Why would I be mad?"

"Because I dragged you into a situation where you were knocked unconscious, stashed in a mausoleum, and possessed. Some people would describe that as a less-than-ideal evening."

"Lucky I'm not some people then, huh?"

"I'm just feeling some guilt," I tell her. "Everything I've gotten you into since we met. All you asked me for was a ride to Ohio. And look where it got you."

"It got me," she interrupts, "right where I want to be. You're forgetting the part where I love you. We may not have exchanged the words 'for better or for worse,' but they mean a lot to me. Okay, I've faced some disturbing things, but I've also felt closer to you than I've ever felt to anyone in my life. And things keep telling us that we're together for a reason. I suspect when we get to Florida, we'll find out what that reason is. I want you to be able to focus when we get there, and not be worried about me. Okay?"

"Okay," I answer. "Thank you."

She puts her arms around me, and I hold her tightly. In the midst of the embrace, she sniffs loudly and asks, "What's that smell?"

The chloroform's effects must be wearing off, and her sense of smell is returning. *How can I put this delicately?* "Dead human," I reply.

"Gross," she says. "How did you get that on you?"

"Umm, I didn't. You did. The last three victims were … stashed in the mausoleum with you."

She gags a little at the thought of it. "Oh, that's horrible! Why didn't you tell me?"

"Kind of hoping to avoid this awkward conversation. They were in a back corner, so I don't think you touched them or anything. Just, ahh, had three very quiet roommates for a few minutes while you took a nap."

"I am *so* burning these clothes," she says.

The ferry docks at the Canal Street terminal, and Bronwyn drives us back to the police station, parking her car in the back lot. As we get out, she says, "I can't thank you enough for your part in this. I suppose when I have a minute to stop and think about everything, it'll hit me that you really did save my life tonight."

"You're welcome," I reply. "I'm still not exactly sure why I get these visions, but every time I can help someone, it brings me a little closer to understanding."

"Do you have to leave New Orleans right away?" she asks.

"Not immediately," I answer, "but soon. Tomorrow, probably. We have someplace to be. For tonight, I'm thinking the Hilton by the ferry dock looked pretty nice."

"It is. And I'll talk to my friend in Indiana about steering the Amber Alert clear of your present location. That should buy you a couple of days, anyway."

"Thank you," Rebecca says.

"That ... *thing* back at the cemetery," Bronwyn says, "said you were going into battle. Is that what's waiting for you in Pensacola?"

"I think so," I reply.

"It also said the three of you would be killed. Do what you can to keep that from happening, please."

"We will."

I give her my cell phone number, in case she has questions for us while she's writing her report. She, in turn, gives me her business card, and I program her number into my phone. We bid our goodbyes and go back to the Sebring. It has been a very long day, and proper lodging will make a world of difference. I'll have to use a credit card at this level of hotel, but it occurs to me now—as it should have last night—that despite the multi-state search for us, no one has tied our names to this event. So they might be looking for the kidnappers of Cassie Haiduk, but they're not looking for Tristan Shays.

I hope.

After confirming that Cassie will be all right in a room by herself, I honor her desire for privacy by getting two adjacent rooms this time, utterly unconcerned about the cost. The hotel is clean and bright, the staff friendly and helpful. It is an oasis after this interminable day. With the car in the hotel garage and our luggage in our hands, we make our way to the fifteenth floor and open up our rooms. The picture windows offer a spectacular view of the river. Rebecca and I take it in for about ten seconds, and then simultaneously fall back onto the bed.

Seconds later, Cassie enters the room, with energy I can't even begin to explain. Clearly, we neglected to pull the door shut behind us. "My God, you guys, this place is awesome. Did you see that view? I'm sleeping with the curtains open. I don't care how bright it gets in the morning. I just love that view."

"That's nice," Rebecca says wearily.

"Can I order room service?" Cassie asks.

"Yes," I reply.

"Can we shop for some new clothes tomorrow?"

"Yes."

"Can I get an in-room movie?"

"Yes."

"Can I get stuff from the mini-bar?"

"Yes." I think about it and add, "But not the booze. I'm checking it in the morning."

"Cool. Thanks, you guys." As she exits, she adds, "This place is so much better than the place last night."

I turn to Rebecca. "Who was that?"

"I'm not sure."

"Did we adopt a child and nobody told us?"

"I think that's what happened," she says with a tired smile. "Mind if I take the first shower? You know, to wash the dead people smell off of me?"

"By all means."

She disappears into the bathroom for a good twenty minutes, during which I am alone with the view. I realize that I haven't eaten anything in the last ten hours or so. But the idea of food is more than I can handle right now, so I content myself with a bottle of water from the mini-bar's refrigerator and lie down on the bed. I try not to relive the events of the past twenty-four hours, but they want to play themselves out in my head, and there's little I can do to stop them.

Granted, I've seen some strange things in the last two years since the assignments have started, but until Rebecca came along, I'd never encountered anything so otherworldly. What happened tonight defies explanation. Was it a genuine warning, like the one I got from the old man in the park in Lawrence, Kansas? Or was it trying to scare me off so I don't help Cassie and her father? The worst part is, there's no way to know until I get there.

And what about the others? Do they share my fear? They heard the prediction of their deaths tonight, just like I did. But neither one of them has asked me to turn us around and not do this. So maybe this is my battle to fight.

Just as I close my eyes and banish these thoughts, Rebecca emerges from the bathroom, wearing only a towel and a smile. "Feel better?" I ask.

"Smell better too," she says. "Your turn."

"I accept. Do me a favor, though. Don't stand in front of the window if you open up that towel. Ship captains will see you, get distracted, and crash."

"I'll try not to cause any maritime disasters while you're gone."

The shower is good and very necessary. Though I didn't endure the level of besmirchment that plagued Rebecca, a day of driving and an evening of battling the forces of evil have left me with a not-so-fresh feeling, and whatever is in this tiny bottle of body wash is like dewdrops from heaven. Though I won't swear to it, I may actually break into song during the course of the bathing ritual.

When I exit the bathroom, the drapes are drawn and Rebecca is on the bed, stretched out in her sleepwear. "You look human again," she says.

"You don't look so bad yourself," I reply, approaching her.

She rises from the bed and stands next to it with me. As she unwraps my towel, she kisses my lips. The feeling is incredible. She feels so warm, so alive. I offer the next kiss and the ten that follow.

"Make love with me," she whispers between kisses.

"Even after everything we've seen tonight?"

"No, *because* of everything we've seen tonight. I need to feel you in my arms and know that we have a shield against everything horrible we've experienced."

I kiss her again. "Love, I do want you. Very much. I'm just so tired. I don't know if I could even get it up."

She fights back a smile. "Uhh, sweetie … it *is* up."

"It is?" I look down. "Oh, so it is. In that case, my answer is yes."

And with that moment of self-awareness, we spend the next hour celebrating each other with the most exquisite lovemaking I've ever known. Every kiss, every touch, every moment spent in each other's embrace refills the emptiness that has been creeping into my soul. Tonight, in this bed, in this moment, I have no doubt that I love this woman and she loves me.

Chapter 4

We sleep in. I can't remember the last time I've had that luxury. When I finally roll over and look at the clock, I see that it is 10:15 in the morning. Rebecca is by my side, sleeping peacefully, and I don't think she's ever looked more beautiful to me than she does right now.

And now we are three hours' drive from Pensacola. From battle, whatever that means. Earlier in the week, it was tornado day. What will today be dubbed? Armageddon? Sounds like the punch line to a bad joke. Knock knock. Who's there? Armageddon. Armageddon who? Armageddon tired of this shit.

Ha ha.

Something catches my eye as I get out of bed and make my way over to the desk. A book I haven't picked up in a very long time. It has a blue cover with gold leaf words on the front: HOLY BIBLE. I open it to a random page and find a heading at the top: The Book of Hosea. *Okay, a little spooky. So, Hosea, you're my ancestor, huh? Let's see what you've got.* A bit of reading reveals that God told Hosea to take a harlot for a wife, and he chose a woman named Gomer. Unfortunate name for a woman.

There's some begetting. Yada yada yada. God is apparently quite pissed. There's some scolding. *My people are destroyed for lack of knowledge,* it says, and these words stand out. Hosea understood that knowing your enemy can save your life. On the way to Pensacola, one of us will need to do some research.

I read through the rest of my ancestor's book and discover to my surprise that I have committed it to memory. This, of course, should be impossible, but I remember what the members of Ha Tesha called me: Hamesh, keeper of the word of Hosea. It's happened—I have his word, his prophecy inside me. If I knew what the hell to do with it, I'd be in great shape.

I am surprised by the sound of Rebecca's voice from the bed. "You're reading the Bible?"

"I just jumped to the end to see who did it."

"And?"

"It was Satan, apparently. But it looks like they have the Hebrews as accomplices."

"I'll wait till the movie comes out," she says, getting out of bed. "How are you feeling this morning?"

"Remarkably well, given the topsiness—and I daresay turviness—of my life of late. Better question is, how are *you* doing this morning after last night's apparent demonic possession?"

"I was doing fine until you called it that. Now I'm not so sure. I'd like to think that's not what happened," she says, approaching me.

"Fair enough. All I know is, you had something big and scary inside of you last night."

"Yes, but enough talk about your penis," she retorts, giving it a little squeeze. "I, for one, am starving."

"Well, the restaurant in the hotel lobby serves Sunday brunch, and I'd like to take you there. Interested?"

"Totally," she says. "Should we wake the cargo?"

"It would be the polite thing to do."

I pick up the room phone and dial Cassie's room number. After three rings, her groggy voice says, "What?"

"Free food, that's what," I answer. "Knock on our door in twenty minutes. Deal?"

"Okay."

I hang up the phone and smile at Rebecca. "I believe we have a date."

We spend those twenty minutes making ourselves presentable. At the appointed time, Cassie knocks on the door. I open it to find her there in familiar clothes, with the exception of a new New Orleans T-shirt.

"Nice shirt," I observe.

"Gift shop," she says. "And believe me, if they had souvenir underwear, I'd be the happiest girl alive. As it is, I had to settle for liquid soap, the sink, and the hair dryer."

"Bordering on too much information, but duly noted. A mandatory stop before Pensacola will be the Gap or Old Navy, or wherever it is you young people buy your garments these days."

"Very cute," she says, entering the room, "and I accept. Traveling light is good, but no luggage is problematic. So, there was talk of free food?"

"Sunday brunch," Rebecca says, emerging from the bathroom.

"Downstairs near the hotel lobby," I add. "I reserved us a table. Even booked it under a funny name for your amusement. Shall we?"

"Hell, yeah," she replies.

After a quick elevator ride, we proceed to the hotel's restaurant, which is as casually elegant as the rest of our surroundings. We stop at the hostess station, where a smiling young woman welcomes us.

"Good morning," I say to her. "We have a reservation for three people."

"All right. Your name, sir?"

"Mr. Panjazooti."

Rebecca and Cassie almost crack up at the absurd name, but the hostess doesn't even blink. "Right this way, sir. We have a table for you by the windows."

And so the Panjazooti party walks to their table, which is indeed right at an enormous picture window overlooking the Mississippi River. It is a beautiful fall day, and a number of ships are making their way up- and downriver. Seagulls and pelicans skirt the water, and pedestrians line the shore. It is a scene antithetical to last night's horrors, and it is just what I need.

"You can help yourselves to the buffet," the hostess says. "Andre will be around to bring you orange juice or mimosas, whichever you'd like."

We make our way to the center of the restaurant's front room and behold the spread. To describe it as an orgy of food would not do it justice. At an orgy, you might get some time with one partner, maybe two or three. But this—each dish is a sumptuous gustatory harlot, beckoning me to partake of her beauty. "You two enjoy Florida," I say quietly. "I'm going to live here."

"Not without me you don't," Rebecca says.

"I'm sure my father will be fine without my help," Cassie adds.

"Ladies," I reply, wide-eyed with gluttonous anticipation, "let's do this."

Sixty minutes later, the repast is past, and I can cross "eat alligator" off my life's to-do list. But the reptile is not alone in the list of animals I have just consumed. I feel like a whirlwind of carnivorous destruction, sampling foods I never knew existed. I am fairly certain that if I lived in New Orleans, I would weigh roughly four hundred pounds, and I would not care.

After a round of moaning—both satisfied and amazed by how much we have eaten—conversation turns back to the day ahead. "So what do we do now?" Rebecca asks.

"Well," I begin, "I owe a certain young woman a little variety in her wardrobe, so a stop at a local clothing shop is in order. After that, I think it's time to head to Pensacola."

"Shall we, then?" Rebecca says, rising from the table.

We get our bags, check out, get the Sebring out of the parking garage, and make our way to a clothing retailer that Cassie approves of (which takes four tries). I purchase about a week's worth of clothes for her, as well as a small suitcase on wheels. A CVS nearby supplies us with all the toiletries the three of us will need, and we head east to Florida.

"So how far away are we?" Cassie asks.

"If we stay on the interstates, only about three hours."

"What do we do when we get there?" Rebecca inquires.

"It seems like the first thing to do is to get the evidence out of the safe-deposit box. After that, I'm not as clear. A trip to the district attorney's office, probably. What do you think, Miss Pre-law?"

"That sounds right. Cassie said it was a federal trial, so we'd have to visit the U.S. Attorney's office for that district."

"Any idea where that would be?" I ask.

"Give me a minute," Rebecca says. Swiftly, she brings out her phone, dials information, and after a couple of questions to the operator, announces, "It's at 21 East Garden Street in Pensacola."

"Well then, it sounds like that's where we're going. Question is: what do we do when we get there? Do we just hand them the evidence and say 'fix this'? Do we walk in shouting 'miscarriage of justice' and hope they'll give us a do-over on his trial?"

Rebecca gets a faraway look for a moment, and then something resembling revelation washes over her. "Oh, I'm so stupid."

"How's that?" I ask.

"Cassie, how long ago was your father convicted?"

"Eleven months ago."

"Good, then we're still in time. Okay, answer me this, either of you: You're about to face federal felony charges for selling secrets. You know you have evidence locked away that could exonerate you, but you can't get to it. What do you do?"

I have to sit there and think about it for several seconds, because the answer in my head is so obvious, it can't possibly be right. But I offer it anyway. "Tell my attorney?"

"Exactly," she says. "The attorney can get an order to have the box unlocked if the contents are material to an ongoing trial. Why would the attorney not do that?"

"I don't know," Cassie says. "I didn't know he *could* do that."

"But your father would know, and the attorney himself would know. The only two reasons for not doing it would be if your father's defense lawyer was unspeakably incompetent …"

"Or involved in the conspiracy," I add.

"Either way, it buys us an in," she says. "We go and file a 2255 motion, citing ineffective assistance of counsel."

"What will that do?" Cassie asks.

"Start the appeal process. As soon as the guilty verdict was handed down, your father's attorney should have filed for an appeal anyway. The fact that it didn't happen strikes me as very suspicious."

"Will we be able to look at documents from the first trial?" I ask.

"They're public record. We should have full access. Tristan, if Mr. Haiduk's attorney was involved in the conspiracy, that means these people have very powerful connections. We may be in over our heads."

"Oh, I've had no doubts from the very beginning that we're in over our heads. The question is how deep, and what can we do about it?"

"Cassie," Rebecca says, "what do you know about the lawyer who represented your father in the trial?"

"Not much. I think it was someone my father knew for a few years. I know he trusted him."

"If there's an appeal," Rebecca adds, "we'll need to find a new lawyer. Tristan, yours is in Maryland, isn't he?"

"Yes, but I think I may have an ace up my sleeve. Does the attorney have to be from Pensacola?"

"No, just licensed to practice law in the state of Florida. Why?"

I get out my phone and look up a number in the address book. "Because I have a friend in Tallahassee who owes me a favor." I dial the number and wait for an answer.

"Foster, Stearns, Dwyer, and O'Malley, may I help you?" a young woman asks.

"May I speak to Kathleen Dwyer, please?"

"I'll see if she's available. May I tell her who's calling?"

"Yes, it's Tristan Shays."

"One moment, please."

Confident, gently patriotic music fills the void as I await a response. After several seconds, a familiar voice comes on. I can almost hear her smirking at me through the phone. "Tristan Shays, I don't believe it. Don't tell me you're languishing in a Florida jail somewhere and you need me to represent you."

"No, that was Atlanta, and it was last week."

"Why do I think you're not kidding?"

"Because you know me too well. I may just need you, Katie, but not for myself. I'm on an assignment, and the person in question has been falsely convicted on a federal felony for selling secrets to the Chinese. We're on our way to Pensacola to try to file an ineffective assistance of counsel motion and get an appellate hearing. If we do, I need a Florida attorney to represent him."

She thinks a moment. "Is he really innocent?"

"Does that matter?" I counter.

"In the final analysis, no. But for my own peace of mind and the likelihood of winning the case, I'd prefer to take it if he really is innocent."

"We're on our way to pick up evidence that is very likely to exonerate him and indict the oil company he worked for."

"*Which* oil company?"

"Consolidated Offshore."

There is silence on the line as she takes this in. Her next statement is conspicuously devoid of her trademark confidence and swagger. "Shit, Tristan. You enjoy fighting dragons?"

"Didn't say I enjoyed it, Katie. Just said I had to."

"Do you know what you're up against?" she asks.

"Somewhat. Though, from the sound of it, you've got some valuable information to share."

"They've been an irresistible force in this state for years now. They're very close to finding a way around the drilling ban that protects the Gulf Coast, and it sounds like they're doing it legally. They're getting some pushback from state legislators, the EPA, environmental groups, and the local fishing industry, but it's just rolling off their back. Nobody seems to have anything concrete that can put a dent in their armor."

I smile at this. "What if I tell you that they're trying to get around the drilling ban *illegally,* and this man might just have the weapon to dent that armor?"

"I'd say go on."

"He worked for Consolidated and gradually built up evidence against them showing that the deal they're putting together with the Chinese is illegal. It was locked away for safekeeping, but his attorney didn't order it admitted into evidence at the trial."

"Hence the 2255," she says. "You thinking stupid or crooked?"

"Stupid always pays dividends, but this is pretty damn stupid for a lawyer who wants to win a case. So I can't rule out crooked. From what I hear, Consolidated has their fingers in everything."

"You're not exaggerating," she says. "I should run screaming from this, because of how dangerous it is. But you're also handing me the chance to take this company down, and I like the sound of that."

"So you'll take the case?"

"I need to see this evidence. How long before you get to Pensacola?"

"About two and a half hours. Then we have to get the evidence and head to the U.S. Attorney's office."

"I'll also want to look at the record of the original case. What was it called?"

"People versus Daniel Haiduk. H-a-i-d-u-k. From last October."

"Okay, I'll look it over, and I'll meet you at the U.S. Attorney's office in Pensacola. If the evidence is as solid as you say, I'll file as attorney of record, and we can file the motion."

"Katie, you're the best."

"The most expensive, too," she adds. "This client better not be indigent."

"One way or another, you'll get paid. That I promise you. I'll see you in a few hours."

I end the call and smile at my passengers. "So she's in?" Cassie asks.

"She wants to see the evidence, but if it's as concrete as you believe, she'll take the case."

"Oh, Tristan, thank you!" she says. "Thank you so much."

"Don't thank me yet. We still have a lot to accomplish before we can call this one a victory."

The road leads eastward. I feel good about having Katie in our corner; she's bold and fearless, two qualities we need when taking on a company this big and powerful. More importantly, she's not for sale. Whatever forces got to Haiduk's original attorney, they won't be able to get to this one.

The sign ahead says Pensacola twenty miles; almost there now. But who will be there waiting for us? Does Consolidated know we're coming? I don't know how they could, since we've kept our plans relatively quiet. But then I think back to the assignment that brought me to Rebecca. Someone in Calvin Traeger's organization planted it in my head, so they could easily know we are coming and what our plans are. And then there's Stelios. It was a risk calling him from Illinois and telling him our intentions. He certainly comes across as no friend of Traeger or Consolidated, but could he be playing us, the way he did when he set me up to take the fall for Jeffrey Casner's murder last week?

It scares me not knowing who to trust or what to believe. Worse still is the fact that the most recent information we've received thus far says we're all going to die in this city. But was that the truth? Or was somebody trying to scare us off because they knew we were going to succeed? The horrible thing that spoke through Rebecca last night was right: I'm not afraid of dying, but I'm terrified of losing Rebecca or Cassie. I feel such tremendous responsibility for their well-being and safety. I can't let that stand in the way of taking care of my own safety as well, though I'm almost certain it will.

We enter the city limits of Pensacola, which looks quite a bit like several other coastal Florida cities I've been to. Cassie gives me directions to our first destination, and soon we are in the parking lot of Panhandle Union Bank. "We should go in with you," I tell her. "If anyone from the other side knows you're coming, I don't want you going through this alone."

"What about the Amber Alert?" Rebecca asks. "Cassie will have to give her name in order to get in, and if they've seen the Amber Alert, we're screwed."

"That's true," I acknowledge. "Trouble is, I don't know a way around it. We can go in with you and hang back, reducing the odds of someone recognizing the three of us together as a unit. But if someone's looking for you by name, they'll know it's you."

"Great time not to be named Mary Smith, huh?" she says.

"One thing I've found," I tell her, "is that you can get away with almost anything if you look like you belong there. People read body language and facial expressions. If you're nervous, fidgeting, jittery, you draw attention to yourself. If you're calm and you look like you belong, people will believe that too, and you usually won't be questioned. Rebecca and I will sit in the bank lobby and wait for you. Get what you need out of the safe-deposit box, and we'll be on our way like it's a day at the office."

"Okay," she says. "What do I do if something goes wrong?"

"Try to get back to the lobby, and we'll improvise from there."

"I'm a little scared," she says.

"That's because it's a little scary," I tell her. "But this was your plan from the very beginning, before you even knew we'd be here with you. Now you've got us, and we've got your back. Show the same confidence you've shown all along, and you'll make this happen."

She nods, takes a deep breath to compose herself, and goes to wait in line to talk to a teller. Rebecca and I sit in the lobby, keeping an eye on her as she makes her way to the head of the line. "I can't hear what she's saying," Rebecca tells me.

"Can you hear what she's thinking?"

She closes her eyes and concentrates. "She told the teller she's here to get something out of the family's safe-deposit box. The teller asked to see some ID. She's getting it out now. The teller is taking it to the back room. Cassie's worried."

Right on cue, Cassie turns to face us, a look of concern evident on her face from all the way across the bank lobby. I gesture to her that it's all right, and use some combination of sign language and semaphore to convey to her that Rebecca is monitoring her thoughts. Amazingly, she appears to get that message, and turns back to wait for the teller's return. About a minute later, the teller does return to her station, accompanied by a man in a suit. Rebecca provides the narration.

"This is Mr. Corrigan. He's one of the vice-presidents of the bank. He's going to accompany her to the safe-deposit room."

"It sounds like her name didn't set off any alarms, real or metaphorical," I observe. "Do you think you'll be able to monitor her thoughts from a greater distance?"

"I hope so. But once she gets into a vault, who knows?"

We watch as Mr. Corrigan escorts Cassie to the back of the bank and out of our view. "He's thanking her for coming in today," Rebecca continues, "but he's not making small talk."

"That makes sense," I reply. "Safe-deposit boxes are a private matter. He doesn't want to risk invading her privacy. Anything else going on?"

"I don't know. I've lost her. They must have headed to the vault area. Do you think we should follow her?"

"No, let's sit tight. I think she's safe."

After a couple of anxious minutes of sitting there, a man in a blue suit approaches us. "Have you been helped?" he asks.

"Oh, we're fine," I answer cordially. "We're somebody's ride today. We're just waiting here for her while she takes care of bank business. But thank you."

It is a perfectly reasonable question, and I should have no reason to feel uncomfortable with it, except that the bank employee next walks over to a nearby security guard and speaks privately with him, including a discreet gesture in our direction. I can only guess that the instruction was along the lines of *Keep an eye on those two, would you?* Perfect in case we need to make a hasty retreat from the bank. Now I can only hope that Cassie's business transaction goes off flawlessly.

Each minute feels endless, with nothing to do to pass the time, and the eyes of a bank security guard on us. "Twenty questions?" I ask Rebecca with a little smile.

"Think I'll pass this time," she answers. "But the first answer you were thinking of was Malaysia."

"You really know how to take the fun out of this game, don't you?"

"God, where is she?" she asks.

"Stay calm. She hasn't been gone nearly as long as it feels like. These things take time. We're watching for trouble. It'll be all right."

More minutes pass, and soon it feels like every eye in the bank is on us. Employees watch us as they walk by. Customers give us uneasy glances. The security guard keeps a steady watch. Ten minutes become fifteen and then twenty. I am even beginning to wonder if something has gone wrong.

"Should we leave?" Rebecca whispers to me.

"No, not yet. We can't leave Cassie, and besides, it'll look more suspicious to leave the bank without the person we're giving a ride to. We need to wait."

Three minutes later, the security guard and the blue-suited man have another quick conference, probably about the fact that the two strangers are still sitting in the lobby, waiting for someone who doesn't appear to be there. To amuse myself, I create dialogue in my head for their conversation.

"They're still here, Charlie," the banker says, because security guards should be named Charlie.

"I know, Mr. Albemarle." No reason; I just like the name. *"What do you think we should do?"*

"Well, they said they were waiting for somebody, but I don't see anybody at the teller windows."

"You want I should call for backup, Mr. Albemarle?" Charlie was apparently hired off the set of a 1940s gangster movie.

"Not just yet, Charlie. Let's go interrogate them. See if their story holds up. I bet if we intimidate them, they'll crack. Not the girl; she looks pretty tough. But the man looks like kind of a pussy. I think we can break him."

To my surprise, Rebecca lets out a little laugh at this point. She must have been reading my thoughts and enjoyed my bank lobby theatre. It gets a little less amusing, however, when the two of them actually come over to us at this point.

"I feel bad that you folks have to wait so long," Mr. Albemarle (who's probably not really named Mr. Albemarle) says.

"Not a problem," I say casually. "This was one of the big errands for the day. Gotta get something from the safe-deposit box, and I guess that can take a while."

He gives a little nod of realization at this information; clearly it explains things for him. His tone softens at this. "Can I get you a beverage or something?"

Before I can answer, Cassie walks up to us, carrying a stack of papers and other items in her overloaded arms. "Hi, guys," she says. "Sorry to take so long. It's like in the bowels of the earth." She looks at the banker. "Funny word. Bowels. Like the earth poops or something."

"On that note," I say, standing, "I think it's time to go. Still a few errands to accomplish today."

Rebecca rises as well, and I turn and smile pleasantly at the men. "Gentlemen, thank you for your hospitality. The seats were very comfortable. Good day."

I lead the group hastily to the exit, realizing precisely how conspicuous we look and how very little—contrary to what I told Cassie—we look like we belong there. If the bankers are in collusion with Consolidated, we have just made ourselves known in a big way.

Clear of the bank and back in the car, we finally have a moment to breathe and to inspect the materials that Cassie has retrieved. There are computer printouts, memos, e-mails, notepads, CD-ROMs. On the surface, it seems that Daniel Haiduk has compiled an impressive array of evidence. The question is, does it prove anything?

"Where to now?" Rebecca asks.

"U.S. Attorney's office," I answer. "We need to meet Katie there and get all this stuff to her."

After gathering the evidence into my briefcase, I start the Sebring and drive us the two and a half miles to the United States Attorney's office in Pensacola. As I pull into the parking lot, I see a Lexus with a personalized license plate that reads: LWYR BCH. I smile; Katie's here.

The three of us enter the facility to find my old friend in the lobby. "You're late, Shays," she playfully jabs at me.

"A wizard is never late, Frodo," I jab back. "Besides, I thought it would be fun if we actually obtained the evidence for you to examine."

"Did you get it all?"

"And then some," I tell her. "This one will be so easy, you should charge half price."

"Ha," she says. "That'll be the day. I got us a conference room. Let's go look this over."

She's all business, I'll give her that. Just five and a half feet tall, Katie is a force to be reckoned with. Sporting a bit of well-earned gray on her head but still full of fire in her eyes, she's got the same spirit I remember from Harvard, when I was an undergrad and she was in law school. We went out on one date, but immediately knew that we were meant to be friends instead. At the moment, she could be a very good friend to the three of us indeed.

"Katie, let me introduce Rebecca and Cassie. Cassie is the daughter of Daniel Haiduk, and she obtained the evidence from the safe-deposit box."

"And Rebecca?" she asks with a certain tone in her voice.

"Rebecca is my traveling companion."

"I see."

"Don't start, Counselor. We're here on business. You can scrutinize my personal life when the meter's not running."

"Fair enough," she replies as we sit at the large conference table. "Show me what you've got."

Over the next twenty-five minutes, we do just that. Katie brings out her records of the original trial and compares them with the printed evidence Daniel Haiduk has accumulated. Occasionally she shakes her head and utters words like *unbelievable, crazy,* or *amazing.* Not wanting to interrupt her, I simply sit back, as do the others, and watch her take notes on what's before her.

After reviewing the printouts, she asks for and receives a laptop computer and a microcassette player with headphones. Ever the multi-tasker, she listens to Haiduk's tapes while looking at the data on the CD-ROMs he provided. Finally, after nearly an hour of review, she takes off the headphones and puts her pen down.

"Your analysis?" I ask.

"Urinalysis is a good word for it," she says, "because I'm pretty pissed."

"Oh. Dead end?"

"Hardly! I'm pissed because a judge let such flagrant abuse occur in the courtroom and because a jury convicted on such flimsy evidence."

"So you're saying we have a case here?" Rebecca asks.

"Oh, yes. I'll file the motion for an appeal today. But—"

"But?" Cassie repeats.

"The quantity of evidence is both good and bad. It's good because it means we'll have an easier time presenting the case. It's bad because the case against your father is so weak, there's very little chance an honest court would have convicted in the first place. Which makes me wonder just how far Consolidated's control goes."

"What are your thoughts?" I ask her.

"Certainly the defense attorney. But maybe some jury tampering, which usually doesn't happen without help from the inside. I don't want to believe that the federal court can be purchased, and I don't know how much I can investigate without jeopardizing my own career. But I do know that we have to be careful."

"What can we do?" Rebecca asks.

"I'll file the motion and get a new trial date set. Do we need to consult with the defendant first?"

"No," Cassie says. "I already have his approval; this is what he wants. Do what you need to do."

"All right," Katie replies. "After that, I need to go and interview his last defense attorney. He won't like what I have to say, but it needs to be said. I want to know just what happened the first time around."

"We should probably be there too," I offer.

She disagrees. "If this process is as crooked as I think it is, it's not safe for you to meet this man."

"Katie," I say, deciding to divulge more, "there's more to this than I've told you. We've had run-ins with Consolidated before, as well as the fishermen who are fighting them. We were called to Florida to help Cassie's father, but also to enter into a battle with these people."

"A battle?" she says. "These people's idea of a battle is to kill you, throw you in the ocean, and shout 'We win!' No offense, darling boy, but a teenage girl and an offensively cute twenty-something blonde are not my idea of the army you need for this skirmish. You and I have had our differences in the past, but I really don't want to see you get chopped into pieces and fed to grouper."

"You don't understand," I tell her. The next words take several seconds to emerge, and when they do, they sound precisely as stupid as I feared they would. "God will protect us."

Kathleen Dwyer is speechless for the first time in all the years that I've known her. "Oh," she finally says quietly, "my mistake then. As long as God will protect you, it's okay. Please, go on into battle."

"Damn it, Katie! Spare me the shit. I know you did your undergrad in religious studies, and I know you're a believer. I don't have time to explain everything right now, but things I've seen in the last two weeks have shown me that there are forces at work here that are bigger than me and you, bigger than Consolidated and the fishermen, bigger than all of it, and they've called me into their service."

She stands there sporting a thousand-yard stare as I finish my rant. "Fishermen," she repeats quietly.

"What?"

"Jesus told his disciples to be fishers of men. When you brought God into it, you made me remember that quote."

"What do you think it means?" I ask her.

"Well, either it means you're entering a battle of biblical proportions or it's a big coincidence and you'll come out of it smelling like mackerel."

"Honestly, I'll be happy if we just come out of it."

"Yeah, there's that," she acknowledges. "So why is it so important for you to meet this other attorney?"

"Information. We're going into this with a deficit of information, and if we're going to stand a fighting chance, we need as much detail as we can get. So I want to hear what he has to say when you question him. Oh yeah, and Rebecca can read minds, so she should be there too."

Katie shakes her head and gives a little laugh. "If anybody else said that to me, I'd tell them they're full of shit. But why do I get the feeling that you mean it?"

"Because," Rebecca answers in my stead, "you had a taco salad for lunch, you need to remember to pick up your dry cleaning, and you've already calculated a $450 invoice in your head for today's activities."

Holding back a laugh, Katie says, "Guess I better watch what I think about you when she's around, huh, Tristan?"

"Oh, I already saw that too," Rebecca says, "and he's taken."

"Don't sweat it, kitten. He's all yours. I'll go file this motion, and then we'll go and visit Mister Owen Casner, attorney at law."

My blood freezes at the sound of the name. "Wait a minute. Owen *Casner?*"

"That's what it says here."

"Oh, shit."

"What?" Katie asks. "What is it?"

"Rebecca, you don't think—"

"You've made me stop believing in coincidences. It has to be a relative, maybe a brother."

"Somebody wanna fill me in?" Katie says.

"Last week, in Atlanta, I was there when one of Consolidated's thugs got blown up, a Jeffrey Casner. I was arrested for it but then released. But if word got to them that I was involved ..."

"It'll make this day even more fun," she says. "*Still* want to go with me?"

"Yes. Now more than ever, in fact. I need to know the connections. Where the lines are drawn, where it all leads."

"Okay. Sit tight. I'll be back in a few minutes with a court date."

Chapter 5

Katie does get a court date for Daniel Haiduk, six weeks down the road. All present wish it could be sooner, but it's important to give the defense time to put its case together. We get into our car and she gets into hers, as we follow her through the streets of Pensacola to the law offices of Owen Casner. Said offices occupy a small brick building on a street called Birch. His sign is hand painted and hangs from the front canopy.

We park on the street and convene with Katie in front of the building. She hands a notepad and a pen to each of us and instructs, "Let me do the talking. You're here to observe. Got it?"

"Got it," I answer.

We enter the small office, and a young woman at the reception desk greets us. "Can I help you?"

"We need to see Mr. Casner for a few minutes," she says.

"Do you have an appointment?" the receptionist queries.

"No, this came up unexpectedly. I'm the appeals attorney for a case he had last year."

"I'll have to see if he's available. Can I give him your name?"

"Kathleen Dwyer," comes the response, but curiously enough, it is not Katie who speaks it. Owen Casner gives the name, as he emerges from his office to stand before us. "I thought I recognized your voice."

There is no warmth at all in his tone. Owen Casner is a short, stocky man in his fifties, starting to lose his hair, and possessing a fashion sense worthy of a guest appearance on a makeover show. Though he is clearly the ugly duckling of the family, I spot the resemblance to the late Jeffrey.

"Hello, Owen," Katie says. "I'm surprised you still remember me. It's been awhile."

"Don't be flattered. They're not fond memories." He eyes her suspiciously. "You're taking on one of my old cases? Which one?"

"People v. Haiduk," she answers calmly.

"Haiduk?" he repeats, sounding surprised. "That traitor? On what grounds?"

"Ineffective assistance of counsel."

"Bullshit!" he counters. "He was guilty. The jury knew it."

"I've gone over the case. I have access to the evidence, the stuff you buried. Best-case scenario, Haiduk walks on appeal. Worst-case scenario, you receive judicial review, maybe lose your license. If I can prove tampering, we might even throw in a free indictment in time for Christmas."

"I want to see this evidence you're talking about," he says.

"You'll get the opportunity during discovery," Katie answers calmly. "For now, it's in a very safe place. Nowhere near you, and nowhere near me."

Casner's face takes on hues of repressed anger and frustration. "So why did you come here?" he asks. "To gloat over your flimsy appeal?"

"No, I came here to hear it from you. The truth about what happened in that courtroom last year. I wish I could present other options besides incompetence and criminal complicity, but after my review of the case, they're the only things on the menu. So how about it, Owen? A little from column A, a little from column B?"

"I think you need to leave here. You and your little entourage, whoever the hell they are."

"Just two paralegals and an intern," she replies casually. "This is a learning experience for them in how not to be an attorney."

Casner looks at us, first Cassie, then me. Then he makes eye contact with Rebecca, and something very unusual happens. A look visits his face, a look of recognition. A second later, Rebecca gets a very troubled expression on her face and I watch her suppress a gasp. This elicits a new expression from Casner, a decidedly worried one, which motivates Rebecca to furrow her brow and narrow her eyes. The whole exchange would be downright comical if I weren't certain that something extraordinarily grim just silently transpired between them.

"The great Kathleen Dwyer," Casner says mockingly. "So superior, so untouchable. You have aspirations of being a judge someday, safe in your little district in Tallahassee. That's no secret. Well, this is Florida, little girl, and the holier-than-thou types don't get far in this state. Just remember that when you're looking down on the rest of us."

Katie looks unfazed by his vitriol. "Owen, that was ... that was really moving. I'm sorry, I didn't write it down, so would you please memorize it for when I put your fat, corrupt ass on the stand? It's the closest thing to a confession I've heard in a long time."

"Get out!" he orders.

"See you in court, sunshine," she calls back as we make our exit.

Back at the car, I can't help but voice my astonishment. "You have got some balls on you, woman."

"What, that?" she retorts. "Just standing up to the playground bully. Didn't you see his face? He got caught and he knows it."

"Yeah," Rebecca says, "well, so did we."

"What do you mean?" I ask. "What was that look you two shared in there?"

"When Katie referred to us as paralegals, Casner looked at the three of us, and he didn't believe it. He looked at Cassie, then at you, and when he looked at me, he put the pieces together. He knows who the three of us are. And then ... and I'm so sorry for doing this ... I reacted to that thought, and he saw me, so he knows I can read him. I'm afraid he's going to tell Consolidated that we're here. Any advantage of stealth that we may have had is gone."

"I suspect it's worse than that," I add. "Katie, you told him about the evidence. That's the one thing they need more than anything else. I'm afraid you've just put your life in danger by making this stand."

"I still had to do it," she says. "I had to hear it from him. And more than that, I need to know if his thoughts betrayed anything. Rebecca, what did you get from him?"

"Guilt," Rebecca replies. "Pretty much a full confession in his thoughts. He was paid off by Consolidated to throw the case, bury the evidence, and let Daniel take the fall. The judge was complicit, and there may have been jury tampering."

"Son of a bitch. I knew it."

"But wait," Cassie chimes in. "If that happened the first time, what's to keep it from happening the second time?"

"Well," Katie answers, "for one thing, your father will have me as his attorney, and there's no way they can influence me. I can ask for a bench trial, so there'll be no chance of jury tampering. And once a judge is named, I'll dig deep to make sure he's beyond the reach of Consolidated's little axis of evil."

"What about what Tristan said?" Rebecca asks. "About your safety? If they think you have the evidence, I believe they won't stop until they get it from you or even kill you."

"I led him to believe it's somewhere else. Besides, if they want me, they'll have to get past Winfield first," she adds.

"Winfield?" Cassie says. "What's that?"

"Not what," I tell her, "*who*. Winfield is her husband. Six feet four, former special ops. Military training in weapons, tactical, interrogation. Man could get a confession out of a house plant."

"Aww," Katie replies, "I didn't know you cared."

"How is the big guy?" I ask pleasantly.

"Big," she answers. "He still won't eat right, no matter what I do, but I think he's in shape to take on anybody who decides to get stupid."

"Warn him about this. Soon. I'd never forgive myself if something happened to you."

She smiles and runs her fingers through my hair amiably. "I'll tell him. And don't expend any energy worrying about me. If they know you're here, it's time to start thinking about yourselves. Something tells me this battle you're entering starts today."

A strange sound breaks the tension following this very somber proclamation, a sound I do not recognize at first. It sounds like electronic music, but I can't figure out where it's coming from. After about ten seconds, Rebecca points to my belt, where my cell phone is clipped. I'm embarrassed to realize that my own phone is ringing; it so seldom happens, I forget what my own ring tone is.

I open the phone. "Hello? ... Yes, yes it's me. Good to hear from you. Where are you? ... Yes, we're in Pensacola too. Can we meet with you? ... Uh-huh ... yes ... okay, that's fine. We'll head over there now.... See you soon."

As I end the call, Rebecca gives me an inquisitive look, which is curious, given her abilities. "You mean you don't already know?" I ask, teasing her gently.

"Humor me. I was respecting your privacy for a change."

"It was Stelios. The *Calliope* is docked at Pensacola Shores Harbor, and he wants to meet with us."

"Who's Stelios?" Katie asks.

"An ally," I reply.

"Maybe," Rebecca adds quickly.

"He came all the way to Ohio to warn us we were in danger," I remind her.

To this, she counters, "Yes, after he set you up to take the fall for that murder in Atlanta."

"So I take it we're a little foggy on where Stelios's loyalties lie," Katie surmises.

"He's one of the fishermen," I reply, "that Consolidated is threatening to drive out of business. When we first met him, he thought we were on the oil company's side, but now that he knows we're fighting against them, there's no reason to doubt his friendship."

"I'll believe that when I see it," Rebecca says.

"Well," Katie says, "much as I would enjoy spending the late afternoon on a fishing boat with you, I need to get going. You three be careful, please."

"You too," I reply. "Make sure Winfield knows what's going on and you're both protected. Your office too. In fact, I think I'd feel best if you left town until this blows over."

She pats my shoulder. "Relax. I'll be fine. This isn't the first time I've taken on the bad guys. Call me on my cell every day. I want to know that you're safe."

"I will." At this, I hug her. "It's good to see you again. I can't thank you enough for taking this case."

"Ahh, you know I have a soft spot for a hard-luck story. If you take a right out of here, you'll see signs directing you to Pensacola Shores Harbor. Good luck with your fisherman."

As the three of us get back into the Sebring, Rebecca looks tense and Cassie is uncharacteristically quiet. It's worthy of an inquiry as we begin our drive. "You okay back there?" I ask our young passenger.

"I don't know."

"You want to talk about it? Or, you know, at least think it loudly so Rebecca can hear?"

"That man could have kept my father out of prison and he didn't. Just because somebody paid him off. My father, the most kind, honest, and decent person I've ever met, is in prison because a corrupt lawyer didn't care about the job he was hired to do. You wonder how I can bring explosives to school? Not think twice about destroying it? It's a sick society, filled with sick people."

"You're right," I reply quietly. "It really can be. You see it day after day after day, and you start to think that's all there is. But there's more, if you look for it. Before our time together is over, I owe you something beautiful."

"You don't have to buy me anything …"

"No, not like that. What I'll give you can't be bought; it has to be found. I don't know when or where yet, but I'll find you something beautiful in this world to counteract all the ugliness."

She hesitates for a moment, taking this in. "Thank you. I think I'd like that."

I next turn to Rebecca. "And how about you? What's on your mind at this hour?"

"Can't imagine," she answers with gentle sarcasm.

"Still no love for Stelios, huh?"

"Tristan, it's not just that. It's everything. Our only weapon was stealth, and Katie's maneuver blew that away. Now they know we're here."

"It was a calculated risk, but we gained valuable information from it," I tell her. "We now know that Casner deliberately screwed his defense. And we have one more piece of the puzzle, linking this case to the car bombing in Atlanta."

"What does *that* give us?"

"Information. After all, 'My people are destroyed for lack of knowledge.'"

"What?"

"It's from that Bible you caught me reading this morning. Our adversary has a network of information and a wall of silence. If we can scale that wall and tap into that network, we stand a better chance of finding out what we need to win."

"Win?" she repeats. "Is that even a possibility?"

"We have to believe that it is."

"Right now," she says, "I'd be satisfied just to come out of this alive. I'm so scared, not knowing what we're going to face. Is Stelios going to help us, or is he part of this too? And then this whole thing with my—with Calvin. Because if he's not here yet, he will be. Trust me."

"I meant what I said earlier about God protecting us. I feel like we're on the side of what's right, and we can endure whatever they throw at us."

"I really hope you're right. I don't want to have done all this for nothing."

A few minutes later, we arrive at the docks and find a parking space. As we get out of the car, I alert Rebecca, "Let's trust him for now, but keep an ear on his thoughts. Let me know if anything feels wrong."

"I will."

The *Calliope* is moored at slip 104, looking much the way she did when we first set foot on her last week in Tarpon Springs. So much has happened since then; it feels like months since we gave Stelios the warning that his boat was in danger of sinking. As we approach the gangplank, the fisherman appears on deck, along with a man in a polo shirt and a pair of white slacks and wearing very expensive L.L. Bean boat shoes.

Stelios greets us as effusively as ever. "Tristan, Persephone! How good to see you! And who is your friend?"

"This is Cassie," I reply. "We're here to help her father."

"Of course, of course," he says through his thick Greek accent. "The daughter. I am Stelios, and this is my boat. You are all welcome here."

"Quid pro quo, Stelios," I tell him. "Who is *your* friend?"

The friend takes the initiative of answering personally, in a refined British accent. "Clive Wolfson. It's good to meet you, Mr. Shays."

It takes a moment for the name to register, but when it does, it sends a chill through me. Something Jeffrey Casner said seconds before his car exploded with him inside: *"You can go right back to Wolfson or whoever sent you, and tell 'em they can kiss my fuckin' ass if they think they're gonna intimidate me."*

This is Wolfson. But who is he? With trust in such short supply, I decide not to say too much at this point, and just see what happens. Wolfson continues speaking as if we are old friends. "Your exploits precede you. We've been following the work you did in Kansas. Very impressive."

"How could you possibly know that was us?" Rebecca asks.

"Persephone, wasn't it?" he says. "As you might imagine, we have an interest in you and Mr. Shays. You've become … shall we say … enmeshed in this unfortunate business with Consolidated. And Miss Haiduk, welcome. I'm so sorry for the indignities your father faced at their hands. But now you're here, and we can set things right again. Why don't we all have a seat."

I'm busy looking for the angle, waiting for another shoe to fall to the deck and the whole thing to turn on us, but it's not there. I turn to Rebecca and my expression inquires *"Anything?"* Understanding my meaning, she just shakes her head. The pair is as clean to her as they are to me. So we sit on deck and Wolfson even brings everyone iced tea.

"It's sweetened," he says apologetically. "I prefer it plain myself, but we *are* in the South, you know."

"I was a bit surprised that you called me, Tristan," Stelios says after Wolfson joins us. "We didn't exactly part on the best of terms."

"I know. But we needed an ally, and I think you hate what Consolidated is doing even more than we do."

"What," he says, "you mean drilling illegally, destroying the ecosystem, and threatening to put us out of business?"

"Yeah, that would be the part I meant."

"Well, you're right about that. So, you went and confronted Calvin, did you?"

"Yes," I answer.

"And what happened then?"

"He tried to shoot me ... a little."

"I take it he didn't succeed."

"No," Rebecca answers. "I stood in his way."

"Good for you, Persephone! Very brave of you."

Wolfson asks, "And just how did you know to find our Miss Haiduk?"

"I got an assignment," I reply. "I was sent to help her."

Stelios looks intently at Cassie and adds, "She was going to blow up her school, apparently, to create a diversion so she could come here."

Panic visits Cassie's face upon hearing this. "How could you know that?"

"I know it," Stelios answers calmly, "because you know it. Don't worry, my girl. You're among friends here. I'm sure if that was your plan, you had a very good reason. Fortunately for you, Tristan here had a better reason to stop you."

It's time to be direct. "You know about Ha Tesha, don't you?" I ask him.

"I don't know them personally, but I know you made contact."

"And?" I prod.

"And what?"

"Come on, Stelios, don't be coy. You've never been stingy with your opinions before. You know I'm one of them. I need to know how you feel about that."

He sputters dismissively. "One of them. Feh. Big fucking deal!" Remembering Cassie's presence, he quickly adds, "Pardon my language."

"Whatever," she says.

Stelios continues. "Bunch of self-righteous old men who take themselves far too seriously. Where is your cabal now? Did they follow you here?"

"No."

"Did they prepare you for what's to come?"

"No."

"But I will," Stelios adds very pointedly. "And yet you still doubt me. Both of you."

"I would apologize," Rebecca replies, "but I think you know where that doubt comes from. And if you say it's completely unfounded, then you're either naïve or stupid, and I don't think you're either of those things."

Wolfson chimes in at this point. "Do you know why you're here? All of you?"

"To help Cassie," I answer, though I know he's going somewhere else with this.

"You know full well that she had plans to get here on her own, without your help. You're not seeing the bigger picture, Tristan. Everything you've been through since meeting your new companion here has been leading up to this. I know you understand this. Perhaps you're not grasping the magnitude of what's about to transpire. This is literally the last chance to stop Consolidated before they proceed with their offshore drilling."

"There are offshore oil rigs all over the coastal waters," I remind him. "What's one or two more?"

"One or two?" Wolfson says with surprise in his voice. "They're planning on three hundred in the next five years."

The number is staggering, and as the look on my face must attest, I had no idea.

Wolfson continues. "I'll take your silence to mean this is news to you. So you see our concern. Not only would the impact be devastating to the fishing industry, but the economic impact would also skew the world economy."

"But Consolidated is an American company," Cassie points out. "I mean, I'm not defending them, but if an American company is meeting our oil needs, wouldn't that reduce the need for imported oil and be good for the economy?"

"Clever girl," he says. "From an elementary economic standpoint, you're correct. But again, we're talking about scale. Those lovely coordinates you received in your mind, Persephone—they represent the largest deposits of oil found in the last century. The yield from these rigs could supply the entire country with oil for the next fifty years. Consolidated would receive massive profits, and OPEC would scramble to keep up. Unless ..." He pauses deliberately, inviting a prompt, which I supply.

"Unless?"

"Unless the rest of their plan materializes. Time for a lesson in political science. If this sounds condescending, I apologize. It's the British accent; it skews everything. America's current enemies are located primarily in the Middle East. Despite the recent flare-ups in Iraq, we are, to some extent, pulling our punches. Playing gentle with our enemies, one might say. And why? Oil. We've been unable to take it by force, so we're working with their governments to root out the undesirable element and keep the access to oil open. The bitter truth is that the military and the American government could give a crap about these governments if oil wasn't in the equation. So, Consolidated stands to profit twice. They have contacts with several paramilitary organizations who stand poised to unleash hell on the OPEC nations— in the name of American victory, of course. Retaliation, patriotism. All the usual rhetoric. So, picture the world in five years. Consolidated's oil rigs are supplying the U.S. with copious oil at gently inflated prices, the OPEC nations are wiped off the face of the Earth, and the rest of the industrialized world finds itself either at Consolidated's mercy or back in hunter-gatherer mode. Getting the bigger picture?"

"Yes," I reply quietly.

"What about China?" Rebecca asks. "How do they figure into this?"

"Excellent question," Wolfson says. "China figures into this from the beginning. After all, the dubious offshore drilling permits are theirs from day one. And China is not stupid. They know much of what Consolidated has in mind, and they see this as their opportunity to achieve irrevocable superpower status, economically and militarily. After the oil starts flowing, China goes public in their role in making it all happen, and presents the olive branch to the United States. Given the inevitable global backlash against America for turning the cradle of civilization into an ocean of glass, we need allies on the world stage. Enter China. We're all friends now. Only they have plans of their own, beyond alliance with the U.S. Plans that make Consolidated's look positively benign."

"How do you know all this?" Rebecca asks.

"My dear Persephone, after all you've seen and heard in the last two weeks, knowledge of future plans and schemes comes as a surprise to you?"

"No, it's not that. It's just … I don't know who you are, I don't know who to trust, and I don't know what our part is in all of this."

Wolfson pauses at this and nods for a second or two. "All right, that's fair. I just presumed that given your gifts, you would simply have lifted any information you needed wholesale."

"I try to be a little more polite than that," she says.

He hesitates a moment and then smiles and replies. "I, however, do not. The real truth of the matter is that you haven't honed your skills enough yet. You've been trying to get that information from Stelios and myself, and you've been unsuccessful. It's because we've learned to block our thoughts in the presence of readers such as yourself. A skill you may want to cultivate, and soon. So it is to be Q and A. Primitive but effective. Who am I? My name you already know, Clive Wolfson. And from my voice, you've gathered that I am UK born and raised. A transplant to this country, though why I chose Florida for a home is a source of constant mystery to me. If they fished for sponges in Seattle or Bangor, I'd be the happiest man alive.

"Stelios and his colleagues work for me. I am the chief executive of a conglomerate that includes more than 90 percent of Florida's sponge-fishing industry, as well as traditional fishing for the local seafood. So, as you can imagine, I have a vested interest in what goes on in the coastal waters around this state. I also have an interest in those coordinates in your head, my dear, the ones you shared with Stelios. Be very cautious about who gets those. Consolidated's interest in them is far greater than mine, and I suspect your knowledge of them may be all that's keeping them from killing you."

"Calvin wouldn't kill me," she says defiantly.

"Maybe not. But if you're wrong, I can't exactly say I told you so. Which brings us to the matter of whom you can trust. In a word, that's us. Stelios, myself. We mean you no harm, and we will offer you our resources. The rather embarrassing confession that accompanies this information is that, frankly, we need you. All three of you."

"*You* need *us?*" I ask.

"Indeed we do. The fact that God or whomever has chosen to plant you in the middle of this imbroglio tells me that you all will have the pivotal part in its conclusion. After all, you have the evidence that can indict Consolidated, do you not?"

"It's in a very safe place," I respond, assuming my best inscrutable face.

That all falls to shit in two seconds when he calmly replies, "Kathleen Dwyer, attorney at law. I hope her custody is more secure than your thoughts, Tristan, otherwise we're all in trouble."

Lovely, psychics everywhere.

"Not everywhere," he says in response to that thought, "but more places than you'd suspect. Which is why trust becomes so crucial. I take it you've informed Attorney Dwyer of the potential peril?"

"Yes. She's prepared."

"Good. They want that evidence, even more than the coordinates. Your barrister needs to lay low until we win this thing."

"She can take care of herself," Rebecca says.

"I certainly hope so. Because Calvin has no remorse about killing absolutely every one of us. You may be surprised, darling girl, at the depths of brutality to which your father will stoop."

And just like that, it is out, the information we've worked so hard to keep secret. Cassie stands up like a shot and looks at Rebecca. "Wait a minute—*father?*"

"Cassie, wait," I say.

"Calvin Traeger is your father?"

"I can explain," Rebecca says.

"Just stay away from me!" she says, tears starting to form in her eyes as she runs to a corner of the boat, far away from us.

I glare at Wolfson. "Nice going. You know, for someone who can read minds, you did a piss-poor job of knowing when something is privileged information."

"On the contrary," he retorts calmly. "I was fully aware of the nature of that communication, and it was a very conscious decision to tell Miss Haiduk of it here and now."

"What?" Rebecca says, astonished. "Why?"

"If I know this is a secret, then certainly our enemy will know it too, and won't hesitate to use it to turn Cassandra against you. By revealing it now, she can process what it means here in a place of safety, and you'll have time to win back her trust. To have it revealed in the heat of battle could be just what Consolidated needs to turn the girl to their side, against you. And then, everything you've worked for would be lost."

I can't argue with his logic. He makes a lot of sense.

"Stelios," Wolfson says with that perpetual irritating calm, "she's had a moment to process it. Go to her with a piece of your baklava, comfort her, and convince her that her traveling companions can be trusted. You remind her of her grandfather, so she'll listen to you."

"Yes, sir," Stelios responds, rising from his seat and heading in her general direction.

At this point, all I can do is stare at Clive Wolfson as he maintains the unflappable aplomb he's displayed from the moment we boarded. I bet he'd be a son of a bitch to face down at poker. And were it not for his earlier confession about needing us, I'd say he holds all the cards.

"So," I finally say to him, "you say you need us, but I still don't know what to do about that. These people are ruthless killers, and we're three unarmed people. How are we at an advantage?"

"Nobody said the word *advantage,* my boy. This will be absolutely grueling for you, and I can't guarantee that you'll come out of it alive. I know for a fact, however, that if I or any of my people were to confront them, we'd be mowed down mercilessly. You three at least will have access to them. Your companions hold both the coordinates and the evidence. That's a valuable commodity, wouldn't you agree?"

"So we're bait?" Rebecca posits.

"Bait is an ugly word," he says. "You're strategic agents in this battle of wits."

"Meaning that your group doesn't care about us either," I offer.

"Not true," Wolfson replies. "Don't fall back on the tired chess analogy that suggests you're as pawns in this. This is a battle, and you will be front-line soldiers, but of the highest caliber. As such, we care very much about your well-being; all of you."

"All right," I respond. "We're making confessions; here's mine: I don't feel ready for this. I feel like we're being asked to get in the middle of this conflict between your group and Consolidated, but I don't know how to fight them. Are you preparing to give us guns? Because I have to tell you, I'm not keen on shooting anybody."

"Guns are crude and ineffective. This battle won't be won by killing the enemy."

Without thinking, I reply, "Tell that to Jeffrey Casner."

The reference does not escape him. "Ah, yes. *That* unpleasantness. Stelios told me that you got caught up in that. It's unfortunate."

"Casner mentioned your name before he died."

"Did he? What did he say?"

"He wanted me to tell you he's not afraid of you."

"Ah, well, the benefits of hindsight," he says. "A bit late for him, but a cautionary tale for us all."

"Did you kill Casner?" Rebecca asks Wolfson.

"That's a bit of a personal question, don't you think?"

She doesn't back down. "You know that Tristan got arrested for that murder. The least you can do is tell us why Casner had to die."

He takes a breath, long enough to contemplate whether this is on a need-to-know basis, and then explains, "Jeffrey Casner was a hired hand for Consolidated Offshore. I believe the crude term they have for his brand of employee is a 'fixer.' He was paid well to eliminate problems. Consolidated considers me and mine a problem. When you encountered Casner in Atlanta, he was planning to come to Florida. There was talk of a fishing trip to the Keys, but we made sure that didn't happen. His next destination was Tarpon Springs, where he was tasked with nothing less than domestic terrorism. He had a list of twenty-one of my company's fishing boats, and orders to blow them all up. The explosion that claimed his life was courtesy of one of the devices he himself had in his car. It was simply a matter of rigging a detonator to the ignition switch.

"So, to answer your question: did I kill him? No, I was nowhere near him. Did I give the order? Yes, my friends, I did. But in so doing, I saved the lives and property of dozens who merely wanted to carry out their business safely."

I take a moment to take all this in, deciding that he's not lying. "What about the damage to Stelios's boat?" I ask. "The damage that I was sent to warn him about?"

"I would say it was a coincidence, but my understanding of the workings of the celestial spheres has taught me there's no such thing. But I *can* say it had nothing to do with sabotage." He gives a little chuckle and gestures to the very craft we're on. "I mean, it's hardly Aristotle Onassis's yacht."

Stelios returns with Cassie at this moment. "I hear what you say about my boat. You be kind to *Calliope*. She is kind to me."

"Of course," Wolfson says cordially.

"I bring you back a friend," Stelios says. "We have talked and eaten baklava, and I think she feels better."

Rebecca and I stand in unison, and I'm surprised when Cassie comes to me and puts her arms around my waist, burying her face into my shoulder. It is the action of a child who needs the reassurance of a loving parent, and I'm the closest approximation to hand. After the initial surprise, I put my arms around her as well, trying to convey that she needn't worry.

"It's going to be all right," I tell her. "You can trust us."

"I'm sorry I didn't tell you," Rebecca adds. "I didn't want you to draw the wrong conclusions. My father is no friend to me now. He chose a side, and it's not the same side I chose. My loyalty is to Tristan ... and to you."

Cassie nods as she releases her embrace of me and then returns to her original seat.

"It's probably an inane and obvious question," I vocalize, "but why don't we just go to the authorities? The police, the FBI, whoever's in charge of this sort of thing?"

"A perfectly valid question," Wolfson replies. "Much like an American horror film. Everyone tries to fight the killer themselves, rather than calling the police. The difficulty is, Consolidated Offshore is not a masked lunatic in the woods, wielding a machete. They've taken great pains to keep everything as legal and above-board as it can appear, while carrying out the nefarious part covertly. If there were something overtly illegal transpiring, believe me, we'd call in the proper authorities."

But I don't believe him. For the first time, I see the deception in his words. As much as this man tries to convince me that his group—whose name, I note with interest, he has yet to divulge—is blameless and on the side of justice, I know it isn't true. They've done things too, even killed when they had to. I suspect no one has gone to the authorities because it would result in convictions on both sides. It is the one piece of information I needed to make my decision.

"Well," I say, standing, "I've heard some interesting things, and I want to thank you for keeping us informed about what's going on. Based on what you've told me, I think we're going to pass."

"Pardon?" Wolfson says with a look of astonishment on his face.

"Pass?" Rebecca says, rising as well.

"Yep. Gonna give 'er a miss this time. Thanks but no thanks. You've told me what's at stake, and I've weighed it in my mind, and in my educated opinion, there's a lot better chance that getting involved will get us six kinds of dead, rather than making a difference. We got what we came here for: Cassie's father will get a new trial. We'll just take her home to her family and let you fine fisher-folk get on with this epic, world-changing battle that has nothing to do with us."

"You're making a mistake," Stelios says.

"Wouldn't be the first time," I tell him. "But this time, I really think the mistake would be getting involved."

"You're already involved. The missions, the prophecies. You're a part of this whether you want to be or not."

I take a few steps toward him, insistent but not threatening. "Maybe so, but you know what you get if everybody decides to say no to a war? Peace. That's what I'm after. Stop Consolidated or let them do their thing; that's your decision. Just leave me and mine out of it."

With that, I head for the gangplank off the boat, with Rebecca and Cassie right behind me. I don't even look over my shoulder to see the reactions of Stelios and Wolfson. Don't know, don't care.

Once we are clear of the *Calliope,* I get an earful from Rebecca. "We're just leaving?" she asks.

"Looks like."

"But what about the mission? What about everything Wolfson told us? We have to stop Consolidated."

Her insistence pushes something in me past my limit of patience. I turn to her, annoyance flooding my tone. "We do? Really? They have a multibillion-dollar plan to establish a domestic oil empire and overthrow Middle Eastern countries that oppose them. What do we have? Your mind-reading abilities? My gift for getting into situations that don't concern me? Shit, if we had thought to keep Cassie's explosive device, we'd have something resembling a weapon we could use against them. But as it stands, we don't. We are go-betweens, so a bunch of corrupt fishermen can take on a bunch of corrupt oilmen and none of them has to get hurt. Well, excuse me for saying it, but I'd kind of like to live this week. And since I'm all sentimental, I'd prefer it if the two of you live as well. Now, if no one else wants to commit suicide today, I suggest you follow me back to the car, and we'll take Cassie home."

Seconds pass, and neither of them utters a word in response. That's all the acknowledgment I need, so I start walking again. No, I'm not proud of myself for raising my voice to Rebecca and Cassie that way, but I'm actually proud of myself for standing up and saying no to the potentially horrible fate that awaited us.

And I have to say for the record that my plan would have been quite good, downright inspired, actually, were it not for the black limo that pulls to a screeching stop next to us in the street. The three men who emerge waste no time with small talk. Instead, each pulls one of us into the limo for an old-fashioned broad-daylight abduction, right there on the streets of Pensacola.

It happens quite quickly, but as I'm being pulled inside the car, I do have time to offer one annoyed musing: "Well, fuck."

Chapter 6

Unsafely inside the limousine, we are shoved into remarkably comfortable seats, opposite our captors, who sit facing us. I feel Cassie reaching for something in her pocket. Before I can even say "Don't," she catches the eye of one of the men opposite. He gets up and pulls away the can of pepper spray, the same one she used to escape her last abductor in New Orleans.

"No no no," the guy says, "we can't have you using that. It's not safe. Do anything else stupid, and you'll find out for yourself."

And so we drive through the streets of this city, now effectively drawn back into the battle we've just excused ourselves from. The silence gets oppressive after a couple of minutes, so I take it upon myself to fill the void with inane prattle. "Consolidated Offshore's welcoming committee, I'm assuming?"

They look at each other but say nothing.

Rebecca takes up the charge. "You're making a big mistake, you know," she offers ominously. This elicits a smile from one and a shake of the head from another. "Do you know who we are?" she asks them.

"No," the middle one retorts, "we go around randomly pulling tourists into the car. Now shut the fuck up."

"Watch your manners," I counter. "There are women and children present."

"Oh, pardon me," he says with all due affectation. "Shut the fuck up ... *please*."

Well played, sir.

Having expended our abductee clichés, the three of us decide that shutting up is probably a good idea. If this plays out as I suspect it will, we'll be taken to someone who will tell us everything we need to know, even if it isn't what we want to hear.

I try to memorize the landscape, in case we find a way to get away, so I can get us back to the rental car somehow. The car should be the least of my worries, but it gives me something to think about, apart from impending interrogation, torture, and death. It's my happy place for the moment. A glance at my companions suggests that they are far from their own personal happy places just now. I put a reassuring hand on Cassie's shoulder, realizing how reassuring it really isn't. I know as well as she does how deep we're in it now.

This fine kettle of fish has just gotten a whole lot finer.

In less than ten minutes, we pull into the underground garage of a tall office building and park in a space set aside for a limousine. I've seen enough movies and detective shows to know that nothing good ever happens in a parking garage, so I am relieved when the three men take us out of the limo and lead us to an elevator. The driver stays with the car; clearly, hostage escort is not in his job description.

All six of us ride the elevator up to the twenty-seventh floor, at the top of the building. As we're getting off, I find the few seconds I need to whisper an important message in their ears: "Hide your thoughts."

It's a tall order, and I know it. Under duress, the idea of protecting our very thoughts from outside attack feels impossible. But in order to survive this, we have to keep some things away from them.

As expected, they take us right to an executive office, identified on the door only by the office number: 2751. The door is open, and the office's inhabitant is standing at the window, staring out at the city of Pensacola, with his back to us.

As we enter, one of our hosts announces, "They're here."

"Wait outside," a familiar voice tells them. "Close the door. I'll call you in if I need you."

"Yes, sir." And with that, the three men leave the room, closing the door behind us.

There is no dramatic musical sting, not even in my mind, as Calvin Traeger turns to face us. Never for a moment did I expect this to be the work of anyone else.

"Well," he says, "of course I recognize my daughter and her kidnapper ..."

"All due respect," I retort, "but I think you've inherited that title ... *Cal*."

He ignores me and continues. "But there's an unfamiliar face in my office. Let's see ... young, vaguely Slavic-looking, and acting very put out. This could only be Miss Haiduk."

Rebecca interrupts him. "Daddy, what the fuck do you think you're doing?"

"I might ask you the same question," he answers. "Did you just happen to choose a vacation in sunny Pensacola after your adventures in storm chasing? Or have you come here to get in the way of my business ventures?"

"You can skip the mustache twisting," I inform him. "We've decided to stay out of this whole deal. Just not interested in what you're up to. You'll get no fight out of us."

"I find that a little hard to believe, given whose boat we caught you leaving today. I think the truth is you've aligned yourselves with Wolf Den."

"With who?" Rebecca asks.

"Spare me the act. My people were watching you on that boat. You were talking with Wolfson himself. You can't convince me that you don't know all about Wolf Den Industries."

"Oh, is that what they're called?" I ask, finally getting the answer I wanted. "Actually, we didn't. Wolfson wasn't very forthcoming with that piece of information. He was far more interested in talking about *you*."

Traeger utters a humorless little laugh. "That's no surprise. Let me guess: he painted Consolidated as the greatest evil on the face of the Earth."

"Not quite," I reply, "but he had a few choice things to say about your plans for world domination. And I have to say, kidnapping us off the street is hardly the way to convince me that you're a philanthropic organization."

"This isn't a kidnapping," he says. "You're free to go at any time."

"Great," I say, turning toward the door and taking my companions by the hand. "Nice talkin' with you."

"But do you really think Wolfson is going to let you live, now that you're in this?"

As God is my witness, I really *really* want to keep going, out that door, down to street level, hail a taxi, and put all of this behind us. But damn it, there's something in Calvin Traeger's tone that suggests that I ought to listen just a little longer. I stop in my tracks, and we turn to face him again.

"Go on," I tell him.

"Have a seat," he offers us, and we do. "I can imagine what Wolfson told you. Stories about cornering the American oil market, driving the competition out of business. It wouldn't surprise me if he threw in tales of international espionage and global warfare." I neither confirm nor deny, so he continues. "I know we're not old friends here, but I think you're smart enough to understand that demonizing me and my corporation is in Clive Wolfson's personal interest. You know what he's capable of. His people killed Jeffrey Casner in Atlanta and set you up to take the blame."

This inspires a response from me. "Way he tells it, Casner was your hired gun, about to come to Florida and blow some shit up."

"He said that?" Traeger says, shaking his head. "Amazing. Jeffrey Casner was on his way to Florida for a fishing trip. He was a systems analyst. If you'd like me to pull up his files, I can show you."

The truth is getting fluid, and it bothers me a lot.

"You think your friend Stelios is really your friend? He was using you all along. He knew Rebecca is my daughter, and he knew how important it was to turn her against me. It looks like he succeeded, too, and that's very upsetting to me."

"Nice try, Daddy," Rebecca interjects, snapping me out of my confusion over his words. "But I know the rest, and the rest tells me you're lying. I know that Consolidated has an illegal partnership with a Chinese oil company to circumvent the Gulf Coast drilling ban."

He doesn't flinch. "You're questioning. That's good. I taught you that a long time ago. Don't just take things at face value. But I also taught you to get all the facts. Yes, Consolidated has a partnership with a Chinese oil company to find drilling sites off the coast, but it's all legal and authorized. The documents are here on site; you can look them over if you want."

This piece of information seems to disarm her. She just stares at him for a few seconds, her face riddled with uncertainty. "But ... but if that's true, then why did you have Cassie's father arrested?"

Traeger looks troubled by this accusation, and I'm glad. Maybe now we have him. But mere seconds later, he explains, "That was an unfortunate thing we had to do. Daniel Haiduk was a valued and trusted employee, with access to some of this company's most confidential information. For years, he served faithfully and without question. Then, last year, he began behaving erratically. He started missing work, questioning corporate decisions. Some of our documents turned up missing. I hired a private detective to observe him, and I was shocked and dismayed to learn that he had been communicating with members of the Chinese government about Consolidated's business practices. I confronted him about it, and he denied it to my face. At that point, I had no choice but to call the FBI, before he could start an international incident."

"That's not true!" Cassie shouts in a voice barely concealing tears. "He would never do that!"

"I'm sorry, young lady. It can't be easy, hearing such things about your own father, but it's true. It broke my heart to have to turn Daniel in to the authorities. I gave him every opportunity to do the right thing, but he refused."

"If all of this is true," Rebecca says, "then why did you pull a gun on Tristan in Ohio a week ago?"

"I overreacted. Try to see it from my point of view. You vanished from my life for years, and then out of the blue, you call me to tell me you're coming back home. Then, when you get there, you're in the company of a strange man twice your age ..."

"Hey!" I interrupt, rising from my seat. "Not twice."

He ignores my protest. "And I find out that he's a suspect in the murder of one of my employees. I really thought he intended to do you harm."

"Why are you in Pensacola now?" I ask him. "You live and work in Ohio. Why did you come down here now, when we would be here?"

"The Ohio office is a satellite office," he explains calmly. "I spend about half the time there and half the time here, closer to the oil interests. I came back down here because I knew that Wolf Den was planning to stir up trouble, and there were rumors that they had involved Rebecca somehow. I had to make sure she was safe."

This is all happening so fast. Every molecule in me wants to distrust this man, but every word he says has the ring of plausibility. I have to ask. "But then ... if that's the case, why did you have your people abduct us off the street and drag us into the limousine?"

Now it's his turn to look astonished. "Abduct you? My employees were under strict orders that you be treated with care and dignity. They met you at the harbor and invited you to come here to meet with me."

In my mind, the strangest sensation overtakes me. My memory of the abduction becomes fuzzy, and I feel light-headed. Then suddenly, in its place, a different memory takes over—the same three men, doing exactly what Calvin Traeger just described: meeting us at the harbor, introducing themselves as employees of Consolidated Offshore, and politely inviting us to visit the corporate headquarters. I now know with certainty that this is what actually took place. I look over at Rebecca, and a similar look of confusion is on her face.

"You're right," I say to him.

"Why ..." Rebecca starts. "Why did I think they took us by force?"

Traeger gives a pleasant little chuckle. "The fellows are a bit on the big side, and they're used to dealing with business types. Even their polite demeanor can look a little intimidating. You'll have to forgive them."

Everything he's saying makes infinite sense, and I'm making peace with the idea that I've completely misjudged him. Then, from out of nowhere, Cassie stands up. "What's going on here?" she asks, sounding panicked. "What's wrong with you two? You know that's not what happened! He's lying. He's lying about all of it!"

Traeger stands and goes to her side. "It's all right, young lady. There's no need to get upset. I know things are happening very fast and you're concerned about your father. I also know that your family is looking for you and they're very worried. If you're ready to go back home, I can put you on a private plane and have you home in just a few hours."

"Stay away from me!" she warns him. "I don't know what you've done to them, but I don't believe you. And I have the evidence to prove it."

Her voice is giving me a headache, and all I want is for her to relax and stop yelling. Calvin Traeger doesn't seem disturbed by her words. Instead, he just keeps trying to reason with her. "Let's get you someplace safe," he says, opening the door to his office. "Rafael, could you come in, please?"

One of the three men who escorted us here enters. "Yes, Mr. Traeger?"

"Miss Haiduk is upset. I'm wondering if you'd get her some dinner and put her up in the executive suites for the night. In the morning, I'd like to put her on the company plane back to Chicago. It seems she's run away from home in order to be here, and I know her family must be worried sick about her."

"No problem, sir. I'll see that she gets everything she needs." He turns to Cassie and politely says, "Miss?"

Cassie runs to me, and—much the way she did on the *Calliope*—she throws her arms around me. But this time, something is different. She whispers in my ear, "You have to remember." As she's doing this, I feel her hand go to my waist and she brushes my hip with her fingertips. Before I can ask her what she's talking about, she pulls away from me and leaves the room with Rafael.

Rebecca and I are now alone with her father. Outside, late afternoon is giving way to evening. In the distance, I can see the harbor where Stelios's boat is docked. Where we almost fell for the smooth talk of a high-powered executive who was trying to use us for his own purposes.

"I owe you an apology," I tell Calvin. "I misjudged you, and I'm sorry about that. I hope you can forgive me. My recent circumstances have made me cynical, I'm afraid."

"Nothing to forgive," he says pleasantly. "And I hope you'll excuse my behavior during our last encounter. I tend to be overprotective. But now I see that you're genuinely fond of Rebecca, and she of you. That's why I wanted you to come here today, to hear it from me. It's not safe for you here. Through no fault of your own, you've gotten caught in the middle of unpleasantness between two very wealthy and powerful corporations. I've tried to make peace with Wolf Den, to find a way for both our enterprises to thrive, but they're extremists. And all my intelligence tells me that they perceive you two as a threat because of your abilities. I have a home here, a private place that no one in Wolfson's organization knows about. Let me put the two of you up there for the night. In the morning, I'll fly you wherever you want to go. I'll return your rental car and pay the fees on it. And I'll even start a false report that the two of you were killed. That way, they won't go looking for you."

"Killed?" Rebecca repeats.

"It's the only way to protect you," he insists. "At least until this skirmish blows over."

"You really aren't doing anything wrong?"

"No, we're not. We're actually paving the way to reduce this country's dependence on foreign oil in a way that doesn't compromise the Alaskan wildlife refuge and doesn't force us to be at the beck and call of hostile nations because of their resources. If all goes as planned, gasoline shouldn't go above two dollars a gallon again in the foreseeable future. And we'll finally be able to pull all our troops out of the Middle East, get them back home where they belong."

The more he talks, the more respect I have for Calvin Traeger. It's like I'm seeing a new side of him, a side I trust and believe. I look over at Rebecca, and I see a similar expression on her face. I watch as her estrangement of several years melts away and she hangs on her father's every word. I actually feel foolish for doubting him all this time.

Rebecca hugs her father, and he reciprocates, holding her for many seconds. When she lets go, he turns to me and says, "Tristan, I hope there are no hard feelings."

"No, sir. I'm actually very pleased by this outcome."

"I'm going to be back at my home in Ohio next week. After you two have had a chance to rest, I'd like you to come visit me for a few days. Let's figure out what we can do about getting Rebecca back in school, taking her law classes, if that's what she wants."

"Really?" she says. "You'd let me take law classes instead of business classes?"

"If that's what would make you happy, then yes. That's what you should take."

"Thank you, Daddy."

Traeger calls to his employee outside the office. "Cornelius, would you come in here, please?"

One of the three men who brought us here enters. "Yes, Mr. Traeger?"

"We're just about done with our meeting. My daughter and her friend are probably tired. Would you please drive them to the residence at Colonial Hills?"

"The limo?"

"Not for just the three of you. The Town Car should suffice."

"Very good, sir."

Calvin turns back to us. "The residence is a fully furnished condo, and the kitchen is well stocked, if you're hungry."

"Thank you," I reply. "For everything."

"You're welcome. I'll leave you two alone for the evening and get back in touch in the morning. Promise you'll behave!" he adds, and I'd swear there's playfulness in his voice.

"We promise," Rebecca says.

"All right, then. Good night, you two."

With that, Cornelius leads us to the elevator and back down to the parking garage. There is a silver Lincoln Town Car waiting, and he unlocks it and opens the back door for us. We climb in, and he gets into the driver's seat.

I suddenly remember, "Our bags are in the rental car. Can we stop off and get them?"

"The condo has everything you'll need for tonight," he answers pleasantly. "In the morning, we can drop by the place you parked and get your things on the way to the airport."

"Thank you," I reply, looking at his reflection in the rearview mirror. I make eye contact with him, and for a split second, something flashes through my mind. It is his voice, but he is saying, *"Do anything else stupid, and you'll find out for yourself."*

The thought is disconcerting; it feels like a false memory, something I thought this man said, but I know in my mind that he couldn't have said it. He sees the puzzled look on my face. "Are you all right, sir?" he asks.

"I'm fine. Just ... just a little headache."

"There's a stocked medicine cabinet at the condo," he offers. "We should be there in about ten minutes. For now, sit back and enjoy the ride."

Clearing the disturbing thought out of my mind, I actually do sit back and enjoy the ride. Pensacola at dusk is quite pretty, and the car is very comfortable. Rebecca rests her head on my shoulder, and I touch her arm. This day has been a whirlwind, I know it has, but when I try to put my mind to why that is, the details are unclear. I know I am not hungry, but I have no memory of where or what I ate today. *I must be more tired than I thought. Sleep will help.*

The thought most prevalent on my mind right now is that it's over. The battle we came to wage has been averted, and Rebecca and I get to leave here in the morning, to go anywhere we'd like. We could take a vacation, or I could show her my home in Maryland. I feel free for the first time in a very long time, and that thought warms me.

A few minutes later, we pull into a housing community called Colonial Hills. Though it has an ornate entryway, it is not gated in the traditional sense—no guards or gatekeeper. On its streets are row after row of well-built, quietly elegant townhouses. Cornelius pulls the Town Car into the driveway of one such townhouse, shutting off the engine and then coming around to the back to let us out.

Afterward, he escorts us to the front door, unlocks it, and turns on the living room lights for us. "Here we go, folks. Welcome to your accommodations. There's some clothing in the closets. I expect there'll be something that fits you well enough for the night. As I said, we'll get your bags in the morning. You have a good night."

"Thank you," I reply.

And with that, Cornelius exits the condo and leaves us alone. The place is peaceful and quite comfortable. After walking from room to room, confirming that, yes, the kitchen is well stocked, there is clothing in the closets, and the medicine cabinet has everything he said it would, we settle in the living room and relax on the couch. It is made of white leather, and it feels like getting a hug from God.

"Screw going home," I purr. "Let's live here."

"I could get used to this," she agrees.

I gesture toward the fifty-six-inch LCD television. "You want to watch anything?"

"No, I really don't. I'm just content to be here."

"Yeah, so am I," I tell her. "That's weird."

"Why is it weird?"

"Because we're us. Since we've met, how many moments of pure relaxation and contentment have we shared?"

She thinks about it a moment. "Two. Maybe three."

"Exactly. And yet, here we are, in your father's condo, supposedly in the middle of this epic battle, but we're safe, we're in the clear, and tomorrow we get to leave."

"I missed the part where that's a bad thing," she tells me.

"Me too. Every inclination of my personality tells me that I should be suspicious and cynical and looking for an angle or a catch, but I don't want to do that. The very fact that I've accepted it is what makes it so hard for me to accept."

She runs her fingers through my hair. "Well, I think that two years of almost nonstop assignments has left you … understandably … jaded and pessimistic about human nature. Finally, someone is treating us with kindness and compassion, and we're just not used to it. I was feeling the same way."

"You were?" I ask, newly interested.

"Yeah. When my father told us all that stuff, I was thinking, *yeah, right,* but the more he talked …"

"The more you believed him," I finish for her. "That's how it happened with me."

She pauses a moment and then asks me, "Are you afraid to go home?"

"Why would I be afraid?"

"Maybe *afraid* isn't the right word. You've just seemed uneasy since we got to my father's office."

"No, that's the problem," I correct. "I'm feeling too at ease. I should be feeling uneasy, with everything that's going on. What I'm feeling feels more like being …"

"What?"

"It's silly."

"What is? What does it feel like?"

"I feel like I'm stoned."

She gives me a quizzical look. "You mean, like in a biblical sense?"

"No, I mean like in a ganjical sense. You know the feeling you get after smoking, when everything's good, and nothing really matters, and all you care about is hanging out with your friends who are also stoned?"

"Umm, in theory, yes, I know how that feels."

"*That's* how I'm feeling now. I've felt this way since shortly after we arrived at your father's office."

"Do you think we've been drugged?" she asks.

"We couldn't be. We didn't accept any food or drink from anyone, there was no gas or injection. But I tell you this: I am barely able to keep from going into that kitchen and seeing if there's cookies."

There *are* cookies, as a matter of fact. White chocolate macadamia nut cookies, and if the couch is like a hug from God, then these cookies are a big, sloppy kiss from Jesus himself. We settle back into the couch with a plate of the amazing things and indulge until a full dozen are gone.

"Do you suppose cold milk would be too much to hope for?" Rebecca asks, standing.

"One way to find out," I reply.

But before we can investigate, we both hear a strange sound from outside the condo, a *thwip* sound and then another soon after.

"What was that?" she asks.

"I'm not sure. Get down, behind the arm of the couch."

Seconds later, as Rebecca tries to hide, I hear someone working the lock to the condo's front door. I'm armed with nothing more than a heightened sense of inner peace, but I'm prepared to go down fighting if I have to.

It takes the new arrival almost no time to open the door and rush into the room. He's dressed in gray, carrying a gun, and wearing what looks like a stocking cap on his head, made of woven metal of some kind. By the time I see his face, the gun is pointed right at me.

"Stelios!"

"Oh, thank God you're all right!" he says, lowering the weapon once he sees it's me. "Don't worry, it's just a tranquilizer gun."

Where does one even get a tranquilizer gun? Are there stores for these things?

"What the hell are you doing here?" I ask him. "And who did you shoot?"

"I'm here to get the two of you out of here. And I shot the two men who were guarding this place, keeping you from leaving."

Rebecca comes out of hiding. "No one was guarding us. We're here because my father invited us to spend the night as his guests before he flies us home in the morning."

"Oh, right. So he's nice now."

"Yes, as a matter of fact," she replies, none too thrilled with his tone. "We misjudged him."

"And this newfound respect and admiration happened, when? Sometime after you got to his office?"

"Yes," I answer.

"And you're still feeling it now, along with an elevated mood and a sense of calm and well-being, yes?"

"Well, yes. What—?"

"Give it a moment and your thoughts will clear," he says.

Suddenly, something in my head changes, as if someone has abruptly shut off the most pleasant music in the world. There is a moment of physical pain, and I see that Rebecca feels it too. Stelios hurries to our side.

"I'm sorry, I'm sorry. You'll feel all right in a moment." He takes off the metallic cap. "Won't need this now."

Amazingly, every good feeling I've had for the last hour is suddenly uprooted and turned on its head. Memories of what really happened rush back at me. "What happened to us?" I ask him.

"Your dear host is to blame. The man who brought you here was emitting a kind of subliminal field that's only perceptible by psychics. He was able to make you believe pretty much anything he wants you to. He was outside of the condo and also outside of Calvin Traeger's office. Once he lost consciousness, the field was broken. My guess is, Calvin knew he couldn't win you over, and he didn't want you siding with us, so he used this trick to convince you that he wasn't doing anything wrong. That way, you'd just go home and never know what he was up to."

"My God," Rebecca says.

"And it worked, too," I add. "I believed every word he said."

"What about the girl?" Stelios asks. "Where is she?"

The horrifying realization hits me. "Cassie," I utter as a gasp. "I … we completely forgot about her. Traeger had one of his people take her somewhere. I don't know what he's done with her. Oh my God, Stelios. She knows about the evidence. If Consolidated realizes what she knows, her life is in terrible danger."

"We have to find her," Rebecca says.

"Yes we do," our rescuer confirms. "But first we have to get you out of here. The guards aren't dead, only unconscious, and they won't be for long. I need you to come with me, and to do that, I need you to trust me. Are you willing to do that?"

Rebecca and I look at each other. We told ourselves we wouldn't get in the middle of this battle, but after Calvin Traeger's betrayal, neutrality is no longer an option. And with Cassie in the hands of the enemy, leaving town is impossible too.

"Yes," she answers.

"All right, then," he says. "Stay close to me."

He leads us out of the condo, past the slumped pair at the front entrance, and to a car waiting several doors down the block. We get in, and he says to us, "Wait here for a minute. I have to go stash those two somewhere. I don't want them waking up and telling Consolidated what's happened. Not for a while, anyway."

He disappears for about five minutes, as Rebecca and I sit nervously in the car, anxious about every passerby and every shadow. Fortunately, Stelios returns and gets behind the wheel, starting the car and pulling away quickly.

"Where are we going?" I ask him.

"Back to the *Calliope*. I've increased security around the dock, so nobody can get access to you again. We need to spend this night strategizing, my friends. I suspect the war begins in earnest tomorrow."

Chapter 7

My head is spinning as Stelios drives us away from the luxury home that was actually our holding cell. Now, it seems, Consolidated has the power to alter our thoughts and our perceptions. Of course, I should have known that from the beginning. It was one of their operatives who sent me the false assignment to warn Rebecca in the first place. All of this makes me even more disappointed in myself for trusting them today.

"There's no escaping this, is there?" I ask Stelios as we head back to the dock.

"You are a free man," he replies. "Unlike Calvin Traeger, I won't hold you against your will. Your rental car is parked near my boat, and if you wish, I will take you to it and let you drive away from here, putting all of this behind you."

"But?" I ask him.

"But to do so would exact a great cost. They have your young traveling companion, and the combination of her unyielding protection of her father and her lack of physical strength is a vulnerability they are certain to exploit. They want that evidence, and while you and I would never dream of harming a young girl, they would do so without flinching. And when she breaks, she'll give up the name of your friend, the attorney who safeguards that evidence. Rescuing Miss Haiduk has to be our first priority. Once she's safe, you can decide whether to fulfill your part in all of this. But know this: everything Wolfson told you is true. If Consolidated succeeds, it will have a lasting impact on the world's economy and political situation, and on the ecosystem of the region. No one should have that much power."

I'm dismayed, as I listen to him, to realize that what he's saying is true, and the only reasons I have for wanting to leave here are personal—fear, apathy, selfishness. And while those are all good survival tactics, they hardly earn me a nomination for the Nobel Peace Prize. I must defer to Rebecca on this. In the end, she has a lot more to gain or lose than I do.

I turn to her. "I won't make this decision without you. This is your father, your life we're talking about. After we make sure Cassie is safe, if you want us to leave here and not look back, I'll honor that. But if you want us to help these people do battle against your father's company, I'll stand by your side."

Her face tells the story of her painful uncertainty. Many seconds pass as she contemplates it, and I wish I had the power to read her thoughts, the way she does mine, so she wouldn't have to voice them. Finally, she speaks. "I wanted to believe him tonight. Mind control or not, I wanted so much to believe everything he said. About accepting me, about welcoming me back, about letting me pursue my studies again. It's been years since he's spoken to me that way, and it was so wonderful to hear him. I felt … I felt like I had my daddy back. And then I learned it was all a lie, like so many lies he's told over the years. Because he thinks we're dangerous. Because he thinks we're a threat. Okay, fine. If that's what he wants, let's *be* dangerous. Let's *be* a threat. Let's fight him with everything we've got."

"You're sure?" I ask.

"Very sure."

"All right, Stelios, you heard the lady. We're in this now. Tell us what we need to do."

"Good. Wolfson will be glad to hear this. He was concerned that he offended you and that offense allowed those men to take you captive."

I'm pleased to see the Sebring still parked near the dock when we arrive. I don't think we'll need to make a hasty escape, but it's good to know that we can.

As we re-board the *Calliope,* Wolfson greets us on the deck. "Welcome back. I'm very glad to see you return safely. We couldn't risk following the car that took you, so we had to rely on Stelios's knowledge of where you might be detained. I'm pleased to see that he was correct."

"We're back in this with you," Rebecca announces. "They've got Cassie Haiduk, and we need to get her back before we do anything else."

He looks quite concerned at this. "I see. That does complicate matters. She holds information they need very much. Do you know where they've taken her?"

His question stirs a memory in me. Something Traeger said when we were in his office. He told one of his associates to take her somewhere, but where? The subliminal field messed with my thoughts and my memories. I can't recall it, not by myself. "Rebecca, help me remember what your father said about this."

She closes her eyes, and I strain to revisit that moment. I can see Traeger in my mind. Cassie is upset and speaking loudly, and Traeger calls in one of his people. He calls the man by name. Rafael, I think it was. He asks her to take Cassie to ... to ...

"The executive suites," Rebecca says. "That's what he said. Take her to the executive suites."

"Well done, Persephone," Stelios says.

"What is that?" I ask. "Is it a local hotel?"

"No," Wolfson answers, "that would be too public. For what they intend, they need privacy. My guess is they have a private place that they call their executive suites."

"What about the place where they took us?" Rebecca suggests.

"No," I reply, "they called that Colonial Hills. It was something different."

"Colonial Hills is the community where they have their long-term housing for visitors," Wolfson explains. "The executive suites would be their short-term housing for dignitaries. Stelios, find out where it is. Use any means necessary."

"Yes, sir." With that, Stelios disappears below decks.

"Any means necessary?" I repeat. "I trust that doesn't mean a Google search."

"It can start with one," Wolfson replies with a hint of a smile. "But it might end other places." As he speaks, I can see that he is giving us a visual inspection. "They didn't harm you, it appears. That's good. It offers me some hope that our Miss Haiduk may yet be alive and unharmed as well."

"Not to be pessimistic," I answer, "but the reason we're unharmed is because Calvin's little mind-fuck games made us agreeable. Cassie doesn't share our gifts, so she may not have the same degree of protection that we had."

"You make a valid point. All the more reason we …" He suddenly stops and sniffs. "Why do the two of you smell like cookies?"

"That's not important now," I reply. "What's important is getting Cassie back. Say that Stelios gets the location where they're holding her. What do we do? Call the police? Storm the place?"

"More likely, the latter. If we get the police involved, the people holding her might panic and hurt her. If we can get in there quietly ourselves, we stand a better chance."

"I was afraid you'd say that," Rebecca says.

Stelios emerges from below with a disappointed look. "Nothing yet," he reports. "Online resources come up empty, and I can't reach anyone who would know where these guest suites are. I can go interrogate one of their people."

Wolfson nods. "Be discreet about it."

"Wait, wait," I interrupt. "I'm not all that keen on interrogation. Maybe there's another way. Let me make a phone call or two." I reach for the cell phone that's clipped to my waist, but as I open the case, I discover nothing inside. "Shit, my phone's gone."

"What?" Rebecca says.

"They must have taken it from you when they brought you to the condo," Wolfson surmises.

"No, they didn't. I would have remembered, now that I have my memory of those events back." Then it hits me—when Cassie hugged me in Traeger's office, she reached for something. "Cassie took my phone. She probably has it on her right now."

"The GPS signal," Wolfson says. "Go below with Stelios and give him your phone number. We have software that can track the GPS signal. From there, we can narrow the radius until we find her."

I follow Stelios below decks to his living quarters and work area. I am surprised (though, at this point, I'm not sure why) to find a very sophisticated computer room, with devices whose function I couldn't begin to guess. He leads me to a terminal and asks for my cell phone number with area code, which I supply, after the requisite period of trying to remember what it is. He enters it into an online software application, and the screen displays first a map of the United States, then a map of Florida. Finally, to my relief, it zooms in on Pensacola. Cassie—or at least my phone—has not left town.

"Can you tell where she is?" I ask.

He stares intently at the screen. "I'm getting an area, but it's a three-block radius at the moment. I'm trying to ping your phone without sending an audible signal that somebody might hear. Give me a moment."

He pushes buttons and stares intently some more, engaging various applications to help filter the signal and close in on where she is. After a couple of minutes, I sense that he is frustrated with the effort and not having much luck.

Fortunately, Wolfson chooses this moment to join us, and he checks in. "Any luck?" he asks.

"Yes and no," Stelios replies. "I have it triangulated to a three-block radius, but I can't get an exact location without sending an audible to the phone, and I can't risk having someone hear it and take the phone away."

"All right, then," Wolfson says, "try this. Save the results and import them into the Consolidated database. Draw up an area map of all addresses within that radius and cross-reference it against any addresses of known Consolidated properties."

Stelios types frantically, and the screen changes to a different application. A list of hundreds of addresses appears. A few more keystrokes, and the list drops to about twenty. "Do a substring search for executive suites," Wolfson instructs.

Stelios makes the entry, and the list of addresses narrows to three. "There," he says. "That has to be it."

"You found her?" I ask.

"I think we have," Wolfson confirms. "It's a property owned by Consolidated. A former hotel. They purchased it and now use it to house short-term visitors."

"A hotel?" I repeat. "But if this is where they keep their guests, would it make sense to keep a prisoner in there? I mean, she could make noise or something."

"It means they've got her someplace isolated within the building," Wolfson surmises. "Soundproof, most likely. And someplace the guests wouldn't encounter her. Stelios, go to the Plantrex app, and pull up the schematic for that address, please."

To my ongoing amazement, Stelios goes to another application, types in some data, and within seconds, the blueprints for the hotel appear on screen. He scans through, floor by floor, looking with Wolfson for a place where they might house an unwilling guest.

"Someplace in the basement, maybe," Stelios surmises. "Or … you don't think—?"

Wolfson realizes the possibility and gives an expression of concern. "I would hope not; I mean, she's only a child."

I don't like the sound of this. "What? What are you thinking?"

"The pool," Stelios says grimly.

Slow on the uptake, I still need more information. "What about the pool? They're going to take her swimming?"

"In a manner of speaking," Wolfson replies, "quite possibly. Water can be very effective in obtaining needed information, Tristan."

Then it comes to me, and I wish it hadn't. "Torture? You're talking about the torture of a teenage girl?"

"We mustn't jump to conclusions. But unfortunately, we can't rule it out as a possibility. If the pool is open to their guests, they wouldn't dare risk using it that way. But if it's closed off, they could very easily adapt it for that purpose."

"Shit, we've got to get her out of there now."

"Steady, Tristan," Wolfson says, putting up a hand. "That is our primary objective, of course. But we only get one chance at it. At the moment, we have the element of surprise. They still think you're stashed away in Colonial Hills and that we don't know where they've got Miss Haiduk. When we play our hand, that all goes away. So we have to make our effort count."

"So what's the plan?" I ask.

"Deception is out, so it has to be speed and force. Stelios, who do we have available right here and now?"

"On this short notice? No one."

"Damn. I was afraid you'd say that. Looks like it's the four of us, old boy. How do you feel about storming the castle?"

This is it. The battle I've tried so hard not to join is bringing me in of its own will and its own power. If I don't fight, Cassie might very well die. "Yeah. I'll … uh … I'll do it. But I'm not good with guns or anything like that."

"Well, then it's a good thing we are," he says calmly. "I'll lead this mission, and Stelios and I will handle the bulk of the unpleasantness. I'll need to know that you can be counted on, should we need you. If I arm you, will you know what to do with it?"

The question makes me feel extremely uneasy. Guns. Never something I've been interested in or comfortable with. But I know which end you point at the bad guy, and I've still got enough of a survival instinct that the answer to the question of them or me is always "them." So I tell him, "Yeah, I'm good," in a tone that bespeaks the tiniest grain of confidence.

"Good," Wolfson says. "I'm glad to hear it. We don't want you shooting anyone, certainly, but it's reassuring to know that if the situation arises, you'll be prepared. I only wish we knew for sure where they're keeping her in the building."

At these words, a familiar phrase whispers through my mind: *My people are destroyed for lack of knowledge.* The words are accompanied by a strange feeling, similar to what I feel when a new assignment comes in. In my mind, I see rooms I've never been to. I am fairly certain they are rooms within the former hotel.

Of course. The assignment. The assignment isn't over. I was sent to protect Cassie Haiduk, and I'm not done protecting her. The same forces that sent me to stop her from blowing up her school are giving me information about her exact location, and it's time to act on it.

"I know where she is," I say suddenly, surprising the two men. "Let me see those blueprints."

I go to the computer and scroll through the different room layouts for the building. Finally, I settle on the basement, and an image is clear in my mind: Cassie, in a chair, surrounded by large, loud machines. Laundry machines; of course.

"She's in the basement," I tell them, "in the laundry room. They're using the noise of the washers and dryers to cover up the sound of what they're doing and to keep her uncomfortable and disoriented."

Wolfson looks truly impressed. "You have a remarkable gift," he says in quiet awe. "Can you see how many people are there with her?"

I close my eyes and try to focus on the room. Never before have I been able to see things of this nature, things that are currently happening somewhere else, and I hope against hope that this isn't just my imagination telling me what I want to see. But I do have an image in my mind, and in that image are four men surrounding Cassie.

"Four," I tell them. "Four that I can see. But it could be more."

"Well done, Tristan," Wolfson says. "We now have the tactical advantage we need. But without their exact numbers, it'll be difficult to know if we have a chance. Still, time is of the essence and we need to move now. Stelios, get me four semi-automatic handguns and one automatic assault rifle."

"Any grenades?" Stelios asks without batting an eye at this shopping list of destruction.

"Only a couple. We don't want to leave a mess."

Stelios leaves the room to go procure the arsenal, and I stare dumbfounded at Clive Wolfson, trying to wrap my brain around what we're about to do. "My God," I say quietly, "who are you people anyway?"

He offers a little nod and a half-smile. "The face of business in a competitive and dangerous global economy. Sometimes the friendly fisherman on the box of fish sticks is packing a little insurance under that raincoat. But hear this: the guns in our hands will not be pointed at you. We're your ally in this. You, Persephone, Miss Haiduk. With your help, we can turn the tide in this skirmish."

Stelios returns with a cache of intimidating weapons and we all return topside, where Rebecca is waiting, having heard only the barest minimum of the conversation that took place below. I brief her quickly on what's ahead, and she takes the news with as much courage as she can muster, expressing some reasonable degree of concern at the prospect of carrying a gun, let alone using it.

The four of us get into Wolfson's gray Lexus SUV, and he drives us toward Consolidated's executive suites, toward the first battle of the war. I'm momentarily startled when Stelios responds verbally to that thought. "Hardly the first battle, Tristan. We've had issues with Consolidated for several years now. It's the nature of the business. We both want the same geographic locations, but for very different purposes. If all goes well, this will be the *last* battle of the war."

"Calvin Traeger feels similar animosity toward you," I tell him frankly. "He considers Wolf Den the enemy."

"I'm not surprised," Wolfson says. "We're an obstacle to him. To all of them. The fishing industry, the laws of the state of Florida and the United States. All of it stands in the way of their making inordinately vast sums of money. So what do they do? They circumvent. Daniel Haiduk threatens to blow the whistle, so they invent treason and throw him in prison. The law says they can't drill off the coast of Florida, so they turn to the Chinese for an unholy alliance. My company fishes in their waters, so they try to destroy us. It's their way."

"And what's your way?" Rebecca asks pointedly. "What do you do in the face of all this?"

"Whatever we have to," he replies. "I won't insult your intelligence by telling you that we're angelic by any means. We've had to do some things I'm not proud of. And the mere fact that we're going into this heavily armed confirms that our hands are not pristine. But we're not run by organized crime ... or even *dis*organized crime, for that matter. We're a private corporation, operating within the law at every opportunity. Once Consolidated Offshore is stopped, we can return to the business we set out to do. Now do you see why you're so important to this mission?"

"Yes," she says quietly, and in her voice, I hear her desire that it didn't have to be.

Ten minutes later, we pull into the parking lot of Consolidated's executive suites. In that parking lot are five cars. Looking up, I see lights in three windows of the hotel, all on the top floor, nine stories up. Wolfson parks us around back, away from the other cars and away from the road, so we can unload discreetly. As quietly as we can, we get the armaments from the trunk. Each of us gets a handgun, and Stelios takes the assault rifle, handing the grenades to Wolfson. We look like we are going to liberate the hotel.

There are several entrances to the building on each exterior wall, but every one has a key-card reader outside, required to unlock it. "What do we do?" Rebecca asks. "Go to the front desk and try to get a key?"

"If this was a regular hotel," Stelios says, "that would work. But Consolidated knows exactly who is supposed to be here. They'd never let us in. Fortunately, they don't have to." He pulls out a small electronic device with a key card attached to it by wires. Inserting the card into the reader, he sets the device to cycle through a range of settings until it beeps and the red light on the card reader turns green. With a victorious smile, he pulls the door open, props it open with one foot, and retrieves the card and the device. "In we go," he says.

But before we can get any further, a man's voice speaks forcefully from the darkness behind us. "Police. Stay right where you are. No sudden moves, any of you."

I put my hands up, and Rebecca does likewise. I don't even want to turn to face the officer, for fear of violating his "no sudden moves" order.

"I can explain," I say quietly.

In response, I hear a different voice, a woman's voice. To my surprise, it is a familiar voice. "Who are you, and what are you doing here?"

Slowly and deliberately, I turn to face the speaker. "Bronwyn!"

"Tristan?" she says, sounding quite surprised to see me.

In a gently comical moment, we both ask, "What are you doing here?"

"Me and the posse are rescuing Cassie Haiduk," I tell her. "What about you?"

"I'm here to rescue her too. She phoned me several hours ago and told me she was in trouble and needed help. She thought the two of you were captured or killed."

"Captured, yes," Rebecca clarifies. "Killed? Well, the night's not over yet, but so far so good. You drove all the way here from New Orleans to help her?"

"It's only two and a half hours on the interstate. She didn't know where else to turn, so she started calling numbers she got off your phone, Tristan. First one she called was mine. I called for some local backup. I didn't realize you'd be here on the same errand."

"Well, we're glad to see you," I tell her, finally putting my hands down. "We need all the help we can get. This is Stelios, by the way, and Wolfson. They're on the side of right, such as it is."

"Captain Bronwyn Kelsey," she says. "New Orleans Police Department. This is Officer Davies and Officer Moffat. What's the sit rep?"

"The girl's in the basement of the building," Wolfson says. "Laundry room. Four hostiles guarding her. Maybe more."

"And we've learned this how?" she asks.

"Courtesy of Tristan's mental abilities. He can ..."

"I've seen him in action," she interrupts. "I'll trust them for now. I'm going to go out on a limb and guess that none of you are in law enforcement?"

"It would purely be a citizen's arrest," Wolfson says.

"All right, then. Let me lead this mission. Do not fire unless fired upon, do you understand?"

"Yes, ma'am," I answer for the group, relieved at the instruction.

"Okay," she says, stepping through the door, "follow me. Stay together. Davies and Moffat, you two take up the rear. Make sure nobody's following us."

"Yes, ma'am," Moffat says.

We enter the hotel and find ourselves in a hallway with no one in sight. With so few guests of the company, staff is kept to a minimum. Good news for us; it means we can probably get to the basement without being seen. There's no effort to look casual now; if we're spotted, the trouble starts. But we catch a break and make our way to the service stairs without being spotted. A second piece of luck allows us to open the stairwell door without a key and without sounding any alarms.

Cautiously and as quietly as possible, we make our way down one flight of stairs to the hotel's basement. This area lacks the bright, clean appearance of the main floor above. Unseen by guests, the basement is dimly lit, cold, and generally dreary. "This is the second dark, unpleasant place I've been with you this week," I tell Bronwyn quietly.

"Let's hope this one works out better than the last one," she retorts. She then turns to the two officers. "Maintain position here at the end of the hallway."

We pass several storage rooms on our way to the end of the corridor. As we proceed, the sound of laundry machines grows louder; this is the place, just like in my vision. I can't hear voices, but I suppose that's good; if we can't hear them, odds are they can't hear us. So we follow Bronwyn into the laundry room, and finally we see them. There are indeed four men standing over Cassie, who sits in a metal folding chair near the big washers and dryers. She looks especially annoyed, but I can see no signs that any harm has befallen her.

Stelios takes a step forward to begin our offensive, but Bronwyn shakes her head and motions for us to fall back. I see the dismay on Stelios's face, but he complies, and we regroup in a storage room down the hall. We close the door behind us, and I turn on the light to see that this room is used to store dry goods for the hotel's breakfast bar.

Stelios immediately confronts Bronwyn. "Why did you stop us? They have no idea we are here. We can take those men out easily."

"It's an unacceptable risk," she says. "Yes, if we go in there with guns blazing, odds are, we can take them out. But that's the last resort, not the first response. Cassie is very close to them, for one thing. And for another, I didn't come all this way to kill anybody."

Before Stelios can retort, I add, "Neither did I."

"Me either," Rebecca agrees.

"Very well then, Captain," Wolfson says. "I trust you have another plan for rescuing this young woman?"

Bronwyn looks around, and something catches her eye. "Anybody got a lighter?" she asks. Wolfson and Stelios both produce lighters from their pockets and hold them up for her to see. "Good. I'm thinking a little homemade flash bomb will be just the diversion we need to extricate her."

"A flash bomb?" Rebecca asks. "What do you plan to use to make that?"

Bronwyn walks over to a counter stacked with dozens of bottles of powdered non-dairy creamer. "Only one of the most flammable substances known to man."

"Outstanding," Wolfson says, sounding impressed.

"Stelios, can you very discreetly get me a few pillowcases from the laundry storage room back there?" Bronwyn asks.

"Of course," he says, ducking out of the room. Less than a minute later, he returns with four pillowcases and hands them to Bronwyn.

"Thanks," she says. "Okay, these burn hot but they burn fast. The idea is to get close, light them, throw them near—but not *at*—the four men, and in the confusion, I'll get Cassie and pull her out of there."

"Works for me," I reply.

"Fill them half-full of the powdered creamer. You need to be able to lift them and throw them once they're lit. And once they *are* lit, you only have a few seconds to get rid of them."

We fill the cases with bottle after bottle of the product I now intend never to put in my body again. I pick mine up and feel that it weighs about six pounds. The others do likewise, and soon we are all armed with our makeshift grenades.

"Follow me out," Bronwyn instructs us. "Stay close to me. When we get within about eight feet of where they are, light them up and throw. Make them land *behind* the people and nowhere near Cassie. We want a perimeter of fire. After you throw, fall back to the storage room. I'll get Cassie out before they know what happened. Any questions?" Nobody asks one. "Good. Let's do this."

I feel my heart start to race as we move slowly out of our hiding place and back toward the laundry room. Underneath everything is the incessant thrumming of the huge, industrial washing machines and clothes dryers, offering a soulless electrical heartbeat to keep pace with my real one. In a few seconds, we can see our targets once again, though we can't hear them well enough to make out what they're saying. They surround Cassie's chair on three sides, bombarding her with what seem to be questions. She remains stony in the face of this treatment, but I can only imagine how scared she feels. We need to get her out of this right now.

Closer and closer we creep, still undetected by the four men who have no reason to suspect they are being watched. When we are about eight feet behind them, Bronwyn gives a nod. Stelios lights his lighter, and Wolfson his. They touch the fabric of my pillowcase and Bronwyn's, and then each of their own. Simultaneously, we let the 400-thread-count Molotov linens fly. They land perfectly, each a couple of feet behind one of the four captors. As the pillowcases land, the flame hits the creamer, and the fireballs are spectacular. The men, clearly startled, whirl around to face the source of the flame. Like a shot, Bronwyn Kelsey breaks down the middle, grabbing Cassie by the hand and pulling her from her chair.

I'm so entranced with watching her that I forget to head back to the storage room with the others. Bronwyn has to put a hand on my shoulder and pull me in that direction. Remembering myself, I run for the room, Bronwyn and Cassie close behind. I make it inside, but before Bronwyn can join us, a voice from behind her orders, "Stop!"

I peer out of the room in time to see Bronwyn stop running and turn to face the man. He has a pistol pulled and aimed at her. She hasn't pulled her own gun, and at the moment, I don't know if that's a good thing or not. In a few seconds, the other three men file in behind the first. "Don't you take her," the first one says.

It's not what I expected to hear; Bronwyn either, clearly, as she replies, "What?"

"The girl. Let her go."

"Let her go?" she repeats.

"That's right. I'm not going to let you take her."

This gets stranger and stranger. "I'm here to take her back from *you*. She's being held here against her will."

"All I know is, we're here to keep this girl safe and ask her where she put some property that was stolen from our company."

I don't recognize this man or any of the other three, so I gamble that he doesn't know me either, and I step out of the room to be by Bronwyn's side; after all, I know more about the situation than she does. "You have to know that she's been brought here by force," I tell him. "Ask her, she'll tell you."

"I've *been* telling them," Cassie contributes at this point. "They don't listen to me."

"Like I said," the man replies, "she has some stolen property belonging to Consolidated. The people who brought her here told me not to let her go to her hotel room until she tells us where it is."

"Until you're done torturing her, you mean."

"Torture?" the man says, sounding genuinely stunned at the word. "We're not here to torture anybody."

"Cassie, did they hurt you?" I ask.

"No, they're just kind of dicks. And I'm sick of being in the laundry room. It's giving me a headache."

Bronwyn intercedes at this point. "I'm a police officer. With my left hand, I'm going to very slowly reach for my badge and show it to you."

The man nods and she removes her badge from her pants pocket and displays it close enough for him to read. "This says New Orleans Police," he observes quite correctly. "We're not in New Orleans. You don't have any authority here."

"I have two Pensacola police officers at the end of the hall who have enough authority to spare. I'm ordering you to release this girl into my custody or face arrest."

They put their guns down and let Cassie walk over to Bronwyn. "What's gonna happen to us?" their leader asks.

"From everything you've told me, you had no idea she'd been kidnapped. I'm going to ask you for your names and contact information, and when we apprehend the people responsible, we'll want to question you, but I believe you'll be clear of prosecution."

It really looks like she's won them over. And believe me, if I had the power to stop time and change things, I would definitely undo what happens next. But I can't, and Stelios and Wolfson walk out of that store room and into the view of the four men. One of the four shouts out, "They're from Wolf Den! It's a trick!"

And things go downhill from there. All four men immediately point their guns at us again. In an instant, Rebecca grabs Cassie's arm and runs with her to the store room, closing the door behind her. Bronwyn draws on the men, as do Stelios and Wolfson. To my amazement, and without even remembering it happening, I find my own pistol in my hand, aimed at one of the four opponents.

Bronwyn calls to the other officers. "Davies, Moffat, we need you!" When the two don't respond, she orders, "Put the guns down." I trust she's talking to them and not us.

"You're with Wolf Den," one of them says.

"I don't even know what that is," she replies. "I'm a New Orleans police detective. I have authorization to use deadly force if necessary, and a very strong desire not to. The choice is yours."

I watch as the men look to each other and then back at Bronwyn, clearly confused about what to do and what will happen next. The one who's been speaking for their group tells us, "I'm sorry. I have my orders. I can't let you leave here with her."

At this already difficult moment, the two Pensacola cops join us, with their guns trained on yet another man. "Captain Kelsey," Davies says, "we stopped this guy coming down the stairs."

"Who is he?" she asks.

One of the original four chimes in, "Walsh, what are you doing here?"—earning a very dirty look from Walsh, who didn't appear to be so forthcoming with that information.

"He's Walsh," Davies says.

"Thank you, Officer," Bronwyn replies. "Does someone want to fill me in on why he's here?"

Moffat replies, "He won't say, but he was carrying this." The officer opens up what looks like a large black medical bag. Our guys cover their guys, freeing Bronwyn up to put her gun down and look inside the bag. She pulls out syringes, vials of liquid, electrodes, and wires.

"Not here to torture anybody, huh?" she asks the original captors. "Then what do you call this?"

The men look genuinely surprised at what she shows them. Their leader asks, "Walsh, what the hell is this? What were you going to do?"

Walsh doesn't answer him, but Wolfson does, calmly asking, "What's your name?"

I'm a bit surprised to hear the man answer, "Lucas."

"And what's your job? What do you do for Consolidated Offshore?"

"I'm head of security."

Wolfson continues pleasant conversation, which sounds immensely odd during this armed standoff. "That's a lot of responsibility. Quite a bit of pressure, I expect. Do you know who I am?"

"You're the president of Wolf Den."

"That's right, Lucas. My name is Clive. I know that my company has been at odds with yours for some time, and you must look upon us as the enemy. Both sides have done things we're not proud of, but we don't have to continue the foolishness here tonight. Captain Kelsey told you the truth. She is a New Orleans police detective, and she was called here by Miss Haiduk to bring her to safety. This is why we're here too. It's clear from your expression that your friend Mr. Walsh has some ideas in mind that don't match up with your orders or your intentions. That's bad news for him, but good news for you. These officers will talk to him about what he was planning to do to her, but he doesn't have to bring you down with him. All we ask is that you put your guns down, let us leave here with Miss Haiduk, and in the morning, report to your superiors that despite your best efforts, a rescue team came in and extracted her."

"They won't let you get away with this," Walsh replies. "Once they find out, they're going to retaliate."

"I never expected anything less," Wolfson says. "That doesn't mean you have to die tonight as well."

Seconds pass without words, and then something remarkable happens: the four members of the Consolidated security team lower their weapons. In response, we slowly lower ours, until we are simply a group of people standing in a corridor, ashamed of what we were almost led to do.

"Take her and go," Lucas instructs. "But understand this: you're not safe. Calvin Traeger wants everyone in your company dead, and what I report to him is only going to make it worse."

"You're a decent man, Lucas," Wolfson says, "and I respect that. Sometimes all it takes is one decent man to prevent atrocities from happening. I want you to think about what happened here tonight. Think about all the parts that don't sit right with you, and then ask yourself if a reputable company doing honest work would ask such things of you. I thank you, gentlemen, for taking the honorable path here."

And with that, we go to the store room, get Rebecca and Cassie out, and make our way out of the hotel and back to the parking lot. The two Pensacola cops lead Walsh out in handcuffs, presumably to answer some very awkward questions.

Back at the car, I ask Cassie, "Are you sure they didn't hurt you?"

"I'm fine. I don't think they were supposed to hurt me, just scare me and upset me until I told them what they wanted to know."

"Did you tell them anything?" Rebecca asks.

"No, nothing. That's why they kept me down there so long. I guess that other guy would have taken over if they didn't get what they wanted."

"I'm just so glad you're okay," I tell her.

"Yeah," she replies. "Me too."

I turn to Bronwyn next. "Thank you so much for your help."

"I don't feel like I did much. It was Mr. Wolfson here who talked us out of trouble."

"I know these people better than you do, Captain. Still, a good deal of luck featured into our fate. Things could very easily have gone differently."

"What are you going to do now?" Cassie asks Bronwyn.

"It's very late, and it's been a long day. I'm going to get a hotel room in Pensacola and get some sleep. I'll stick around for a while tomorrow before I head back, just in case you need me. Where will you all be?"

Stelios answers, "We're going back to *Calliope*. My boat. There is room for everyone on board, and it will be safer for them than any hotel."

"That's good," I reply. "I could really use some sleep."

"Sleep?" Stelios says. "Who said anything about sleep? Tonight we train, if there is to be any hope of surviving tomorrow."

Chapter 8

Back on board Stelios's boat, the mood is tense. No one speaks as we gather on deck. I'm very tired, and if the faces of my companions are any indicator, they share that feeling. It's been a very long day for us all, and Stelios's promise of combat training does nothing to lift my mood. But he's right—by morning, Consolidated will know what we've done and they won't be any too happy about it. Whether that results in a heart-to-heart talk or a volley of gunfire remains to be seen, but it's certainly not the night for sound sleep.

"I'll make coffee," Stelios says, heading for the galley.

"What happens now?" Rebecca asks Wolfson. "Stelios talked about training. I can't imagine anyone around here wants us firing guns off all night."

"Quite right," he answers. "That's why we won't be using them. There may be a physical battle that transpires, but they have equally dangerous weapons at their disposal—weapons of the mind. And tonight, we will train you in the defense against them."

"So you're going to teach me how to use my own brain?" she asks, a tone of disdain in her voice. "And just why, precisely, do you th—"

Without a hint of warning, her words are interrupted as she's knocked backward onto the deck. Startled, I begin to move toward her to assist, but Wolfson is between us and he waves me off, gallantly bending down to offer her a hand up. She accepts, but she definitely doesn't look pleased.

"I'm very sorry, my dear, but I was detecting doubt in you, and I felt a gentle demonstration would be quickest."

"That's what you call gentle?" she retorts, rubbing her lower back.

"Compared to what you may face? Absolutely. You ended up on your back because I pictured you that way. Consolidated has individuals who can picture things far more grisly to do to you. I want to prevent them from being able to succeed."

Cassie has been watching this exchange, and she asks, "Does that mean *you* have the ability to do grisly things too?"

All eyes turn to Wolfson, who looks uncomfortable for the first time since I've met him. He hesitates for several seconds before quietly responding, "In theory, yes. I've never tried, and believe me, I never want to. We should get started."

On that somber and gently frightening note, our training begins in earnest. Our hosts have quite a challenge, given the considerable difference in Rebecca's and my psychic abilities. As they stand before us, I can feel them visiting my thoughts, sizing me up, learning my strengths and weaknesses. They stand in front of Rebecca and do the same thing as she watches. Then they move on to Cassie, and something strange happens. As Cassie stands in front of the two men, they concentrate on her, looking deeply into her eyes, past her eyes; but something is different. Wolfson looks puzzled, then curious, then frustrated.

"Stelios, anything?" he asks.

Stelios shakes his head. "Nothing. I don't understand." He reaches out to Cassie and puts two fingers on her neck. "She's alive, she's human, but nothing."

Alive? Human? He says this as if there's reason to think some alternative is possible. Now I have to ask. "What's going on? What is it about her?"

Wolfson explains, "Every person alive has thought patterns—a psychic signature, if you will—that makes that person distinctively him- or herself. If I stand in front of you or Miss Traeger, I can detect your thought patterns and even interact with them, manipulate them to some degree. But Cassandra here is somewhat of a mystery. Even in her immediate presence, I'm picking up no thought patterns, and neither is Stelios."

"Sure she's not wearing a metal hat?" I ask snidely.

"Very droll," he returns, "but I'm quite sure."

"So then why?"

"Yes, why indeed? That's the question. This talent of hers may have saved you all during her interrogation. Her captors were unable to lift the information they needed. Hence the session in the laundry room. They had to resort to old-fashioned methods, and they weren't very good at it, fortunately."

"Told ya I didn't tell them anything," she says.

"I've never encountered anything like it," Wolfson continues. "I apologize for what's to come, but I need to test something."

As soon as he stops talking, the most excruciating headache comes over me. It's so bad that I drop to my knees and clutch my head in agony. Through crossed eyes, I glance over and see that Rebecca is right beside me, sharing this lovely experience. From above us, I hear Cassie's voice insisting, "Stop it! You're hurting them!" She stands in front of us and it stops.

Regaining control of my faculties, I see that Cassie looks fine, an observation that does not escape Wolfson and Stelios either.

"Remarkable," Stelios says.

"Unprecedented," Wolfson adds.

"It didn't even hurt a little?" I ask Cassie.

"No. You know, other than seeing my friends being melted."

Rebecca and I stand again, with help.

"Another one of the weapons they can use against us?" I ask.

"I'm afraid so," Wolfson says. "And again, one of the milder ones. Yet Cassandra is untouched by it." He looks at her again. "Are you doing anything deliberate to shield yourself?"

"I don't know. I don't think so."

"And you have no psychic or extrasensory abilities that you know of?"

"No. Until I met these two, I didn't really believe in that stuff."

"Well," Wolfson says, "I think, if nothing else, your resistance to outside influence earns you a good night's sleep. Stelios, please show her to a cabin below decks so she can rest up."

"Yes, sir." And with that, Stelios leads Cassie away.

"And then there were two," Wolfson says. "Are you ready?"

"That depends," Rebecca answers. "Are you going to keep doing things like that to us all night?"

"No, that won't be necessary. Instead of pain, I can send you visual or auditory stimuli. We'll work on becoming aware of them as external and then finding ways to deflect them or suppress them completely. Tristan, this should help keep you from getting false assignments in the future."

"Couldn't we just wear the metal hats like Stelios had?" I ask.

"Those work at very close range and only marginally well. It's too big a risk, given the stakes. It worked for Stelios tonight because he wasn't their target. By tomorrow, we'll all be their target. Let's begin."

The overnight hours pass with exercise after exercise. Mercifully, the attacks they mount against us consist of mental images, sounds, smells. It's remarkable the things they're able to make us perceive completely against our will. I realize during our training just how dangerous a weapon this ability is. To know that there are people out there who can control others is extremely disturbing. I think of how many people are considered insane for believing that other people can manipulate their thoughts, and I now know that they are the sane ones, the cautious ones. I'll never scoff at someone in a tinfoil hat again.

Around 4:00 in the morning, fatigue is getting the better of us, so our mentors give us a break. I go to the rail of the boat and look out at the marina. The city itself is quiet, but already the first signs of life are appearing on fishing boats all over the dock. Fishermen eager to get a jump on the day's catch are prepping nets and cranes and traps. I hear faint conversations in English and Spanish, Greek and Portuguese. There is laughter and camaraderie, and it buoys my soul for reasons I don't even fully understand.

The sun isn't up yet. I want to watch it rise, because somewhere in the dark places of my mind and my spirit, there is a powerful fear that I may never see it rise again. I truly don't want to believe that this is my last day of life, but I know it is possible. As much as I want to be brave and heroic and strong, I am afraid. And I am surrounded by people who can pull that thought out of my mind as easily as if I'd spoken it.

Stelios approaches me. "Not if you use what you've learned tonight, my friend."

I give him a little laugh. "Hey, I thought we were on a ten-minute break."

"We are," he says pleasantly. "Here and now. But once day breaks and this battle begins, there is no respite. You must stay focused and vigilant at all times. Don't let our adversary know of your fear. They'll exploit it, use it against you in cruel ways."

"Stelios, why is this happening?" I ask. "All this strange activity? Psychics and messengers and mental warfare. It's bizarre, and yet here we are, surrounded by it. Why now?"

"I really don't know," he says. "It's been around for thousands of years. The soothsayers of the ancient world had it. As you've come to find out, the prophets of the Bible had it." Rebecca approaches us and listens as he continues. "In a way, it's part of our heritage all throughout our human history. We're such magnificent creatures, Tristan, capable of astonishing wisdom, intelligence, compassion, beauty. But at the same time, capable of horrors unrivaled by any other living thing. The gifts that we have set us apart, but they also bring us together. After all, here we are. Is there a reason why we were chosen? I wish I knew."

"Stelios," Rebecca says, "two days ago, in New Orleans, something happened to me. Something bad."

He looks intently at her for several seconds, and just like that, her memories are his as well. "Something very bad," he confirms. "You're fortunate to be here. Did it hurt you?"

"Not physically," she replies. "But the things it said to me ... it said that we were all going to die here. It knew things about us."

"There are others in the world who share our gifts," Stelios explains. "Some have darker intentions. This man ... this thing ... wanted to feed on your gift to save its own life. It was dying, trapped in a host it couldn't get out of. It saw you, touched you, felt your energy, knew of your abilities. And it wanted in. It wanted to introduce doubt and fear in you, to take down your guard so it could continue living inside of you. But you escaped."

A look of relief washes over her. "So it wasn't telling the truth about what will happen to us?"

"I wouldn't worry about that at all. It was a being of malice and lies. Anything it told you was for its own benefit."

To my surprise, she puts her arms around him. "Thank you, Stelios."

"Don't thank me yet. Your break time is over, and the lessons continue."

"More lessons?" I reply, trying not to whine about it.

"Of course, more lessons. You've learned the art of defense. Now you must learn the art of counterattack. Positions, please. Let's begin."

Stelios teaches us well. In the hour that follows, I learn things about my own mind that I never thought possible. Things about human thought in general, and the illusion that it is truly private. Our thoughts, I discover, are like our voices, and sometimes they can be heard, even when we think we are whispering.

At sunrise, I look to the east, watching the sky brighten over the city. If I were a man of prayer, this would be the time for one, but despite my lineage, the best I can muster is a resolute promise that I will stay strong, brave, and honorable in everything I do today, no matter what the cost.

Shortly after 7:00 in the morning, I realize just how well Stelios's lessons have worked. I become aware of a presence—thoughts that I recognize. Seconds later, a car pulls to a stop near the marina and two men get out—two of Consolidated's men.

"Wolfson," I call out, "we've got company."

Wolfson and Stelios join me on deck, and we watch as the two men stand on shore, facing the *Calliope*. One of them calls out, in a voice louder than it needs to be, "Wolf Den Industries! We are here to formally charge you with wrongdoing against our company. We demand that your representatives accompany us to our corporate headquarters, where you will make a reckoning of your crimes and unethical business practices."

Clive Wolfson looks unimpressed. He calls back, equally loudly, "Spare us the dramatics. If you're trying to influence our fellow fishermen against us, you're wasting your breath. Here, I'll show you." He raises his voice further still. "These people are from Consolidated Offshore, the oil exploration and development company. Please let them know how welcome they are here."

What follows is a chorus of profanity and vulgarity in myriad languages. I don't recognize many of the words, but the tone is clearly not a rousing round of "Good morning to you." Some suggest creative places where Consolidated can put their oil wells. Others unleash a virtual ballet of obscene gestures at them. As a matter of politeness, I restrain my laughter.

"There, you see?" Wolfson says. "Now that we're done playing games, why don't we skip to the point of this little breakfast meeting?"

The second man answers, "You and your representatives are to come with us to Consolidated's offices. Bring the Haiduk girl with you. If she doesn't return the materials her father stole from us, she'll be arrested for possession of stolen goods, and the people who brought her here will be arrested for kidnapping. Once those materials are returned, we're prepared to negotiate a cessation of hostilities between our two companies."

"Brilliant," Wolfson calls back. "But bullshit. There's no chance in hell that we're going to your corporate headquarters, given that the last time, you took three of our associates prisoner. We agree to your little meeting, but it has to be on our terms. Two of our people will meet two of your people in a public place in one hour. I choose Bayview Park, at a picnic table just east of the main playground. Nobody comes armed. Then we can compare our lists of crimes and unethical behaviors and see who has the most to say. Accept these terms, and there is hope for a cessation of hostilities, as you put it. Reject these terms, and the war begins in earnest. What say you?"

I watch as the two men confer quietly regarding Wolfson's terms. The first responds, "We accept. Bayview Park, one hour."

Without another word, the two get back into their car and drive away. I'm impressed, and my tone in speaking with Wolfson shows it. "You did it."

"Don't schedule any parties yet," he replies, and I'm momentarily amused to hear him pronounce it *shed-yool.* "A lot is riding on this meeting, and if we muck it up, we could be in for a world of hurt."

"We," I ask, "as in Wolf Den?"

"We," he answers, "as in you and I, Tristan. We need to be the ones to face them."

"Doesn't it make more sense for Rebecca to attend, instead of me? She *is* his daughter, after all."

"Remember how this whole thing started for you: you were summoned to bring her to him. I don't want to risk delivering her into his hands. Besides, you're a stakeholder in this now."

"I appreciate your confidence, but I'm not sure I know what to say during this meeting."

"It's a reading of grievances. I'll present mine and you'll present yours."

"What if it's an ambush?" I ask him.

He nods in acknowledgment. "It's not beyond the realm of possibility, but I very deliberately chose a public park, not far from a playground. It should help our chances of keeping this meeting legitimate."

An idea comes to me. "Bronwyn is still in town. What if I call her and ask her to keep an eye on things, from a safe distance?"

Wolfson ponders this for a moment. "We would be violating the very terms we set up. But if she can perform discreet surveillance, it would give us a margin of safety. All right, invite her."

I bring out my cell phone and call Bronwyn at her hotel, forgetting for the moment just how early in the morning it is. She answers her phone on the third ring. "Bronwyn Kelsey."

"Bronwyn, it's Tristan. I'm sorry for calling so early ..."

"No, it's all right. I usually get up early anyway. Is everything all right?"

"Yes, we're fine. But we've had another visit from Consolidated, and if you're able to stay in Pensacola a little longer, we could use your help."

"Of course. What can I do to help?"

I brief her on the interaction with the two men and the meeting that Wolfson has set up. "I'd feel safer if I knew you were there, watching covertly from a distance."

For several seconds, I hear nothing on the other end of the phone, to the point where I am uncertain if she's still with me. "Bronwyn?"

"A park," she says.

"Yes. Is something wrong?"

"No, it's just ... this is strangely reminiscent of something that happened to me ten years ago. I was running surveillance for a friend—well, not even a friend, really—I had just met him a few days earlier.

He had arranged a meeting with some dangerous people in a park in New Orleans, and I was there to make sure nothing went wrong. Well, something went wrong. He was all right, but the people he went to meet were killed. I couldn't stop it. And it haunted me for a long time. Your request brought back those memories, that's all."

"If you can't do this, I'll understand."

"No, it's not that. You saved my life two days ago, after all. I owe you this. I'll be there, and I'll stay out of sight. Do you want additional backup from the Pensacola Police?"

"No, just you, please. The more police presence, the more chance we'll be spotted."

"Fair enough," she says. "Makes me wish I'd brought the radio equipment we used at the cemetery. Tristan, I know I don't have to say this, but please be careful."

"I will. I'll see you in an hour."

"If all goes well," she replies, "you won't."

I end the call and return to Wolfson and Stelios. "She's in. She'll watch from a distance and only intervene if things go wrong."

"Good," Wolfson says. "We should leave in about fifteen minutes."

"Leave for where?" The question comes from behind me, and I turn to find Rebecca approaching with a cup of coffee in her hand.

"Wolfson and I have to go," I answer. "While you were below decks, two of your father's people came here looking for us."

"Is that what all the shouting was about?" she asks. "Where are you two going? Not back to their offices …"

"No, nothing like that. We're meeting them in a public place. Both sides will air their grievances, and the goal is a cessation of hostilities. That's what they said, and it's what everyone wants."

"And you believe them?" she asks.

"Yes," I answer, as Wolfson simultaneously says, "No."

I turn to him. "No? You don't think this meeting is legitimate?"

"I certainly don't think the one they proposed was. You know what happened last time they brought you to them."

"But that's why we moved it …"

"Precisely. It was the only hope of removing their advantage."

"And even with all that?"

125

"You don't know them like I do, Tristan. No offense intended, Miss Traeger, but right now, your father is like a wounded, frightened animal. The evidence Cassandra has picked up could send him to prison for the rest of his life, and he has one single thought in his head: get it back. If he has to kill ten people to do that, he will."

This is too much. I pick up my phone again. "I have to warn Katie."

"No," Wolfson says sternly. "Don't call her. Don't say her name; don't even think about her. Consolidated's operatives might be able to pick up that information. I'll have two of my own people go to her and help her find someplace safe to be until this blows over."

"How will she know to trust them?" Rebecca astutely points out.

"Tristan, you know this person. Give me a phrase, something that only you and she would know. They'll present that to her."

I think about it for a moment. Then it comes to me. "Give her these words: traying on the Charles. She'll know what it means."

"Traying, you say?"

"Yes. She'll understand. Please keep her safe."

"Stelios, see to it, won't you?" Wolfson says.

"I'll call our team."

"Do you need help gathering weapons?" Rebecca asks Wolfson.

"No," he answers, "we're going in unarmed."

"What? You remember the part about them killing ten people to get what they want?"

"I'm counting on their need for the location of the evidence. As long as we have that, they shouldn't want to kill us. They'll try to steal the thoughts from us, but we won't let them. Isn't that right, Tristan?"

"Uh … yes." *Confidence. Nice.*

"I want to go with you," Rebecca says.

"I'm sorry, but I can't let you. Tristan and I have to go alone. Two of ours meet two of theirs. That was the arrangement. Stay here with Stelios and go over what he's taught you, in case things don't go well for us. And keep Miss Haiduk out of sight and safe."

"Wolfson, please," she insists. "You know my father on a professional level, but I know him on a personal level. Let me go with you, or at least let me go in Tristan's place. I can read his thoughts. He'll find ways to shield them from you, but he won't be able to shield them from me."

"It's out of the question," he says. "Your emotional connection to your father could be used against us. Tristan and I will be fine." He shuts down further discussion by walking toward the gangplank.

Rebecca holds me back for a moment. "Please don't get hurt," she says.

"I'll do my very best."

"And be careful around my father."

"I'll do everything I can, love," I answer honestly.

"So … traying on the Charles?"

"Back in college, we would borrow cafeteria trays in winter and use them to go sledding on the Charles River when it froze over."

She laughs a little at this. "You're full of surprises."

"That's me."

She kisses me. "Come back safely to me. There's a lot more I want to hear."

"Tristan, let's go," Wolfson says. "I want to get there early, get a feel for the location."

I follow him down the gangplank and we go to his car, which is parked near the marina. He unlocks it and we get in. "She's upset," I tell him.

"I'm well aware, which is another reason why she shouldn't be there." He starts the car and we pull out. "Tristan, this isn't an easy question, but I have to ask: how well do you trust her?"

I don't even have to think about my answer. "With my life. Why?"

"I'm afraid she may become a liability in this contest. For all her loyalty to you, she is still our enemy's daughter, a fact that could be used against both her and us. I can't let that stand in the way of what needs to be done."

"I hope, Mr. Wolfson, that you're not asking me to choose between Rebecca and your corporation, because you can't expect me to choose you."

At a red light, he turns to me and says very seriously, "I have to know that you won't be distracted, whatever happens to her. Today is the day; I'm certain of it. If there is to be violence, it will happen today.

You love this woman; I know that. But you can't let that interfere in the heat of battle."

"Wolfson, this isn't Normandy," I remind him. "This is a major American city, and the marina is filled with people. If Consolidated comes in with guns blazing, someone will call the police, and they'll be stopped. They're not going to take that chance, just for the possibility of maybe killing one or two of us."

"There are things more dangerous than guns," he replies. "I told you last night. Their attack can be both brutal and subtle. If they bring out their most dangerous weapon, no matter how prepared you think you are, you won't be ready. Not even Stelios and I could withstand it."

"What kind of weapon are we talking about?" He doesn't answer, and as the light turns green, he drives on. "Wolfson, I need to know this. What are we up against?"

"A psychic so powerful, he could kill us all just by wanting to."

I pause to take in the implications of that, waiting a good long time before asking, "And what do we do against that kind of power?"

"We die," he answers.

This cheerful bit of news shuts the conversation down for the fifteen minutes it takes us to get to Bayview Park. We arrive a little more than ten minutes early for the meeting and proceed to the picnic table near the main playground. I'm relieved to see that we've arrived first. "Let me take the lead," Wolfson says. "If they ask you something directly, you can answer if you feel comfortable doing so. If not, then refuse to answer. I'm almost certain they'll send a psychic, so be very guarded with your thoughts. Don't let them upset you. If you get upset, your concentration may slip, and you might inadvertently give something away. At all times, maintain your composure."

I look around, hoping to catch sight of Bronwyn, but then I quickly catch myself and put any thoughts of her out of my head. I can only pray that she's here, hidden away out of sight.

In the distance, I see a car arrive in the parking lot. Two men get out: Calvin Traeger and a man I don't recognize. "Wolfson," I say quietly, "they're here."

"I can't see them from where I'm sitting. Who is it?"

"It's Traeger. But I don't recognize the other man."

"Describe him."

"White, looks like mid-thirties. Maybe five feet ten, 180 pounds or so. Reddish-brown hair. No facial hair."

"Jordan Blaylock," Wolfson says.

"Is that bad?"

"It's not good. He's Traeger's second in command. He can be very dangerous when he wants to. Be on your guard. Come on, stand up. We'll face them as they arrive."

We stand, and Wolfson turns to watch the two men approach. When they're about twenty feet away, Traeger calls out to us. "You're early."

"So are you," Wolfson retorts.

"Got lucky with traffic."

"Do we need to search each other for weapons?" Wolfson asks them.

"That doesn't exactly bespeak an atmosphere of trust," Traeger answers. "We're here to talk. Nothing more."

Wolfson waves them over and then comes to sit with me on my side of the table. Traeger and Blaylock approach and take seats on the other side.

"I have a list of grievances," Wolfson says.

"As do we," Traeger replies.

"Let's get to the point, Calvin," Wolfson says. "We can sit here all day and read grievances. You know what Consolidated has done. The attempted sabotage of my fishing fleet, the illegal pact with the Chinese, and the plans for offshore drilling in protected coastal waters. Add to that the fraudulent prosecution of Daniel Haiduk, and the kidnapping of his daughter as well as your own."

"Quid pro quo, Clive," Traeger replies calmly. "Shall we start with industrial espionage? Restraint of trade? Intimidation, extortion, assault? The murder of Jeffrey Casner? Your companion here looks surprised to hear this. Have you been telling him you're the good guys?"

"I can make up my own mind, thank you," I tell him.

"You want a cessation of hostilities," Wolfson says, "fine. So do I. To achieve that, we'll need impartial binding arbitration."

"With full disclosure," Traeger adds. "But I won't enter into arbitration with this so-called evidence hanging over my head. The stolen materials from Consolidated. I want them back."

Wolfson stares at him for several seconds before answering, "All right, but there are conditions. You'll get the materials back only after both parties participate in arbitration and that arbitration leads to a cessation of hostilities and a withdrawal by Consolidated from protected offshore waters." He pauses a moment. "And an agreement to speak to the Justice Department to have Daniel Haiduk released from prison."

"And what do we get in return?" Traeger asks.

"An end to all of this," Wolfson answers. "You go your way and we go ours. Your people will proceed unmolested, and you'll be free to conduct your business as you see fit. Nobody else has to get hurt."

Now it is Traeger's turn to stare. Seconds pass and nobody speaks. Finally, he says, "I accept."

Before I can even breathe a sigh of relief, a voice from behind me surprises me and everyone at the table. "Well, I don't!"

To my amazement, Rebecca comes out from behind tall bushes, approaching us.

"What the fuck is *this?*" Blaylock demands angrily, producing a pistol that he points at her. Trager puts a hand up, apparently to prevent the man from firing.

"We agreed no weapons," Wolfson says.

"We also agreed two people from each group," Traeger counters.

"Rebecca, don't!" I caution her. "It's under control. You don't have to do this."

"You used me," she tells her father. "You used me, and you used Tristan. And I'm tired of it."

"We came here to work this out," he says as calmly as he can, "and that's what we've agreed to do."

"It's a lie," she spits back at him. "It's all lies, just like it's been all along with you. You and your lapdog here ..." She points at Blaylock, who looks none too pleased at the comparison. "You say you'll work things out, but then you'll find a way to make more money and more trouble, and nothing will change. You'll just find a way to get that evidence and then you'll use those coordinates you sent to me ..."

"Rebecca!" I say again.

"What coordinates?" Traeger asks. "What are you talking about?"

"Oh, like you don't know!" she says.

"Site 603," Blaylock says to him. "Whitmire had them, and before his little *accident,* he must have sent them out to a reader for safekeeping." I notice that at these words, Traeger casts an accusatory glare at Wolfson. Blaylock continues. "It was her. She has the coordinates. Sir, this could be the opportunity we've been waiting for. If we have those coordinates and the evidence, we don't need arbitration, we don't need any cessation of hostilities. Odds are good she knows where the evidence is too. We need her."

Wolfson tries to intercede. "Calvin, don't throw away what we've agreed to here just because your daughter made a hasty decision."

Blaylock continues, "They're obviously not interested in working things out."

"That's not true!" I counter.

"Get the coordinates from her," Traeger instructs Blaylock.

"I can't. She's blocking me somehow."

Traeger is staring at Rebecca; his face looks as if he's heard nothing that's been said. "Site 603, and the coordinates have been here all along. Well, my darling daughter, it looks like you might be of some use to me after all. Why don't you come with me." He takes a step toward her.

"Don't come near me," she warns. "I can hurt you if I have to."

"Take her with us," Traeger tells Blaylock. "Get rid of the other two."

At that moment, a shot rings out, splitting the air between both parties. To my relief, Bronwyn comes out of hiding, ready to fire again. "Police!" she announces. "You two stay right where you are!"

Traeger, uncertain who she's addressing, looks at me. "Sorry, Cal," I reply, "she means you. This one's mine."

Contrary to orders, Traeger and Blaylock run. "Go!" Bronwyn tells us. "Get to safety. I'll go after them. Go!"

Wolfson and I run back to his car, as Rebecca makes her way back to the Sebring. She calls to me. "Where are we going?"

"Back to *Calliope*!" I tell her before getting into Wolfson's car. "And we are going to have a long talk about this if we're not killed horribly first!"

Chapter 9

My ride with Wolfson back to the boat is not among the more pleasant experiences I've ever had in my life. It involves frequent repetition of the apparently rhetorical question, "What was she *thinking?*" and includes, well, let's just say more vulgarity than I've ever heard emerge from an Englishman ... and I've seen a lot of Guy Ritchie movies. I suspect that if Wolfson owned a guillotine, he would put Rebecca in it—face-up so she could see the blade coming.

I'm startled by the ringing of my cell phone. I unholster it, as Wolfson warns, "Don't answer it."

Looking at the screen, I inform him, "It's Bronwyn. I have to take this." I answer the phone. "Bronwyn, what happened?"

"I lost them," she says. "I'm sorry, but they got away. I'm not authorized to give chase in a private vehicle, so I had to let them go."

"What do we do?" I ask her.

"Just be careful. They're probably coming to find you. I'm going to coordinate my efforts with the Pensacola P.D. and the FBI if necessary. I'll try like hell to get you some backup from law enforcement, but I honestly don't know how long it'll take. Be careful. Stay away from them if you can."

We park at the marina, and I scramble to keep up with Wolfson as he bounds up the gangplank to *Calliope*. Stelios meets us on deck. He quickly asks, "What ...?" but then after only a moment's pause to read us, he quietly adds, "Oh, shit."

"You!" Wolfson says to him, barely containing his rage. "You let her off this boat!"

"She hid her intentions from me," Stelios replies. "By the time I knew what her plans were, she got past me and was on her way there. Her abilities are getting stronger."

"Perhaps we've trained her a bit too well, then. Let's hope so, anyway. After what happened at that park, conflict is imminent. But I won't let it be on their terms. Make ready to cast off. I want us out of port the minute that girl is back on board."

"Aye, sir." With that, Stelios heads to the engine room.

A terrible silence follows, during which Wolfson and I stand on deck, knowing what is coming but not knowing when or how. "Please don't blame her," I entreat him.

"And why not? She brought this upon us. Compromise was at hand, and she blazed in on her own personal vendetta, ruining everything."

Before I can speak in her defense, we both see the Sebring pull into a parking space at the marina. Rebecca gets out, locks the car, and hurries on board. Immediately, Wolfson glares at her, meeting her with such force that it sends her sprawling backward onto the deck without him laying a hand on her.

Defiantly she gets up, offering a volley of her own that sends him tumbling into a bulkhead. "Enough!" I snap. "Both of you. Stop this. We can't be fighting each other."

"If not for your little girlfriend here, we wouldn't have to be fighting at all," Wolfson retorts in a petty tone that is beneath his supposed dignity.

"Suck it, Clive," she fires back, unleashing some of the tough girl she's been keeping in check. "Spare me your bullshit. I saved you from arranging a lot of useless arbitration that would never happen."

"Your father and I had an agreement."

"He was lying!" she shouts. "He never intended to go through with any arbitration. He would trick you into believing him and then have his people get the evidence, get the coordinates, and blow up every single one of your precious boats!"

"And how, precisely, do you know he was lying?"

"Because his lips were moving. The two events tend to coincide!" He doesn't reply, so she continues. "You were right there with him,

Mister Big Powerful Psychic who can knock girls on their ass with his brain. What did your psychic abilities tell you about Calvin Traeger then?"

Quietly, he answers, "Not to trust him." This answer leaves everyone silent for a moment. "I'm sorry. I wanted to believe him. I wanted to think there was a chance for peace between the two groups. Please forgive me."

She nods a little without answering. "So what's the plan?" she inquires.

"I'll go to the authorities, tell them about what Consolidated has done. And if necessary, about what Wolf Den has done. But we need to buy some time so we can do this. So we're going to cast off, put out to sea for a couple of days until things cool off here."

Stelios returns from the engine room at this inopportune moment. "No, I'm afraid we're not."

"What do you mean?" I ask.

"There's a problem with the boat. I think it may be the fuel pump. I'm sorry."

"How serious is it?" Wolfson asks. "Can you fix it yourself?"

"Probably, but it would take at least two hours."

"Get started. We may have that much time until they return. I'll give a shout if we need you."

Stelios heads below again. I turn to Wolfson. "What's going to happen? You know these people. What do you think they'll do next?"

"A three-pronged attack, I suspect. They'll try to find your attorney friend and see if they can get her to tell them where the evidence is. At the same time, they'll try to re-acquire Miss Traeger for the sake of getting those coordinates. And while they're here, I expect they'll want to kill Stelios and myself once and for all."

"I can draw them out," I suggest. "Take Rebecca and leave here. Get the heat off of you until you can contact the authorities."

"No, no, my boy," he answers. "That's very generous, but I can't let you take them on yourself. Your training went well, but for what they're likely to do, you'll need us here."

At that moment, in my head, I hear Rebecca's voice again, desperate this time, coming from far away. *Cat's eye.* I repeat the words. "Cat's eye."

Wolfson looks surprised. "So you know, do you?"

"No, not really. It's no more than words to me. Is that their weapon?" He nods gravely. "What is it? What does it do?"

Before he can answer, Cassie appears from below decks. "Hi, guys," she says sleepily. "Sorry, I kinda needed to sleep in a little. Is everything okay?"

Rebecca walks over to her and puts a hand on Cassie's shoulder. "Some men are coming here. People who want to hurt us. I don't want you anywhere near here when they get here." She looks at Wolfson. "Let me take her someplace safe. You must know someplace."

"I'm sorry," he says, "but it's too dangerous. If they can track you, they'll follow you wherever you take her. Besides, we need you and your abilities right here. Take her back below decks, into the computer room. The door locks, and it's the most secure room on the boat. It's the best we can do for now."

"I can help you," Cassie says. "I'm not afraid."

"That's very good, young miss," Wolfson replies gently, "but I suspect you're the only one among us who isn't. You may yet be able to help us, but for now, stay safe. Persephone, take her, please."

Rebecca leads Cassie down to the computer room. Alone again, Wolfson resumes what he was telling me. "Tristan, about the weapon, where did you hear that name?"

"Rebecca and I both heard it in our heads during our trip down here, each in the other's voice. I just heard it again, seconds ago."

"Then it's true," he says. "They will use the weapon."

My cell phone rings, and I answer it as quickly as I can. "Hello?"

"Tristan, it's Bronwyn. I'm at Pensacola Police headquarters, trying to get you some help, but I'm getting tangled up in jurisdictional issues. It's slowing me down. Are you safe?"

"For the moment, but I don't know how long. They have a weapon … something they're bringing. Everyone here is afraid of it, and I don't know what to do. I think we might need you."

"I'm trying to expand my jurisdiction by connecting this case to the one from New Orleans—the cemetery case—but they're questioning the connection. Once I get the authorization I need, I'll come and help you, and I'll bring backup. You're on the boat, at the marina?"

"Yes. Pensacola Shores Harbor, slip 104. Please come quickly. And be careful. Whatever they have in store is more dangerous than guns."

In the distance, I see a sight that makes my heart sick: cars, three of them, all headed toward us. Large, elegant cars that speak of power and privilege and imminent danger. "Oh, God, I think they're here," I say into the phone.

"What? What do you see?"

"Three cars. Consolidated's cars."

"Stelios!" Wolfson calls. "We need you up here."

"I have to go," I tell Bronwyn, as I feel an icy chill sweeping through every vein in my body. "Please hurry."

Stelios returns quickly to the deck with Rebecca right on his heels. "Is Cassie safe?" I ask her.

"She's locked away in the computer room," she answers, looking with the rest of us at the approaching vehicles. "As for safe? I don't think any of us can make that claim."

"Bronwyn's coming as soon as she can," I tell her.

The three cars park in the marina parking lot, and two of them open up to let their occupants out. Calvin Traeger is there, to no one's surprise, and with him is Jordan Blaylock. From the second car, three members of Consolidated's security team emerge, faces we've seen before. I look at the third car, but no one gets out. *Who's in there? What's in there? And why aren't they coming out with the others?*

Traeger and his entourage calmly make their way over to the wharf, approaching the slip where *Calliope* is moored. "What do we do?" I ask Wolfson quietly.

"Stand your ground. No sudden moves. Let them make the first move. Stelios, no luck on those engines, I take it?"

"No, sir," he answers quietly. "Not enough time."

"Don't think about it again, any of you. I don't want them knowing."

I can feel my heart pounding, even as I struggle to control it. They just keep approaching, these five men. So calmly, so steadily. Finally, they stop, standing on the pier. On the boat's deck, we are at least ten feet above them, looking down at them, and yet I feel like they are in the position of power.

Traeger is the first to speak. "We tried it your way. We tried diplomacy, and you responded with violence."

"I have it on good authority that your diplomacy was false," Wolfson replies. "That you had no intention of entering into arbitration with us."

"So you're questioning my integrity now too?"

"Calvin, I questioned your integrity from the first time I met you. And don't speak to me of violence when you and your group are here to start a war."

"The war started a long time ago," Traeger says. "I'm here to get my daughter away from you. And the Haiduk girl too. It's time for her to go back to her family."

"And if we refuse?"

"Then we will board this vessel and extract them by force."

"We're prepared to defend them and this boat with our lives. Leave now. Accept the offer of arbitration that we agreed upon, and we won't bother you again."

"We don't need your arbitration," Blaylock answers. "You're an inconvenience at most. When we have the coordinates and our property back, you'll be nothing more than a footnote in all of this."

Stelios pulls a very large handgun out of his waistband and points it at them. "Come on and try it then!" he growls.

Effortlessly, Blaylock points two fingers at him, and the gun is ripped from his hand and flung over the side of the boat and to the bottom of the harbor. "We will," he says calmly.

"You know what we've brought here," Traeger says. "You know what we'll use against you if you don't cooperate. Are you prepared to risk that?"

I'm not sure where the answer comes from, but I hear myself tell him, "Yes. We're ready for whatever you use against us."

"Then you've brought this on yourselves." He turns to Blaylock. "Bring him."

Blaylock walks away from the dock and back toward the third car. Traeger continues to stare at us from below, unflinching, emotionless.

"What did I just do?" I whisper to Wolfson.

"Stay calm," he whispers back. "No matter what happens, stay calm."

My pulse is racing, despite my best efforts. I made the choice; I said the words. Have I doomed us all? *Bring him,* Traeger said. Not *bring it.* A person, a man. But who?

Blaylock reaches the third car and opens the back door. My eyes widen as a figure emerges. As I see him rise to his full stature, fear starts to fill me. I see a similar fear in Rebecca's eyes as the man stands in the parking lot, dwarfing those around him by almost a foot. "My God," I say quietly, "what is that?"

"You said you knew," Wolfson replies in hushed tones.

"Cat's eye?" Rebecca asks.

"Anatoly Katsai," Wolfson says. "Their most dangerous weapon. Perhaps the world's strongest and most dangerous telepath. They went all the way to Russia to obtain him. All your training, everything you've learned—it is for this. You must resist him. Now, before he gets too close, use what you've learned. Try to send yourselves a warning about him, any detail you can, to the time when you were on your way here."

"But if it's already happened ...?" I point out.

"Just try it. Quickly."

I close my eyes and try to send a mental telegram, with any details about this man I can gather. I want it to say: *Anatoly Katsai, powerful psychic. Consolidated's weapon. Attacking us on the dock. Six and a half feet tall. Come prepared.* But with each step this man takes closer to us, my thoughts become scattered, and the only thought that I feel making it through is a single word: *Katsai.*

I feel pain starting, a different pain than the kind that preceded each new mission over the past two years. This pain is unique and unbelievably strong. It feels like someone has inserted a sharp spike into my skull and is stirring my brain itself. I feel warmth on the lower part of my face, and I reach a hand up to realize that blood is trickling out of my nose. A quick look at Rebecca tells me that she is suffering equally. Wolfson and Stelios have their hands on their temples, but they seem to be better at resisting the full impact of this onslaught. Traeger and his people are fine. Katsai can obviously direct this at whoever he wants.

Still the terrifying giant approaches. Step by step, he and Blaylock get closer to the *Calliope,* and a pain that I thought couldn't get worse does. On a scale of one to ten, this one is a "fucking kill me now," and I'm very frightened to understand that this is what he means to do.

What this situation *doesn't* need is commentary, but unfortunately, Calvin Traeger steps up to meet that need anyway. "It will only get worse," he informs us. "The closer he gets, the stronger the agony will be. Give me what I asked for, and all four of you will survive this. Refuse me, and only one of you will."

Amazingly, Wolfson chooses dry British wit as his counteroffensive measure. "Calvin, sorry to bother you, but do you have any aspirin on you? I have a slight headache."

Through blinding pain, I barely discern Traeger's reply. "As you wish."

Their attack is perfectly executed. At this hour of the morning, most of the fishing boats near us are out in the Gulf, pursuing their day's catch. The few that remain, though they would undoubtedly be sympathetic to our cause, are filled with individuals who are unaware that we are suffering a worse agony than any bullets could inflict. Katsai now stands side by side with Traeger and Blaylock, and just by facing us, he is tearing us apart.

I manage to look at his eyes, and I realize to my amazement that they are cloudy, useless orbs. "He's blind?" I shout out, stupefied.

"Believe me," Stelios replies through his personal agony, "he doesn't need his eyes. He sees everything he needs to with his mind. Focus on resisting. Try not to talk."

I wish it were that easy. The force of Katsai's will is overpowering. His every thought feels like electricity surging through me. I try to focus on resisting, but I can't. So I next try to focus on my own breathing, on getting each individual breath out. In doing so, I hear my breaths, sounding pained and ragged, like each one might not get another to follow it. Again I look over at Rebecca, and I see how hurt she is too. I project a thought, hoping that she can hear it: *I love you. I'm so sorry I got you into this.*

Moments later, she looks over at me, and in my mind, I hear her voice: *It's not your fault. If anything, I got you into this.*

Too late I realize that these private thoughts may not be private after all. Whether by coincidence or strategy, Traeger chooses this moment to change tactics. "Rebecca, you alone can save their lives.

Come down off that boat to me, and their pain will stop instantly. Stay there and you will watch your friends die horribly while you survive. And then I will get the information I want from you, with no regard for your comfort, your safety, or even the lamentable fact that you are my daughter."

Seconds later, I watch in horror as she starts to walk toward the gangplank. The most I am able to say is, "Rebecca ... don't—"

"I have to," she says. "I can't let them kill you."

I am too weak, mentally and physically, to try to stop her. All I can do is watch her take five more halting steps in that direction. I feel consciousness start to slip away from me, and I know if I pass out, any hope of resistance is over. Suddenly, from the haze of semi-nothingness, I become aware of a figure rushing past me. The hazy blur physically takes hold of the other hazy blur that is Rebecca, and begins stacking the four of us, including Wolfson and Stelios, in a straight single-file line. The first hazy blur then stands between us and Katsai's blind gaze, and like a genuine miracle, the pain is blocked.

I regain my faculties sufficiently to see and address my savior. "Cassie!"

"Yeah, hi. I figured out how I can help," she says. "Human shield. The pay sucks, but the look on your faces makes it all worth it."

I glance down at our assailants and find them mystified at the sudden impotence of their weapon. Katsai looks puzzled; Traeger and Blaylock look genuinely pissed.

Cassie isn't done. She picks up a blunt object she'd placed on deck and holds it in her left hand. "Hey, assholes!" she calls out to the attackers. "How are you with rocks?" And with that, she hurls the object with magnificent accuracy straight at Katsai's bald head. It makes contact, knocking Katsai backward. Had this been a Warner Brothers cartoon, there would have been a huge cloud of dust, an enormous crater, and the water level in the harbor would have crested. In actuality, the man-thing stumbles backward, landing on the pavement stunned and tending to his bleeding head.

"Fuck this," Blaylock sneers, pulling out a pistol with a silencer.

Traeger pushes the weapon aside. "No, Jordan, no guns. We can't risk hitting my daughter." Regaining his composure, he addresses us. "Very good, Miss Haiduk. You're the first person I've ever met who can withstand Katsai's abilities. That makes you very special. But unfortunately for you, I don't think you're impervious to the effects of physics. Jordan, move her."

Blaylock focuses on Cassie, and in an instant she is thrown across the deck like a doll, crashing headfirst into a bulkhead. She looks too stunned to get up right away, which is more than I observe about Katsai. The behemoth is back on his feet, ready and newly inspired to hurt us again. "This time we won't pull punches," Traeger says.

And it begins again. Without Cassie to shield us, all four take the full brunt of his mental assault. Fueled by his anger, he mixes the pain with powerful hallucinations, and I fall to the deck, certain that poisonous spiders are stinging me and ripping my flesh off of me. To my eyes, they are real, and as they attack me, I begin to see my own bones and organs emerge through what remains of my skin. I feel my blood pouring out of me and onto the deck, and though in the deepest, most reasonable part of my brain, I know this isn't real, can't be real, the feeling is so overpowering, it drowns out all reason. There must be a thousand unspeakable ways to die, and at this moment, I would trade my current situation for any one of them. Because I know that this man can and will leave me alive as long as he wants to, enduring suffering that would take the life of anyone who experienced actual physical injuries of this kind.

A further thought from Katsai, and in my mind, flames are consuming my body, leaving the attacking spiders unharmed to continue ravaging me. Strangely, a new element enters my thoughts—a sound, distant at first, but building in volume and intensity. It sounds like shouting, emphatic, powerful shouting. As it builds in intensity, the suffering I'm enduring begins to ebb. Soon the sound matches the other sensations and then overpowers them. I struggle to reclaim my thoughts, and I soon realize that the sound, the shouting is a chorus of voices, all speaking—

Hebrew.

"It can't be ..." I say softly, scrambling to my feet. I stagger to the rail and look down at our attackers. Praying that I'm not still hallucinating, I see a ring of four men surrounding Katsai, all with their palms outstretched as they chant loudly in Hebrew. Only now, it is Katsai who is suffering, his own power reflected back at him. The brotherhood has come to save me; Ha Tesha is here.

Rebecca, Wolfson, Stelios, and Cassie all struggle to stand and watch this unbelievable bit of good fortune unfold. I smile a little at Stelios through the residual pain. "To answer your question from earlier, *there's* my cabal now."

They are winning—these four old men are overpowering this unspeakable weapon of a man. But then, the tide turns, and Katsai realizes that he himself is giving them the ammunition to harm him. With a massive yell, he switches off the force that is being used against him and raises his arms, sweeping them left and right. The result knocks the four men backward to the pavement as if Katsai had swung a giant club in a 360-degree arc.

Ehad looks up at the *Calliope*. Making eye contact with me, he calls out, "Tristan, we need you! Help us, Hamesh."

Without even giving it a thought, I rush down the gangplank and help my friends to their feet, taking my place beside them. I stand between Ehad and Arbah, opposite Sheva and Tesha. "I've never been so glad to see you guys," I tell Ehad. "What do we do?"

"Stand strong against him," he replies. He and the others hold their arms forward, palms out, so I do likewise. I'm not sure what this does, but I don't want to be the only guy not doing it, so I join them. "If he attacks again," Ehad explains, "turn it back against him."

Katsai looks like a caged animal, turning in lumbering movements, trying to find a weakness in our defenses. Finding nothing, he emits a series of panicked cries of rage. From this distance, he appears immense, more topography than man. He is like some sort of mythical troll or ogre, exploited by Consolidated for his abilities. Do they pay him? Do they keep him chained up somewhere until they need him? Does this man have a family? A mother who loves him in spite of everything? Does he even know where he is or what he's doing, or is he like a slave, mindlessly obeying Consolidated's commands? Though he has hurt me more than anyone in the world ever has, I can't help but feel pity for Anatoly Katsai.

In less than two seconds, I realize that this is precisely the weakness in our defenses that Katsai is looking for. He takes this opportunity to throw me across the parking lot into the side of a parked car. It happens so fast, I can't even be sure if he did so with his hands or with his mind. Only one thing is clear at this moment: parked cars are hard, and they hurt. As I shake my head and remind myself not to do *that* again, I blearily see my comrades in arms punishing him for this maneuver. Once I can stand, I rejoin them in encircling him.

Wolfson picks this delightful moment to offer some taunting from above. "You're defeated, Calvin!" he calls out. "We will not give you what you want. Leave now, before they destroy your man."

Blaylock again pulls out his pistol and points it directly at Ehad. "Let him go!" he orders.

Ehad turns to Blaylock and gives him a resolute expression. "No weapon formed against us shall prosper." And with that, he puts two fingers on the barrel of the gun.

Blaylock pulls the trigger, but nothing happens. The gun jams. He tries again and again, always with the same result. Finally, he calls out, "Fall back! Everyone, let's go!"

Consolidated's forces retreat and make their way back to their vehicles. Last to leave is Traeger, who turns to us and says, "This isn't over."

After what I've been through, his words strike me as absurd, and they trigger a desire to mock him. "Really?" I say to him as he's walking away. "This isn't over? You sure you don't want to go with 'You haven't heard the last of me' or 'I'll be back'? Ooh, how about 'You'll pay for this!'"

"Go fuck yourself!" he calls to me over his shoulder.

"That one's good!" I call back. "You work on that. I tell you what, if you come up with a really good one, you can e-mail it to me."

I don't know where this exuberance is coming from, but I suspect it has something to do with the cessation of the agony I was certain was going to kill me. I turn back to my four allies and rush to them for a group hug, which is odd, because I am not the group hugging type. They seem equally delighted to see me.

"I can't thank you enough," I tell them. "But I have so many questions. Here, come aboard the boat and we can talk."

They follow me up the gangplank, as I bask in the absolute relief of being out of pain. "How did you know where to find me?" I ask.

"Well, Tristan," Ehad says, "the simple fact of the matter is, you were our mission."

"I was?"

"Yes. The four of us had a vision of you here, in this place, in great danger, so we boarded a plane and came here to help you."

"I don't know what to say. I've always been the one to deliver the messages. I never thought I would be in need of saving. But here you are."

"Don't thank us yet," Arbah warns. "We aren't out of danger. Your enemies didn't leave because they were beaten. They're regrouping, finding ways to shield and protect themselves. This strike was to assess your strengths. Now they know, and they will come back even stronger. We don't have much time, and there's much we need to share with you."

The others meet us as we reach the deck. "You remember Rebecca and Cassie. These are our friends, Clive Wolfson and Stelios Papathanissou. These men are from Ha Tesha in Chicago. This is Ehad, Arbah, Sheva, and Shmoneh."

"Actually, I'm Tesha," he corrects me.

"Sorry, sorry. I'm terrible with numbers."

Stelios looks at them with disbelief in his eyes. "You came all this way to do what you just did?"

"That and more," Arbah says. "Tristan is one of our number. His arrival was written of many years ago, and as we dug deeper, we learned that this battle was too."

"It was?" Rebecca says. "In those scrolls you showed us? Does it say what will happen?"

"We've brought transcription of the prophecies with us," Tesha replies. "And we should look at what is said. Some things are clear; others less so."

"We have to use our time wisely," Wolfson decides. "We don't know when they'll be back. Stelios, see to the engines. You men … tell us what you know. You saw what we're up against. We need all the information we can get."

Chapter 10

Before we can sit down to discuss prophecy, Wolfson puts a hand on Cassie's shoulder. "We all owe you our thanks, Miss Haiduk," he says. "It seems you have gifts we never suspected, including a good throwing arm."

"Sorry about your rock," she says. "It was the least-expensive-looking thing in that room I could find to use as a weapon."

"Ironically enough," Wolfson replies, "it's a ten thousand-year-old geode, absolutely priceless."

She looks away, her face a picture of embarrassment. "Oops."

He gives an amiable little laugh. "And I hope it hurt like a son of a bitch when it hit him. Please feel free to use it again, should the opportunity arise."

"I guess I should get off the boat and get it then," she says.

"Just be back quickly. We're going inside to talk with these men. You're welcome to join us there when you return."

As Cassie makes her way to retrieve the ancient projectile, Stelios leads the rest of us into the dining room, where we all sit around a large rectangular table. Ehad pulls a small stack of papers out of the inner pocket of his windbreaker. I'm gently amused to see that he's wearing a windbreaker in Florida in September, but I politely put that aside and listen to what he has to say.

"We were all very saddened when you told us you were leaving, Hamesh," he tells me, placing the papers onto the table. "We had hoped that your arrival would bring unity to us, as the scrolls foretold. But they also foretold of your departure for a great battle. So we knew that you were not ours to keep. But then, last night during prayer and meditation, Arbah, Sheva, Tesha, and I all received an identical vision. We saw you and Persephone in great danger, here in Pensacola, at the hands of her father."

"All four of you saw the same thing?" Rebecca asks.

"Yes, we four and only we four. That was how we knew who should come here. So, while Shteim made travel arrangements, the rest of us pored over the prophetic scrolls in detail, transcribing into English everything that touched the foretelling of your arrival, your foray into battle, and the conflict you were to endure."

From behind us, Cassie's voice chimes in, "Spoiler alert, huh?" She enters the dining room and hands the geode back to Wolfson. "I found your rock. It's not in bad shape, all things considered. It didn't hit the ground too hard after bouncing off the troll."

I look at the stack on the table. "So you're saying those papers are a detailed history of my future?"

"Hamesh," Ehad says, "you know how prophecy can be. Sometimes it's accurate, and sometimes the interpretation is incorrect. There's no guarantee that what we share with you today will actually come to pass. It's important that you know this. If we rely too heavily on what is foretold, we forget that God gave us the greatest gift of all: free will. We will need that free will along with this prophecy, in order to emerge victorious."

"Remember how long ago this was written," Sheva adds. "Hundreds of years."

"But it knew about us," Rebecca replies. "It mentioned us by name. Read the part you read to us before, about us. Tell Stelios and Wolfson what it says."

Ehad finds the appropriate page and begins to read. "And as the new days commence, from the west shall come Hamesh, keeper of the word of Hosea, he who will bring wholeness to The Nine. Upon the tail of a mighty wind will he arrive, fresh-steeped in grief and newfound wisdom. And by his side shall come Persephone, fair of face and possessed of fire."

148

"You see?" she says. "Persephone. That's me. I'm fair of face, and possessed of fire, whatever that means."

"Your presence in the prophecy was a source of interest and concern to us," Ehad tells her. "Particularly that last part about being possessed of fire. After you left, we searched the scrolls for similar wording, and we found it at least fifteen times, from beginning to end."

"But ... how can that be?" she asks. "I'm only twenty-one."

"Yes, you are. But just as each member of Ha Tesha is descended from a biblical prophet, so it seems are you, my dear Persephone. If our interpretations are correct, you are descended from Miriam, sister to Moses himself, and the first prophetess of the Old Testament. You are the keeper of her sacred word, just as we believe your grandmother on your mother's side was as well. Tell me, was her name Deborah?"

Rebecca looks astonished at this. "Yes. How could you—?"

The four members of Ha Tesha share a look of excited agreement. "You see?" Sheva says. "I knew it had to be. The grandmother, and down the line from her. Persephone is the singularity."

"I'm the what now?"

"All along," Tesha says, "we thought Hamesh was the center of these prophecies as they pertained to us. But when we read further, we realized that it is you, Persephone. You are the key to all of this. Do you know what a quantum singularity is?"

Rebecca and I try to look intelligent in the face of this. Fortunately, Cassie steps in to save the day. "It's a black hole," she answers. "A gravity well. A force so powerful that nothing can escape its pull, not even light itself."

"In this world of prophets and seers," Tesha says, "you are a quantum singularity, a force so powerful that all forces nearby are drawn to you. Miriam's life was turbulent and dangerous, and as her heir, you have inherited some of that turbulence. Call it destiny or whatever you will, but Hamesh—Tristan—had to find you and bring you here, to engage in this battle as the prophecies decreed."

"Wait," I interrupt, "decreed? What do you mean?"

"There is more that we didn't read to you earlier," Ehad tells us. "It continues: Brief shall the unity be, for the true sins of one father and the false sins of another shall align. Oil and water shall combine with blood, and set the messenger adrift into battle."

"You knew," I say, amazed to learn this.

"Everything happened so quickly. Your arrival and then your sudden departure. It didn't give us proper time to study the ancient writings. Not until after you left."

I piece it out. "The true sins of one father—that would be Calvin; and the false sins of another—Cassie, that must mean your father. Oil and water shall combine with blood. Consolidated's oil and the waters of the Gulf where Wolf Den fishes. It's all here, and it's accurate. We have to believe that whatever follows it is accurate as well. Don't you see what this means? We have a battle plan for what they're going to do next."

"Hamesh, please," Ehad says in a voice of entreaty, "I know that's how it must sound, but I can tell you stories of prophecies of old where too much foreknowledge led to defeat and ruin."

"Not this time," I reply. "Since the last time I met you, I read the book of Hosea just once, and it was committed to memory. My ancestor's words, Ehad. Given to me as a warning. 'My people are destroyed for lack of knowledge.' Sound familiar?"

"Of course," he says quietly.

"Well, not this time. This time, my people won't be destroyed, because we've got the knowledge the others lack. I've given up two years of my life to be Jehovah's telegram boy. Never once did I ask for payment. Today, I'm presenting the invoice, and the payment is written on those sheets. You came here with them for two purposes: sharing what you've learned and helping me to win this war. Okay, I accept. Don't back out on me now; that's all I ask."

I watch as this kind old man hesitates, taking in everything I've said to him. He looks like the burden is great, perhaps more than he's capable of accepting at his age. "I will share these words with you, Tristan Shays, because you are a good man, an honest man, one who gives of himself. But understand this: the prophecy you receive is a gift from God. Not a payment, not a fulfillment for services rendered. The Almighty owes you nothing. He gave you life, and he gave you the gift of saving lives. Do not stand at the altar with your hand outstretched and ask, 'Where is mine? What have you done for me today?' The Lord does not owe you or any man such an answer."

He's good with the guilt, I have to give him that. I go from self-righteous to feeling like shit in nothing flat. I could defuse the moment with a witticism, but since he's got me 100 percent dead to rights, contrition seems to be the order of the moment. "Forgive me," I say humbly. "All of you, please. You're right. It's just been such a long journey, and I'm very tired and more than a little scared. I *am* grateful. For your help, for my gifts. For those who care about me, and for my life itself. If you choose to share these prophecies with me, I'll go forward understanding that there is a plan and there is a reason for what's to come. And I won't question the way of things."

Ehad smiles and nods his head gently. "Now you are ready to hear."

He nods to Tesha, who takes over the reading of the prophecy. "Upon the shores of the great peninsula shall the battle commence. Hamesh shall encamp under the banner of the wolf, though it be stained with blood. Though few in number, still shall they defend mightily the stronghold of their people. Far from home are they, with no land, no fortress to protect them. Wood and steel, net and trap alone speak for them in this hour of dark need."

"*Calliope*, it has to be," Stelios says. "Wolf Den has no offices in Pensacola, and *Calliope* is all we have to defend, and all that is here to defend us. Where did you say this prophecy came from?"

"It was found in a cave," Sheva says, "in the Holy Land in the year 1763."

"How is that possible?" Wolfson asks. "To have this level of detail—names, places?"

"It is God's work," Ehad answers plainly. "It is through gifts such as this that Ha Tesha was formed. We are keepers of this sacred prophecy, along with the new gifts of foresight bestowed upon us. This is why Tristan is so important to us. He completes our number, and his fate is tied to the prophecy itself. Never in all the years of the society has a single messenger been so important to the destiny of all."

I shake my head and smile, hearing that. "You see, *you* can talk like that and make it work. If I were to say things like that, I'd just sound like an idiot."

Rebecca gives me a little slap on the back of the head. "Ignore him. What else does it say?"

Tesha returns to the transcription. "This part of it is less clear-cut. It says, Hear, O Israel, and tremble. For beneath the water, darkness sleeps, a blackness that, awakened, shall set brother against brother and scorch the desert sand under a despot's greed. Beneath the banner of the eagle crawls a serpent from out of the waters of the Jordan to strike with tooth and firebrand. In a shower of blinding light, the standard-bearer shall see the serpent in its true form."

"What does all that mean?" Cassie asks. "Why Israel?"

"Consider where the scroll was found," Ehad replies. "At that time, America was little more than a troublesome English colony, unknown to the scribes and prophets of the Holy Land. Any prophecy shared would have been assumed to be for the people of Israel."

"And the sleeping darkness?" Rebecca asks.

"Oil," I answer, as things become clearer to me. "The oil under the water at the given coordinates. If it's awakened—brought to the surface—it'll ignite the sociopolitical struggle that Wolfson told us about. Is there an eagle in Consolidated's logo?"

"No," Wolfson says, "it's a stylized C-O for Consolidated Offshore."

"Money," Cassie says. "There's an eagle on the dollar bill. Maybe that's Consolidated's banner; they're in it for the money."

"That just leaves the matter of the serpent," I add. "Should we assume that it's Calvin Traeger himself?"

"No," Stelios replies, "in this situation, he would be the standard-bearer, the leader of the organization, who sees the serpent in its true form. So, who is the serpent?"

"Blaylock," Wolfson says in a moment of epiphany. "Of course. 'From the waters of the Jordan.' Jordan Blaylock. He's the serpent, so he's the key to all of this."

"I need to know more," I tell them. "So far this is accurate, but it tells us mostly what we already know. What else does it say?"

Tesha continues. "From under the banner of the eagle walks a giant, one who shall see without eyes, speak without voice, smite without hands. Lo, though his force be great, still shall the wolf rise up to strike, with earth and air, fire and water. Through pain and despair shall the wolf endure. And God shall summon forth a force of righteousness and peace to prevail, and its number shall be six and twenty."

"Six and twenty?" I ask.

Ehad explains, "Ehad, one; Arbah, four; Sheva, seven; Tesha, nine; and Hamesh, five. So you see why we four were called to your aid. The prophecy says that the five of us together are needed to prevail over Katsai."

"So the prophecies talk about Katsai," Rebecca says. "Do you know him?"

"Not personally," Ehad answers, "but his story is near legendary. So much so that I began to wonder if he really existed. Now that I've seen him, I'm in awe at what he can do."

"The more we know about him," I reply, "the safer we'll be when he comes back."

"Safe? No, none of us are safe. But I'll tell you what I know about him. Anatoly Katsai comes from a village in Ukraine—a village called Pripyat, several miles outside of Chernobyl. On April 26, 1986, Katsai's mother Svetlana was seven months pregnant with him, and living in that village. That night, the nuclear power plant suffered the horrendous disaster. The people of Pripyat weren't told initially, and so they were exposed to terrible levels of radiation. Katsai's father Sergei would die of radiation poisoning within a month. After a few days, Svetlana was evacuated to someplace safe. Doctors were certain that she would lose the baby, but she carried him to term, and when he was born, he appeared normal in every way."

"Wait a second," I interrupt. "He's only in his early twenties? He looks twice that age."

"Patience, Hamesh," Ehad continues. "All will be revealed. As the boy grew, it became more and more apparent that this was no ordinary child. For one thing, he appeared to age much faster than normal. By the age of six, he had lost his sight, but he began to compensate for it in strange ways. Though his intelligence was average at best, his perception became unprecedented. He could describe colors, even without the use of his eyes. As the years went on, his mother worked with Soviet scientists to develop his abilities. He could touch light bulbs with his hands and they would illuminate. He developed great physical strength, and even greater mental strength, until he could not only see the thoughts of others but interpose his own thoughts into the minds of anyone he chose.

153

"This was certainly a great opportunity for whoever got to him first. Scientists wanted to develop his gifts. The Soviet government wanted to use him as a spy. The military wanted to use him as a weapon."

"And what did *he* want?" Rebecca asks.

"He wanted to take care of his mother. The radiation exposure was taking its toll on her, and her health was failing. Seven years ago, she died, leaving Anatoly all alone in the world. What happened next is the subject of debate. Most stories say he went insane with grief and rage. Of course, that was very convenient for the government. It meant he became a ward of the state, subject to their complete control and jurisdiction. And for five years, he disappeared from public view. Most likely, he was crafted into an even more powerful weapon. The next time anyone even heard his name, he had re-appeared in the United States, two years ago, as a member of a psychic collective under the control and guidance of Calvin Traeger. Today, my friends, you saw what he can do. The most powerful psychic the world has ever known. With the mind of a young boy—lost, alone, probably frightened. Lashing out at anyone who stands against him."

"I felt it," I say quietly. "When we were fighting him. I felt this overwhelming sense of pity toward him. It made me let me guard down, just for a second, and that's when he threw me like a wadded-up piece of paper. How do we fight that?"

"With unity. The prophecy says that we five will stand against him. Persephone, Stelios, Mr. Wolfson, if you were to join us, it would help our cause."

"Certainly we'll help," Wolfson says.

"I will too," Cassie adds.

I shake my head at this suggestion. "I don't think that's a good idea, Cassie."

"Hamesh," Sheva says, "I might remind you that of all of us, Miss Haiduk has had the most success in fighting Katsai. Her unique thought patterns make her immune to his particular weapon of attack."

"Yes," I reply, "but only to that particular weapon. He can still hurt her in many other ways. And he knows that she's a threat to him, so he'll want her out of the way first. Cassie, I don't want to diminish your contribution in any way, but I promised I'd keep you safe, and I don't think I can do that with you fighting this man and the others. Besides, what does the prophecy say? Does it mention her?"

Tesha returns to the prophecy. "The part that follows is less clear. Ere the sun sets, the shadow of the giant shall again darken the banner of the wolf as the eagle circles to strike. Through smoke and shard shall the wolf tread in pain and hardship. Shields once wielded shall be shattered, and many will weep. From the west, a warrior will ride, carrying a talisman of lead. Full circle shall fortune then turn, as the saved becomes the savior."

"Savior?" Rebecca asks. "Like in … *that* … savior?"

"No," Ehad says, "these prophecies are from out of Judaic writings. They wouldn't refer to that. I believe it's speaking of an actual person engaged in this battle."

"There's more," Tesha says. "In the final hour shall the standard-bearer look beyond the great light and find salvation. But just as in the Garden of old, the serpent shall strike at his heel, driving its venom deep into generations. And with peace forestalled by no more than a breath, blood shall be spilled again, and the Nine shall mourn."

As his words end, a terrible silence falls over all who hear them. *The Nine shall mourn.* But mourn who? One of our own? One we were sent to protect? Or is it me? This portion of the prophecy deals with my arrival. Does it also foretell my downfall? Am I having my own murder read to me on the day it's going to happen? The worst part is, I don't know. Like the rest of the prophecy I've heard, it's just detailed enough to scare the shit out of me, but not specific enough to spell things out exactly as they'll happen.

My words come out quietly. "So that's it then."

"But …" Rebecca falters. "I don't understand. Do we … win?"

"Don't you see?" I reply. "Nobody wins. And now we find out that we don't even have to do anything. It's all written out here, nice and neat. Hundreds of years ago, some friendly people sat around and wrote down everything that's going to happen to us today. How convenient! In fact, let's go have lunch. I'm a little hungry, and apparently, this shit's going to happen whether we do something or not. God's just going to fuck with us …"

"Hamesh," Ehad interrupts, a tone of dismay in his voice.

"It's Tristan," I reply pointedly.

"I thought we'd come so far on your path to understanding," he says. "Your faith is being tested. Don't lose it now."

"Well, I guess I fail the test then. Or better yet, I don't even show up to take it."

"Prophecy is a gift," he says gently, but I'm in no mood for gifts or lectures. "It is sent to help steer the faithful toward making the right decisions."

"Why bother?" I ask him. "It's all written out, down to the very end. And maybe I don't like how it ends."

"Would you walk away from Persephone now? Leave her to whatever future awaits her, simply because of words written long ago? Especially now that you know her importance in all of this—her importance to you?"

"No, of course not."

"Her fate is tied to yours, just as yours is to hers. You may not know exactly why you met, but centuries ago, someone with a gift similar to yours looked into the future and saw that you two would meet, and that this meeting would bring about a set of events that would prevent a catastrophe on a global scale."

"Now you're being overly dramatic."

"He's not," Arbah tells me. "What he says is true. If your enemy succeeds, it will impact the world economically, socially, and politically."

"More prophecy to support that?" I ask, incredulous.

"No. Research. When I learned who we would be fighting, I checked with many sources about Consolidated Offshore's business plans for the next five years. Their ambition and scope is staggering. They project meteoric growth in the industry, even in times of economic downturn. They will absorb rival companies worldwide and obliterate those who don't join them. Their goal is to eliminate the need for imported oil—not reduce it, eliminate it. Doing so would create a chain reaction in the world markets. They need the information that Persephone protects. Without it, they won't succeed."

"Maybe you missed the part of the prophecy where we lose," I remind him. "The part where we mourn for somebody. Is it me? Is it Rebecca?"

"I don't know," Arbah answers.

"What about you?" I ask Ehad. "You seem to have all the answers. Who will it be? Who doesn't get to walk away from this?"

"I don't know either. But with so much at stake, how can you turn your back on it now?"

"In the last two hours, I've come closer to dying than I've ever been before. I watched people I care about suffer. I don't know if I can do it anymore. There are people here who are much better at this than I am. Let them take up arms if there's a war to be won."

"You tried stepping away yesterday," Wolfson reminds me, "and you saw what happened. You were brought right back into it. For good or ill, Tristan, for reasons we're not allowed to understand, you are at the center of this, you and Miss Traeger both. Now, I don't know much about prophecy, but I do know this: with your help, we may lose and we may prevail. Without your help, defeat is certain."

I look around at the faces of everyone assembled in that little room, and it's clear to me that the only person who's not prepared to wage this battle is me. "Why can't it just tell us how to beat them?" I ask anyone who can answer.

"The frustrating answer," Ehad says kindly, "is because that's not how it works. We're given glimpses, bits of information that we can heed or disregard. And then we're given the task of deciding what to do about it."

Stelios rises and comes to sit next to me. "Tristan, I know what a burden this is for you. It's in your thoughts and it's on your face. I know you're feeling cowardly right now, but I can see beneath that, and I know that you're truly afraid for Persephone and for Cassandra. You see yourself as their protector, and you think if they're in danger, you've failed somehow. Why don't you ask *them* what they think about this?"

"You keep telling me how you got me into this," Cassie says, "but let's face it—you wouldn't be here right now if I didn't get *you* into this. I came down here to clear my father's name, and to do that, I need to stand up to the people who wronged him."

Rebecca takes my hands in hers from across the table. "Two weeks ago, I was a stranger to you. I insinuated myself into your life, asked you to drive me across country when I had no business doing that. These have been the most remarkable days of my life. I know you might find this hard to believe, given everything we've been through, but you're probably the best friend I've ever had. It's so noble of you to want to keep me safe, and there are times and places for that. But this isn't one of them. This is the time to get our hands dirty. My father orchestrated this whole thing, tricked you into bringing me to him. Well, here I am, and now he has to deal with me. Maybe I'm here because I'm the one who has to stop him. I'm possessed of fire, remember? That's gotta count for something. So I'm going to try. If you're too tired, too injured, too anything, I swear to you I won't think less of you for sitting this one out. You've done more than your share all along. But if you're up for it, I'd be honored to fight by your side."

There are no words to express what I'm feeling. A dozen emotions are competing in my mind. I want to laugh, cry, run away, make a stand, shout to the skies. Most of all, I want this battle to be over.

"Then I'm with you," I answer, and my answer re-energizes the assembly.

It is a hallmark moment and I truly wish we could take a minute to relish the camaraderie and unity we're all feeling. But life has other plans, which becomes very apparent when a window to the room smashes violently and a canister hits the floor. Almost immediately, the air becomes thick and acrid.

"Gas!" Stelios calls out. "Everybody out now!"

Chapter 11

The air itself has become our enemy. In a matter of seconds, every room on the boat has filled up with a thick cloud of gas that burns my eyes and my throat. I try hard not to breathe, but fear is starving my lungs of oxygen, and I can't help myself. I regret each shallow breath I take as I follow the others toward the main deck and fresh air.

The sight that awaits us is almost as lethal as the one we just fled. On shore, Consolidated has returned in force. A dozen armed men stand facing the *Calliope*, flanking Calvin Traeger, Jordan Blaylock, and a fully recovered Anatoly Katsai. I recognize several of them as Consolidated's security team from the executive suites. With our group's arrival on deck, all weapons are pointed our way. Katsai glares at us through empty eyes, and he does not look forgiving. In our haste to go topside, no one stopped to grab a weapon, not even Cassie's favorite priceless throwing rock.

"Do I have your attention?" Traeger asks calmly. No one replies. "I'll take that as a yes. The time for negotiation is over. Our demands are as follows: First, you will turn my daughter, Tristan Shays, and Cassandra Haiduk over to me immediately. Second, you will give me the location of the offshore drilling area identified by us previously as Site 603, including latitude and longitude. Third, you will return the materials stolen by Daniel Haiduk and drop the appeal that you filed to re-open his case. And finally, you'll all come down off of that thing you call a boat, so that it can be impounded while Wolf Den's executives face prosecution for the crimes they've committed."

A lengthy silence follows, long enough that I begin to wonder who will speak next and what will be said. After about twenty seconds, Wolfson finally replies, "Oh, I'm sorry, Calvin, were you speaking? I got a bit distracted by the mention of Wolf Den's crimes when you're standing here with twelve armed men and a kidnapped mutant, trying to steal my boat and cover up the evidence of your company's corruption. All of this, of course, after you filled the boat with poisonous fumes. I won't give you what you want. None of us will. These people here have come a very long way just to help us stop you, because they know we're on the side of right."

"Clearly they don't know you very well then," Traeger retorts.

At this wildly inopportune moment, my cell phone rings. I make a motion to take it out of its case, and six guns are suddenly pointed directly at me. I catch a glimpse of the screen and notice that it is Bronwyn calling. "I'm sorry to interrupt the whole about-to-kill-us thing, but I really need to take this."

"Put it down," Blaylock instructs. "On the ground."

"Won't be a minute," I answer, accepting the call. "Hello?"

"Tristan, it's Bronwyn."

I make a particularly big show of who I'm talking to. "Oh, hello, police captain Kelsey, who's come to Pensacola to help us."

Not being deaf or developmentally disabled, she catches on quickly. "I take it you're not in a good place at the moment?"

"Why, yes," I say, continuing the show, "about twelve of Consolidated's people are here at the boat with us right now. Thank you for asking."

"I'm almost through the red tape," she says. "I should be able to get to you with some Pensacola P.D. backup within the half hour."

"Just a few minutes away, you say? That's terrific. Police and FBI too? Thank you for being so thorough."

"Is there an immediate threat to you?" she asks.

"Yes," I reply, still for everyone's benefit. "Yes, indeed."

"God damn it, I'm sorry about this. I'll be there just as soon as I can. Hold them off for as long as possible."

"Very good," I answer. "I'll tell them. See you in a couple of minutes. Thanks so much." I end the call and turn back to Traeger and company. "Sorry about that. That was the police. They're on their way; be here in a couple minutes. They're very eager to meet and arrest you all. They asked me to see if you'd be willing to lower your weapons and put your hands behind your heads, so we can save a step when they get here."

Traeger listens patiently to this award-worthy performance until I'm done speaking, and then turns to Blaylock. "Jordan?"

"He's bluffing," Blaylock says calmly. "There's no FBI, and the police aren't on their way."

Fucking psychics. Can't trust any of 'em. So much for plan B.

"Well then," Traeger says, "now that the bullshit is done, can we please continue? Make your way quietly onto the dock."

Ehad steps forward, pauses for a moment, and then turns back to us. "Follow me and trust me," he says quietly. With that, he continues to the gangplank and walks toward the pier. The rest of us look to each other, unsure of what to do. The other Ha Tesha members follow Ehad. That's good enough for me, and I'm next to go. Rebecca follows, and then Stelios, and finally Wolfson. I look around for Cassie, but she is nowhere to be found. I can only guess that she has chosen to hide on board the boat, someplace where the gas hasn't reached. For now, it seems to be a good decision. They have asked for her specifically, but her liberty buys us some more time until Bronwyn really can show up.

The four members of Ha Tesha lead the charge. Simultaneously, they begin to utter the same words, calmly but forcefully, again and again: "No weapon formed against us shall prosper." With that, they make their way over to the security team, and each places two fingers on the barrel of all of the guns. And just as before, every armed man finds himself carrying a useless weapon. This does nothing to brighten Blaylock's already sunny disposition. "Katsai!" he calls out. "Now!"

The blind giant extends his unnaturally long arms out from himself, and the men of Ha Tesha end up sprawled on the ground. I rush to help them up, and Ehad whispers to me, "We have a plan. Tell the others—open your mind up to what we'll be thinking, and then project it, as strongly as you can, at Katsai. Go, quickly. We have one opportunity to make this work."

I finish helping all four to their feet and then return to Rebecca and the others. Out of the corner of my eye, I watch Consolidated's security force all taking apart their weapons, trying to figure out how they all could have jammed at the same time. But it effectively gets them out of our way while we work on Katsai. I share Ehad's instructions, and in a matter of seconds, I feel a thought creeping into my mind: *Anatoly Katsai, hear me. These men you serve are wicked. They do not care for you. They have made you into a slave, into a weapon. Resist them. They have no right to control you this way. Your mother would weep to know what you have become.*

As the thought begins again, I project it outward. I see the rest of our foursome doing likewise, and I watch Katsai's face as the message is received. Clearly used to being on the giving end, he appears surprised to be receiving a message of this nature. The surprise turns to a look of horror as the words hit home for him. There is no counterattack—and thank God, too, because I don't honestly think I could handle another round of the patented Katsai mind rape. This time, the good guys are on the offensive, and it seems to be working. Katsai stands staring into space, hearing our words, even though none of us is speaking. It looks like it's a private message, too, because Traeger and Blaylock are looking at each other, wondering why we're not writhing in agony on the ground as they had hoped.

The message repeats, and when we project the words *Your mother would weep to know what you have become,* Katsai lets out an anguished cry. I actually see tears running down his face as we tell him what no boy wants to hear—you're a disappointment to your mother. But I can't pity him; not again, not after what happened last time. It's all the opportunity he needs to play volleyball with my body, and Tristan Shays is done being sporting equipment. So it is to be no pity, no mercy. Both barrels of the mind, and don't let up.

Time loses meaning for me. I can't tell if we repeat the message three times or thirty, whether it is just a minute that passes or an hour, but I watch as this man, this weaponized human being who can kill with the power of his thoughts, succumbs to the gentle insistence of ours. *Your mother would weep to know what you have become.* Would my own mother, gone for ten years now, think likewise of me? If she could see me on this pier in Florida, joining forces with a large, corrupt corporation to combat another large, corrupt corporation, would she weep and wonder what I've done with my life? At the moment, I have to wonder.

I feel my train of thought slipping from the all-important message, and I re-focus my efforts. Eight of us are sending this same litany of shame and rebellion to this man, and I have to believe that in his head, it sounds like a choir of angry voices condemning him. In a way, it is nearly as cruel as what he did to us, but with help so far away, we have to continue.

Within another minute, Katsai puts his massive hands up to his massive head and again lets out a cry that shakes me to the core. What happens next is a source of amazement and horror for me. He takes a lumbering step forward, and then another, and then another. It appears he is coming toward our group, but then he diverts, heading toward the wooden dock. His tears continue, and I see before me a beaten man, awakened at last to the reality of the travesty that his life has become through no fault of his own. On and on he continues down the wooden dock, one at which no boats are currently moored. He stops at the end of the dock and hesitates. Turning his head skyward, he lets out a single word, the first any of us has heard him speak since he arrived. *"Maht!"* Without understanding a word of Russian, I understand without question that he is crying out to his mother.

Then, without another word, Anatoly Katsai steps forward once again. It is not the accidental course of a blind man who has found himself in a dangerous place. Rather, it is the deliberate steps of a powerful psychic, a man who does not need the benefit of his eyes to know where he is and where he wants to be. The step propels him off the pier and into the waters of the Gulf of Mexico. Instantly, the message we've been projecting stops, and we all stand transfixed at the spectacle. For a few seconds, the natural buoyancy of the salt water brings him bobbing to the surface, but he makes no effort to save himself. His great weight pulls him down, and for an instant—though I can't swear to it—I think I see relief on his face as the sea consumes him.

A new feeling sweeps over me, an anguish born entirely of my own feelings. I have just participated in a conspiracy to commit suicide. Rebecca grabs onto my arm and my shoulder. "Tristan … what—?"

To my amazement, I begin to hear music, a chorus of four men's voices, all chanting the same words. Again, I lack the ability to translate, but in my heart, I know what we are all hearing from the members of Ha Tesha: kaddish, the Hebrew prayer for the dead. It is simultaneously beautiful and terrible.

But there's still work to do. Blaylock and Traeger move from confused to amazed to seriously pissed in record time. "What the fuck did you just do?" Blaylock demands.

Never one to miss an opportunity, Stelios takes command of the moment. "We killed your man!" he bellows powerfully. "Look at this and ask yourselves if your cause is just. With nothing more than our thoughts, we've disarmed your men and shown Katsai the error of his ways, an error so great that he chose to end his life, rather than live the rest of it in your twisted service. Now, the rest of you—you could very easily be next. Is your mind so strong or your path so true that you could withstand the same? If you don't want to join the Russian at the bottom of the harbor, you have one choice: lay your weapons on the ground and form a line over there."

It doesn't take much thought for the twelve-man security team to do as they're told. Pistols hit pavement in short order, and within a minute, Stelios, Wolfson, Rebecca, and I are escorting the men to a part of the pier far away from *Calliope.* Once they're out of the way, we can focus on the two in charge. But even they have to understand that it's over for them. Even now, I can hear several police sirens approaching. Bronwyn's cavalry has arrived. As I see the cars make their way toward us, I wave to get their attention. Officers get out of the three Pensacola police cars, followed by Bronwyn from her own vehicle.

She approaches me at a fast clip. "Tristan, thank God. I was afraid we would be too late. How did you manage to hold them off?"

"Let's call it the power of positive thinking," I reply. "These twelve are on Consolidated's security team. They didn't mastermind this, but they're certainly complicit. Four of our colleagues have the two top men over there, closer to the boat. They'll be the ones to talk to about everything, and believe me, there's plenty."

She looks past me. "Two top men? I only see one, and the four people you mentioned are over by the pier ... singing or something."

"Only one?" I turn around quickly and realize that she is correct. Traeger stands alone, looking confused. Jordan Blaylock is nowhere to be found. And the members of Ha Tesha are still reciting their prayers, near the water and far from the two men I had hoped they would guard.

I rush over to Ehad. "Where's Blaylock?" I ask, trying not to sound frantic.

"Who?" he asks.

"Blaylock, the other guy. The ... the-the-the *serpent!*"

He looks around. "I don't know, Hamesh. We were in prayer."

"But you were supposed to be watching him!"

He sounds surprised to hear it. "Were we? You didn't ask us to."

"It's expected. The good guys watch the bad guys. I thought you all were able to read minds. I must have at least *thought it*. We have to find him."

As the Pensacola officers lead the security team away, Bronwyn hurries over to join me. "What's the story?" she asks.

"We've got one," I tell her, "but the other one got away. The one from the park who had the gun. He's dangerous, and we have to find him."

"What's his name?" she asks.

"Jordan Blaylock. I don't think he could have gotten far."

A voice calls out from an unexpected place, asking, "Looking for me?" It is Blaylock, and to my horror, he is on the deck of the *Calliope* with a small box in his hand.

Bronwyn pulls her gun and aims it at him. "Jordan Blaylock, you're under arrest. Come down off of that boat with your hands empty and raised above your head. I want no sudden movements out of you, do you understand?"

His reply is positively pissy. "You know something, lady? You are turning out to be a real bitch." And just because things aren't quite screwed up enough, the next words out of his mouth are in a voice different from his own, but still familiar to Bronwyn and to me. "We should have killed you when we had the chance."

The sound freezes me in my tracks, and I have no idea when my next breath comes. I have heard this voice before, just days ago, in a cemetery in New Orleans. Recognition hits Bronwyn at the same moment. "Kalfu …" she says in a terrified whisper.

Whatever is residing in Jordan Blaylock decides that it is now in control of the moment. Defying her orders to stand down, it produces a sickening smile on his face. "Did you miss me?" it asks. "You broke my last toy, but I want to keep this one, so I'm not going to let you do that again."

I watch as Bronwyn tries to remain strong in the face of this threat. "Whoever you are—whatever you are—if it's me you want, come down and we'll talk this out."

"Talk this out?" it replies, sounding simultaneously angry and amused. "I don't talk, I *take*. And yes, it's you I want. But not you alone. Where is she? The one I tasted." His eyes scan the pier and settle on Rebecca. As she makes eye contact with him, there is a moment of recognition. Even as far away as she is, she knows what has returned.

Rebecca's eyes widen as Kalfu communicates silently with her. I watch as she walks toward us, toward the boat—toward him. "Rebecca, don't!" I call out to her, but it is no use. She continues to walk, drawn to this thing that wants to own her. When she gets a little closer, I rush to her side and physically restrain her from moving further.

"Let her go!" Kalfu orders, but he holds no sway over me, and I don't release her, not for anything. In response to my defiance, he makes his way off the boat and onto the pier, stopping a few feet in front of us. Bronwyn raises her weapon, but he doesn't even flinch. Finally, I can clearly see the object he holds in his hand. As I hoped it would not be—but feared it would—it is a detonator. It takes me no time at all to realize that in all the confusion, Jordan Blaylock had slipped quietly aboard *Calliope* and planted a bomb. And despite what I thought just a few minutes ago, this whole thing is far from over.

The Blaylock-Kalfu thing smiles at me. "Quite right," it says, clearly privy to my thoughts. "It's over when I say it is. And you can still walk away from this. Give me Traeger's daughter. Give me the annoying little girl. Give me the materials that were stolen from Consolidated Offshore, and I won't kill you and the police bitch. And maybe, if I'm feeling *very* generous, I won't blow your boat up either. So you see,

Bronwyn Kelsey, we're not going to talk anything out. You're going to do exactly what I say or you're going to die."

Bronwyn doesn't flinch. "I'm not afraid of you," she says. "Hand over the detonator and show me where the bomb is, or I will shoot you."

The thing inside the man is equally relentless. "I know what you fear. Your memories are mine to visit. You think you can defeat me—that if you defeat me, it will atone for mistakes of your past. Ten years ago, such a long time to nurse a wound."

The members of Ha Tesha gather around me, staring in wonder at this new enemy that seems so very old. "The serpent of the prophecy," Ehad says quietly.

"Jordan Blaylock," I tell them. "Second in command at Consolidated, and currently hosting a very ancient force, one that we faced in New Orleans this week and only thought we defeated."

The four men close their eyes, and in a moment, I hear and share their thoughts: *Jordan Blaylock, you must resist this darkness that controls you. There is goodness in you, and you cannot give your life over to one so steeped in evil.*

"Oh, please," Blaylock says dismissively. He raises one hand and sends the four messengers sprawling backward. "Spare me your little tricks. Katsai had the mind of a child. You know how strong I am. I see your weaknesses like they were written on your forehead. They make me happy. You traipse around saving people as if it matters, when all along you're all hiding your own flaws and shortcomings. Especially you."

He directs those last two words at me. "Who, me?"

"Oh, yes. Tristan Shays, the conflicted hero. Poor little rich boy, so lost in his own thoughts, trying to find a purpose in life. If this is your calling, messenger, then why did it bring you such pain? What are you running from?"

"I don't owe you an explanation. What are you, anyway, but some dark thing that hides inside people and uses them to do your bidding?"

"You think this is about good and evil, don't you? And very conveniently, you've convinced yourself that yours is the side of good and mine is the side of evil. Look around you. The two words are meaningless. Believe me, I've been around long enough to know."

"So you're what, then?" I ask him. "The devil?"

He laughs heartily at this. "The devil? I thought you were smarter than that. There's no such thing. Just a convenient excuse made up by so-called holy men so they'd have someone to blame when they inevitably slipped from their self-proclaimed piety."

"I guess next you're going to tell me that God doesn't exist either."

"Hamesh," Ehad says, "don't engage it this way. It's full of nothing but lies."

"Don't interrupt, *Tzvi*," Kalfu snaps at him, calling Ehad by his given name. "We're having a conversation." He turns back to me. "You realize that by asking me that, you're admitting that you accept that I am who I say I am."

"I listen to whoever's making sense, and at the moment, that's you. Besides, you're the guy holding the detonator. That makes you the center of attention at the moment. So I'm listening."

He laughs a little bit at this, using the borrowed vocal cords of Jordan Blaylock. "I knew I liked you. You're different from the rest of them. I could use a man like you. It's not too late to change sides, you know."

"*So* not interested. You're dodging the question."

"Oh, that. The whole God question. You really want me to stand here and spoon-feed you the answer to a mystery that's divided humanity for thousands of years?"

"Sure," I reply, "that'd be great."

"Hamesh," Ehad interrupts again, "please. This is very dangerous. We should leave this place."

"Honestly," Kalfu says in response to this, "I've never seen four old Jews so eager to get out of Florida."

I actually have to stifle a laugh at that one, out of courtesy for my friends. He may be an agent of darkness, but that was a good one. "You know I can't trust you," I tell him. "I look at you, and I see you poised to kill everyone I care about."

"Doesn't have to be that way, Tristan. Everyone you care about has something I need. If I get that, they're free to go. The site coordinates from Rebecca, the stolen materials from Cassandra."

"And what do you want from me?" I ask.

He smiles as he regards me. "Yes, what about you? Each to his talents, I suppose. I could use a faithful messenger. I would see to it that you wouldn't feel the pain you used to feel. You'd be well rewarded for serving me. I could give you anything you wanted."

"If I go with you, will you disarm the bomb on the boat?"

At this, Rebecca speaks up. "Tristan, no! You can't—"

I put a hand on her shoulder to keep her from stopping me.

"If I get what I need, I disarm the bomb and take it far away from here."

From behind him, a voice says, "What, you mean *this* bomb?"

We all turn to see Cassie standing in a far corner of the parking lot, calling to us. In her hands, she holds an electronic device covered in multi-colored wires. It is smaller than the one she herself had brought to her school just a few days ago, but placed inside the hull of a boat, it would certainly sink it. That is, were it not currently in the hands of a brave but very foolish fifteen-year-old.

"That's not yours, young lady," Kalfu tells her calmly. "Someone needs to have a talk with you about boundaries."

"Save it, asshole," she says. "I'm not going to let Tristan go with you for the sake of a boat. Not if I have anything to say about it."

"Tristan and I are coming to an understanding. So why don't you come over here, hand me that device, and stand with the others before you get hurt?"

"No!" she says defiantly. "I'm the reason they're all here. I came here to help my father, after what you did to him, and I'm not going to just give up and give you what you want now. I know a little something about explosives myself, and I know that if I pull out this green wire ..." She pauses long enough to disconnect it. "... your little bomb here is useless."

"Cassie!" I call out. "Put it down and run." She remains where she is, holding it.

"Are you sure about that?" Kalfu asks her. "You're pretty good with plastic explosives, I'll give you that. But you're holding a fragmentation pipe bomb. Tricky things. Sometimes they have false fuses. And you got a B-minus in chemistry, isn't that right? You still feeling confident in your skills?" He holds the detonator up higher. "Maybe we'll have

169

a pop quiz right here and now. I'll press this button, and if you don't explode, we'll bump that grade up to an A. But if you do explode, well … the best I can offer is a C-plus."

"Run, Cassie!" Rebecca shouts to her. "Throw it and run."

Though she is far away, I can see a resolute look in Cassie's eyes. "Tristan," she calls out.

"Yeah?"

"If I'm wrong … if this doesn't work … make sure they don't win. Make sure my father will be okay."

"You don't have to do this," I tell her. "Just get as far away from it as you can! There's still time."

"Just promise me," she says.

"I promise," I answer, feeling every drop of blood within me turning ice cold.

Like something out of a nightmare that can't be stopped, I watch as Cassie lowers her head and clutches the bomb tightly to herself. I know she believes she's successfully disarmed it, but there's something in Blaylock's expression that looks like victory, and I think she knows it too. I don't want to believe she's throwing her life away like this. Something has to be done, but I don't know what it could be. Spread throughout the parking lot are some of the strongest, most determined individuals I've ever met, and not one of us can say or do a single thing to change what is to come. We stand, frozen in fear and disbelief, our minds bracing for the unimaginable thing we are about to witness.

Without another word, Kalfu moves Jordan Blaylock's thumb down a fraction of an inch to depress the black button on the hand-held detonator. I am aware of Rebecca pressing herself into me, hiding her face, and turning her back to the rest of the world, and then a moment of absolute silence—a sensory void that feels as if time has stopped. I can feel it so clearly that I wonder if someone has successfully stopped time itself. But then it ends, with a bright flash of light and an overwhelming amount of sound, a powerful boom followed by a rush of air and pressure. I close my eyes against the reality of it, and I become aware of a flood of sound—car alarms, sirens, panicked voices, someone's scream, and worst of all, the calm, almost joyful voice of Kalfu speaking through Jordan Blaylock, a single word that I will never forget.

"C-plus."

As much as I can't bear to open my eyes and face what's occurred, I know I have to. This isn't over, and Blaylock still has a gun in his hand. I open them and look immediately at the place where Cassie was last standing. She is gone. Not lying delicately on the ground, looking like she's sleeping. Not badly hurt but hanging on long enough to make one more brave speech. She is simply gone. The area where she was standing is littered with debris from the explosion, which has destroyed several parked cars. But *Calliope* is safe. At my side, the members of Ha Tesha are dazed by the blast. Rebecca is sobbing into her hands, and—to my shocked dismay—Bronwyn Kelsey is on the ground, knocked out by the effects of the explosion.

I hear my own voice, ragged and in a whisper, utter, "What have you done?"

"Just the beginning," he says. In a flash, he grabs Rebecca and pulls her away from me. "Give me the coordinates to Site 603," he snarls at her.

"You killed her," she says through her tears.

"Yes, and you should pay very close attention to how easy it was for me to do so. Give me those coordinates or I will spend the next six hours killing you."

"Let her go!"

I turn at the sound of the voice and see Calvin Traeger standing twenty feet away, holding a pistol on his senior vice president. "Jordan or ... whoever you are ... it's over. No more killing."

But Blaylock does not back down. "You useless old piece of shit. You really think you run this company? It's mine. I've let you stay long enough. Once I peel the information I need out of your little slut daughter's head, I'll have everything I need to start the joint operations with the Chinese. Within five years, I'll have every industrialized nation in the world begging to be in my good graces."

"Not if I have anything to say about it."

"Well then," Blaylock says, "it's a good thing you don't. Sorry, Calvin, but you're fired." With that, he takes aim and pulls the trigger, and I watch as Calvin Traeger falls to his knees, blood leaking out of a brand-new hole in his lower chest.

Rebecca lets out a scream. "Daddy!" Breaking free of Blaylock's grip, she runs to her father's side.

Blaylock turns to me. "That just leaves you. It's a shame, really. We could have been a very powerful team."

I watch helplessly as he levels his gun at me. But at the moment I fear all is lost, I hear Bronwyn's voice from the ground near my feet. "Blaylock!"

Two gunshots rip through the air, and I watch as Kalfu loses yet another plaything. Jordan Blaylock staggers for a few seconds and then falls backward to the pavement, ending this ordeal at last.

I'm light-headed with all the fear and the sudden onrush of relief. I look down at myself and see that some of his blood has gotten on my clothing. At first glance, it looks like just a little, but strangely, with each passing second, more of it appears. Suddenly I'm struck with the realization of just how cold it feels for a Florida autumn day, and I feel the need to lie down, right here and now.

Immediately before darkness washes over me, I hear Rebecca's panic-stricken voice as if from a very long way away. "Tristan, no!" And then there is nothing.

Chapter 12

I am nowhere. That's the best way I can describe my present state. My body and mind have lost all sense of place and time. Darkness swirls with light in my thoughts, but I can't open my eyes to perceive them. I am aware of sound, but it is warped, flanged. It feels wrong. Smell and taste are dimly perceptible, but they too are wrong, as if I'm holding an old penny in my mouth. I may be floating; I can't tell for sure. I have lost the sense of the ground beneath my feet. *Or was it beneath my back? Did I fall?*

Awareness. Sounds. They are voices; familiar, I think, but I don't know who is saying what.

"We're with you."

"What do I do?"

"Keep moving forward."

"Why isn't he responding to me? Last time, in the dream, I could see him and talk to him."

"Don't lose faith. We have work to do here before he can see you and hear you."

"I'm scared. What if I do it wrong?"

"You must believe in your ability to succeed. Search for what you need to find."

"I feel like it's dark here."

"You can control it. Believe there to be light and there will be."

"It worked. Now I can see what I'm doing. Oh my God. Look at that. Do you see that?"

"We see it."

"How am I supposed to fix that?"

"From what I understand, you have the ability to go to it, physically interact with it, and with your thoughts, begin to undo the damage it has done."

"How could I possibly do that? Look at what it did to him. I can't fix that. I'm not a doctor."

"The abilities you have are more powerful than surgery. Use the power of your will to obtain it."

"How?"

"See it in your hand. Command the damage that it has done to heal. Most of all, believe with every bit of your will that you are stronger and you will prevail."

"Okay ... I guess. Here goes."

"Very good."

"I can feel it."

"How does it feel?"

"It's still warm."

"That's understandable. Try to dislodge it."

"I think it's stuck. I don't know if I can get it."

"Don't think of picking it up, like you would an ordinary object. Instead, believe that you already have it. See it in your hand."

"All right. I have it. What do I do now?"

"You must leave here and take it with you. Bury it in the ground."

"I will. But I need to know if he's all right first."

"There's reason to make haste."

"I know. But I have to hear his voice."

Through the dampening haze, one sound becomes clearer. It is Rebecca's voice. "Tristan?"

I want to speak, to call out to her, tell her where I am, but I can't speak. All I can do is think her name. *Rebecca?*

Again I hear her. "Look at me. I'm here."

I can't see. I can't open my eyes.

She hears each thought as clearly as if I'd spoken it. "Look with your mind. Focus your thoughts on the sound of my voice and see me right in front of you."

Though I'm not exactly sure what she means, I try it. I look without the use of my eyes, and an image comes into focus in my mind. She is there, standing above me. Behind her is blue sky, and silhouetted against it are the four members of Ha Tesha. It was their voices I just heard. I couldn't be further from understanding.

Where am I?

"You're in the same place you were. In the parking lot of the marina."

And where are you?

I hear a hitch in her voice as she is barely able to suppress tears, but I am surprised to realize that they sound like tears of joy. "I'm inside of you."

Inside of me? What do you mean?

"You remember back in Kansas, when I entered your dream and I came out with smoke and soot on me?"

Yes, of course. But what—?

"Ha Tesha guided me how to use this. Remember what Jason taught us about the Hopi Indian medicine men? Well, I did it. I was able to enter your body and bind my thoughts to yours."

That's amazing, but I don't understand why you would choose to do that now.

"Because I had to get *this*." I watch as she holds something up in her hands. Weary as I am, I can see the object, but I can't make anything meaningful out of it. It is a piece of metal, jagged and twisted, but lacking the shape of anything recognizable. It could be a piece of abstract sculpture, but the way she holds it, so carefully and almost proudly, it must have some special significance for her.

I see it, but I don't recognize it. What is it?

Now unable to hold back her tears, she answers, "It's the bullet that almost took you away from me."

Bullet?

From the haze, I try to piece together my most recent memories. I remember Blaylock shooting Calvin Traeger. Then he turned to me, and I thought he was going to shoot me too. But Bronwyn must have regained consciousness, and she shot Blaylock. I saw it clearly. She shot him twice.

Then I realize the truth. No, not twice. She only shot him once, at the same moment he fired at me. Bronwyn took him down, but not before he shot me. The blood I saw on my clothing was my own.

Returning to the present moment, I look over at Rebecca again as she holds the instrument of my fate. *You're holding my life in your hands.*

"Yeah," she says, trying to contain her tears. "Pretty fucked up, huh?"

What happens now? I ask her.

"Well, if Ehad is right, I hold on to this bullet and I leave your consciousness. According to Hopi custom, I have to take the bullet and bury it in the earth, as if it were a disease. If the spirits accept it, you should recover just like you'd never been shot."

I feel weariness washing over me as I struggle to stay with her. *Be nice to those spirits, then,* I tell her with a little smile.

"I promise," she says.

I'm so tired. I don't think I can stay awake much longer.

"You rest, my love. I'll take this thing far away from you and bury it deep. You rest, and when you wake up, we can be …"

Blackness returns, and with it all sound fades away. Sometime later, I'm not sure how long, I open my eyes and feel relieved when an image appears. The first thing to reach my eyes is fluorescent light; it is almost painfully bright, and it's difficult for me to focus on my surroundings. I see whiteness—white paint on the walls, white curtains on a window. I'm on my back, in what appears to be a bed. I hear beeping, a regular, steady beeping that does not sound like an alarm; I soon realize that each beep represents a beat of my heart. *Okay, hospital. Not especially where I want to be, but there are worse alternatives.* I cough a few times, and the first sound that follows it is Rebecca's voice. "He's awake."

I become aware of a great deal of shuffling. Rebecca's face enters my field of vision as she stands over my bed. She smiles, and suddenly nothing hurts. Within a few seconds, I'm aware that Bronwyn is here, as are Stelios, Wolfson, Katie, and even the four members of Ha Tesha.

"How you feeling?" Rebecca asks.

"I had the strangest dream," I answer. "And you were there, and you were there …"

She fights back a little laugh. "Easy there, Dorothy. Don't get yourself too worked up." She nods to the others. "Yeah, he's all right."

"How long was I out?" I ask groggily.

"Twenty hours," Stelios answers.

I'm silently amazed at this. I don't *feel* like I've been asleep for twenty hours. But after everything I've been through, I guess I really needed the sleep. I try to move to a seated position, but several of those standing over me hold me down.

"Whoa, not so fast," Katie says. "You're not ready to get up yet."

"Have you all been here the whole time?" I ask.

"Rebecca stayed overnight with you," she says. "The rest of us got some sleep and came back in the morning."

"Is it over?" I ask, fearing the answer.

Bronwyn supplies the best guess. "From what we can tell, yes. Jordan Blaylock seemed to be pulling the strings for the whole operation, and my shot was lethal." There's great sorrow in her voice as she says these words.

"Are you in trouble for this?" I ask her.

"I'll have a lot of paperwork to fill out, and a lot of explaining to do, but Blaylock actually did me a favor, ironically enough, when he started talking in the persona of the suspect from the cemetery. It allows me to link the two cases together, and it means I'm here following up on an active investigation."

"Yeah, about that …" I add. "Somebody want to tell me just what the hell happened out there?"

"I'm not sure anyone here can, completely," Ehad answers. "In Jewish folklore, there are tales of a *dybbuk,* the dislocated soul of the dead, returned to this world to attach itself to a living person. The one you called Kalfu spoke and acted in the manner of a *dybbuk*—someone with a grudge, a task to complete. When Blaylock was killed, the spirit may have fled his body, or it may have returned to Gehenna, the netherworld from which it came."

"What did it want with me?" I inquire.

"We can't be sure," Tesha answers. "It spoke of you, and it certainly showed an interest in you. But it also suggested that it was many hundreds of years old. Perhaps it had a score to settle with one of your ancient ancestors."

"So I might see it again? Is that what you're saying?"

"All things are possible," Ehad states plainly.

I look back at Rebecca, standing over me. "Bec ... your father?"

The words bring a pained expression to her face. "I couldn't save him, Tristan, the way I saved you. That ... *thing* made me choose. It knew I couldn't save you both. He lived long enough to say goodbye to me, and for me to forgive him for everything he put me through." I see the tears begin to fall down her cheeks, and I reach up and take her hand.

"You saved my life, and as long as I live, I'll never be able to thank you properly for that. I'm so sorry that it had to be at the cost of your father's life. If I could change places with him ..."

"No," she interrupts. "Don't. My choice was deliberate, and I didn't even have to think about it. If I had it to make again, I would still choose you."

"Thank you. I don't know a single good thing to say that would make this any easier, but if you can take any comfort in knowing that at the end, he showed you that he cares, let that be the memory of him that you keep."

She kisses me. "Thank you for that," she says quietly.

Wolfson takes a few steps over to my hospital bed. "I owe you quite a debt of gratitude," he tells me. "I know this isn't a battle you chose, and I also know that you have issues with some things my company has done. But I hope, when all is said and done and you're able to look back on this time, that you'll believe in your heart that you fought on the side of right."

"Well," I reply, "your company had fewer demons from the netherworld on the payroll, so that right there is an indicator. What happens now for the Wolf Den?"

"Business as usual, I suppose," he says. "Consolidated should be less of a problem now. Blaylock was to blame for the majority of the company's illegal and unethical dealings. The police arrested those who supported him, and now those coordinates won't get to them, so our fishing grounds will be safe. It's given me something to think about, certainly. I have some priorities to examine. You've granted me a fresh perspective on it all, I have to say."

I glance at Stelios at the foot of the bed. "And what about you, you salty old sponge rancher? Back to business as usual for you too?"

He shrugs his shoulders. "Hard to say. It's been a very strange month. Maybe I'll actually consider retiring."

"Not because of me, I hope."

"No. I'm just finally ready to admit that I'm not as young as I used to be. And I came awfully close to dying yesterday. Gives a man pause to reflect. Maybe it's time."

"Look on the bright side," I tell him. "You're already in Florida."

He gives a little laugh, but then his face turns serious. "Tristan, I want to apologize. The things I said and did before I knew who you were ..."

"Stelios, I appreciate that, but it's all right. Even after all of that, I believed I could trust you. It's why I called you when I knew we were coming back to Florida. I consider you a friend, and I'd be glad if you didn't disappear from my life when this is all over."

He touches my shoulder warmly. "Of course. Well, now that we know that you're all right, we should be on our way. You stay in that bed until you're well again. Persephone, make sure he does."

"I will," she answers.

"Take care, old boy," Wolfson says.

"You too," I reply. "Thanks for coming to the rescue when we called."

"I might say the same thing. Goodbye for now."

Stelios and Wolfson leave the room, and the four members of Ha Tesha approach my bedside. "I think we should be returning home now as well," Ehad says.

"Well, if I'm Dorothy in this little extended metaphor, I guess that makes you the Scarecrow, because I'll miss you most of all."

"You don't have to," he replies. "Now that you know your ancestry and what the prophecies foretell, you know that you always have a place within our group. When you're well again, come back to Zion and be a part of our circle."

His invitation is not surprising. And with their belief in prophecy and destiny, it's perfectly natural for them to expect me to be with them again. But is it what I want? After this whole ordeal, I feel different inside. I've spent the past two years constantly on the go, protecting people I'd never even met. Now—well, now I'm not sure.

"Ehad … thank you for that offer. I know I barely know you all, but in a very short time, you've really made me feel like part of a family again. Both my parents are gone, and I've been on my own for quite some time. The warmth and caring that you showed me and Rebecca both will stay with me for a lifetime. For now, though, I think I have to decline your invitation. I need some time to remember who I am, and to get my life back on track. That's not to say that I'll never knock on your door again, so don't retire my number, but for now, I need to be me for a bit."

He nods, his face a picture of kindness and understanding. "I hope you find what you're looking for."

"And I hope you find a new Hamesh to complete your group."

"You forget," he says with a knowing little smile, "we have the prophecy to fall back on. A new Hamesh will come. Maybe even someone you know."

Intriguing. "What aren't you telling me?"

"Give it time," he says. "Besides, we can't give you *all* the answers up front. What fun would that be? Be well, Tristan. I suspect we'll see each other again."

And with that, the four men offer their goodbyes and leave the room.

Katie is close by, and I see something I'm not used to on her face. Her trademark confidence is overshadowed by a look of concern, and I need to bring back the cockiness that I've grown to admire so much. "Well, at least my attorney is here," I say with a smile. "Because I think somebody might have to get sued for all of this."

"Just tell me when and where, baby. I'll sue the shit out of 'em."

"Hey, wait a minute … have you been on the clock this whole time?"

"Don't worry, cheapskate," she says with a smirk. "I have a special coma rate for the hours when you were out."

"You're safe, Katie? They didn't hurt you?"

"Never even came close," she replies. "A couple of Wolf Den's people came by to tell me the latest developments. Even gave me the secret password. I'm amazed you still remember traying with me on the Charles."

"How could I forget?" I ask. "What about the evidence?"

"Safely locked away. Tomorrow, I'll introduce myself to Daniel Haiduk and let him know what to expect in the weeks ahead."

Haiduk. The name stirs my thoughts in a direction I've been trying hard to avoid. But now it is all I can think about. Cassie is gone, and nothing anyone can tell me will convince me that it isn't all my fault. I need to say something, anything to end this building silence that is oppressing me, but I don't have a single word to start the impossible conversation. Instead, I feel tears start to flow from my eyes, and I become aware that my breathing has turned to sobs.

Rebecca hurries to me and embraces me the best she can, given my current position. "Shh, love, don't cry. I know how you're feeling right now, believe me. I'm feeling it too. And I can stand here all day and tell you not to feel guilty, tell you it's not our fault. But I know that as long as we both live, we're going to feel some responsibility for what happened. It's natural. Just remember this: from the very beginning, Cassie made the choice. We stopped her from doing something really terrible that could have killed her or made her a criminal and an outcast. We gave her a way to come here and rescue her father, and because of what she did—because of what we helped her to do—he's going to get a new trial, and Katie feels certain that he'll be released."

"But she's still dead, Bec," I reply weakly through my unabated tears. "She was under our care and we stood there and watched as—"

"I know. Trust me, I know. It's an image I'll never be able to shake. But once again, she made the choice to take the bomb off the boat. By doing that, she saved the *Calliope* from sinking. I talked with Bronwyn about this last night. Because of the type of bomb and how close we were standing to the boat, if it had gone off, odds are good that you and I would both have been killed. So she didn't just save an old fishing boat, she saved both of our lives, and probably Bronwyn's too."

The thought had never entered my mind. "Really?"

It is Bronwyn who replies. "I really think so."

"Couldn't she have just thrown it into the ocean?" I ask.

"Maybe. But salt water does strange things to electronics. By throwing it, she may have accidentally detonated it. We'll never know.

Just like we'll never know her full motives for holding on to it the way she did. But because she made that choice, we're all still here."

"What about the Amber Alert? There have to be consequences of all of this."

"I spoke to the Chicago field office of the FBI," Bronwyn says. "Talked with them yesterday for a full hour and briefed them on everything that happened. They sent local police to inform Cassie's grandmother. Last night, after she had a chance to deal with the news, I called her myself, tried to put everything in the light in which it happened."

"How is she?" I ask, afraid of the answer.

"She's devastated, of course. And the first instinct is to blame. I won't lie to you: a good deal of that was pointed toward you and Rebecca. But we talked, and I explained to her what your role was in everything that happened. I told her how hard you worked to protect her, and in the end how courageous and self-sacrificing her granddaughter was. And while none of that can bring her back, at least I was able to help her understand."

"Is she going to press charges?"

"I didn't discuss that part with her. Since it's a federal matter, it was outside of my jurisdiction. The FBI will have some questions for you once you're feeling better, but by that point, they'll have my full report, so they'll know that your motives and intentions were honorable."

"I'm just so tired," I say, realizing the truth of it even as I utter the words. "Twenty hours unconscious and I still feel like I could sleep for days."

"You almost died out there," Bronwyn replies. "I have no idea how Rebecca did what she did, but I know it saved your life. I was standing there, watching her. It was the most amazing thing I've ever seen. She shut her eyes as she stood over you, and then she closed her hands tightly. When she opened them up again a few seconds later, she was holding the bloody remnants of the bullet that was inside of you. The surgeon here at the hospital confirmed it. There was no exit wound on you, and he spent an hour searching your abdomen but found no trace of a bullet. You're very lucky to be alive."

"I guess I just choose my friends well." I squeeze Rebecca's hand at this, and she squeezes back.

"I suppose I should be getting back home," Bronwyn says, with a twinge of regret evident in her tone. "Didn't expect to be away for three days."

"I can't thank you enough," I tell her.

"Me? I'm the one who should thank you. I wouldn't have made it out of that cemetery if you hadn't come along."

"Well, you certainly returned the favor," I reply. "And I'll never forget it."

"You folks take care of yourselves. Take some time off. Sounds like you could definitely use it."

"I'll walk out with you," Katie says. "Tristan, I want you to call me once you're out of here. We'll talk about what happens next."

I nod, and the two women leave the room. Now, only Rebecca and I remain. A wave of quiet washes over us, interrupted only by the regular beeping of my heart monitor. "I wish I knew what to say," I tell her.

"Say what you're thinking," she offers.

"I thought you already knew what that was."

"Actually, I don't. I can't hear it now. After everything we went through with Katsai, and then the effort of getting the bullet out of you, I can't hear your thoughts."

"Oh, honey, I'm so sorry …"

"Don't be," she says. "I'm not. This … gift … wasn't something I asked for; I don't even think it was something I wanted. It just … *was*. Now that it isn't, I can't feel very broken up about it. I think maybe I was supposed to have it for this period of time, when it was most needed. A little gift from my ancient ancestor."

"If you want to talk about yesterday, we can," I tell her. "I can't even imagine how agonizing the choice was, knowing you could only save your father or me."

I watch as she fights back a tear. "The agonizing part is that at the time, the decision *wasn't* agonizing. I watched you both fall, and my mind and my heart both told me that I had to save you, even if it meant losing him."

I hold her hand tightly. "Without you, I wouldn't be here. Nothing I can say can express my gratitude."

"One thing you could say would express it," she corrects me. "Say you'll stay with me. I'm not asking for forever. But after everything that's happened, I can't imagine spending the next part of my life without you there. God, that sounds needy. I'm sorry. And it's entirely up to you. I mean, it's not like I'll put the bullet back in if you say no ..."

"Rebecca ..."

"And I understand that you'll have more assignments, and if you don't want me to go on them with you, I won't ..."

"Rebecca." This time, she stops, realizing that she is rambling. "Of course I want to stay with you. I'm in love with you, and I can't think of anyone I'd rather have by my side."

She bends down and squeezes me, probably harder than she should.

"Ow, ow, love you, ow."

"Oh God, sorry. I forgot."

"Quite all right. Those ribs should grow back." She gives an embarrassed little laugh at this. "So tell me, what was it like being inside of me, getting that bullet out?"

"It was scary. I knew how important it was, but I didn't really know what I was doing. The guys were there with me, and they helped a lot. I can't tell you how relieved I was to hear your voice in my head. It's what gave me the confidence to continue. After that, I just went looking for the bullet until I found it."

"What was *that* like?"

"I ... I guess I didn't realize that something so spiritual could be so gross. It's not every day you get to be inside your partner's intestines."

"So you don't want to make regular visits to my colon? To make sure it stays healthy?" I ask with a little smile.

"It's a nice place to visit, but I wouldn't want to stay there. Let's put it that way."

"Okay, it's a deal. No more field trips to my bowels. We'll take vacations like a real couple."

"I'd like that," she says. "So, can I get you anything?"

"A grilled cheese sandwich with sliced tomatoes on it, on sourdough bread."

"Hmm. That sounds good." She holds up an IV bag on the end of a pole, the same bag that is draining into my arm. "But for the next day, *this* is your grilled cheese sandwich."

"My arm doesn't taste grilled cheese."

"What does it taste?"

"Warm, salty water, one drip at a time." I slide over a little and pat the bed to invite her to come up and join me.

"Won't we get in trouble?" she asks.

"Rebecca Traeger, ponder the last week we spent together and then tell me you're concerned about upsetting a nurse."

She climbs into bed next to me and curls up in the crook of my arm. "Much better," I tell her.

"It feels like forever since we held each other," she replies. She feels so warm and so alive next to me. "I want a life again. A life with you. A life without bombs and guns, without giant mutant psychics and demons, without waking up each morning wondering if someone will try to kill us."

"I want that too," I tell her.

"Is it possible? Can we have that?"

"I don't know. I hope so."

"And what about the FBI?" she asks. "What are they going to want?"

"I guess we'll find out when they come."

The FBI does, in fact, come to my hospital room the next day. Rebecca is asleep in a chair in a corner of the room when the two agents enter. I'm dozing lightly, but at the first sight of them, I am wide awake. I was expecting men in suits, but this is Florida, after all, so it doesn't really surprise me that they arrive in slacks and shirt sleeves. One of the pair looks to be about forty, the other in his late twenties.

"Mr. Shays?" the older man asks. "I'm Special Agent Jefferson Deckard. This is my partner, Special Agent Tom Bryson. Are you feeling well enough to answer some questions?"

"Yeah, I think so."

"Good, thank you. I want to start by telling you that you're not under arrest."

"Good start," I reply. He smiles, but just barely.

"So any information you choose to share with us is at your free choice and your discretion. Understand?"

"Yes."

"We also would like to speak with Rebecca Traeger."

I point to the sleeping form in the corner who is, surprisingly enough, still sleeping. I grab a rolled-up Ace bandage from my bedside and lob it gently at her. It bounces off her head, rousing her quite abruptly from her sleep.

"Dude, what the fuck!" she calls out before realizing we have company.

"The FBI is here to talk about your alien abduction."

"You do know I was five when that show came out, don't you?"

"The reference wasn't lost on you. Come meet agents Deckard and Bryson."

She stands and comes over to sit on the edge of my bed. "Hi," she says to them. "Sorry. I was sleeping."

Agent Bryson informs her, "We were telling Mr. Shays that we have some questions for you, but you're not under arrest, so you're welcome to speak freely as much as you feel comfortable."

She asks, "Do you want to interrogate us separately, to make sure our stories match?"

"Interrogation is a harsher word than what we're here for," Deckard says. "We've already spoken at length with a Captain Bronwyn Kelsey of the New Orleans P.D. She briefed us on the situation as much as she knew it, but there are still some parts of it from before you joined forces with her that we need to ask you about. How and where did you first meet Cassandra Haiduk?"

"It was last Friday," I explain. "We were in Illinois, visiting some friends of mine." I decide not to bring Ha Tesha into this if I don't have to. I don't know what Bronwyn has or hasn't told them, and I figure it'll be easier if I don't start rambling about secret societies. "I know this might sound strange, but for the past two years, I've received … I guess you could call them visions. Warnings about people who are in danger. And I go to find these people and give them the warnings."

The FBI agents don't respond, but they don't start laughing or look at me like I'm insane, so I figure that's a good beginning. "I received a warning about Cassandra Haiduk on Friday morning."

"What kind of warning?" Bryson asks.

I have to be very careful here. I don't want to damage Cassie's character, even now. I decide how I can tell the truth without telling the truth. "I had reason to believe that there was going to be an accident at her school. A small explosion in the chemistry lab that could have left her injured or killed. So Rebecca and I went to the school to talk to her."

"We spoke with officials at the school," Deckard tells me. "According to the office secretary, you were in Leonard High School in the early afternoon, posing as audiologists. Is that correct?"

Shit. Didn't expect them to have that level of detail. Let the tap dance begin. "Yes, that is, in fact, correct."

"Complete with appropriate attire and—even more interesting— audiology equipment. Can you explain why that is?"

Rebecca takes up the charge. "Part of conveying the message to people is putting them at ease. Sometimes that requires assuming the role of someone they'll trust. In this case, posing as audiologists allowed us to talk to Cassie in a quiet, neutral place in her school."

"And what is *your* role in all of this?" Bryson asks her.

She tells them of our first encounter, and how she asked to travel with me. Without mentioning a romantic relationship, she describes our interactions as a very close friendship. This seems to satisfy the agents, and the questions continue.

"Okay," Deckard says. "It's Friday afternoon. You're at the school, dressed like you're giving a hearing test. You've found Cassandra Haiduk, and you gave her the message about the explosion. What happened then?"

I pick up the story from there, explaining how Cassie told us about her father and her desire to go to Florida to help him. "She said she was planning to run away and either hitchhike or hop a freight train to Florida to help him. Rebecca and I discussed it, and we knew she meant it. We didn't want to see her put herself at risk that way, so we offered to accompany her to Florida by airplane."

"So, wait," Bryson interrupts. "Here's this girl you just met, and you're going to give up your current plans and fly with her to Florida, just because of a story she told you?"

"I know how that sounds," I tell him. "But when I get an assignment, like the one I got with Cassandra, I get protective feelings for the person. I had the time and the resources to help her, and I really couldn't live with myself if I had ignored her and she'd gotten hurt."

"You talk about flying there with her," Deckard says, "and yet you drove her to Florida. Why is that?"

"The Amber Alert," Rebecca says. "Cassie called her grandmother to let her know she was safe, and the grandmother called the police. So we knew we wouldn't be able to fly."

"And why didn't you turn the car around at that point and take her home?"

"We offered to," I answer, "but Cassie insisted. She said she was the only hope her father had. And she did have sole access to the evidence that will be used to exonerate her father in a few weeks. She most likely saved him from a life in prison."

The two agents look at each other as they hear this part of it. "You understand the delicate position we're in," Deckard says. "The moment you learned about the Amber Alert and chose to continue with your plans, you violated federal law."

"Yes," I reply. "We did."

"The girl's good intentions aside, she was a minor, and in the eyes of the law, not able to make decisions of this nature. You transported her across state lines, and placed her in not one but two life-threatening situations."

"Bronwyn told you about the cemetery, huh?" Rebecca asks.

"Yes, she did," Bryson says. "According to her statement, Cassandra accompanied you in pursuit of a serial rapist and murderer, and in so doing, she briefly ended up as his captive, while he threatened to kill her."

After several very awkward seconds of silence, I weakly offer, "We got him."

"I think you're missing the point, Mr. Shays. We're trying to determine what, if anything, you and Miss Traeger might have done to put Cassandra Haiduk in jeopardy. From everything we're hearing, there was considerable risk of danger. And I apologize for being blunt, but Miss Haiduk was killed while under your care and supervision."

Deckard's words slice mercilessly through my concerted efforts not to think about the reality of what happened. Instantly, my thoughts return to that marina, to the sight of that young woman standing in the parking lot, clutching the bomb to herself. What was she thinking? Was she terrified? How could someone in that situation not be? In my hours of semi-consciousness that followed, my mind constructed dozens of scenarios for how everything could have played out differently. But it didn't, and she's gone. No, not gone. A fashion trend is gone, your favorite childhood cereal is gone. A good-luck charm is gone. Cassie Haiduk is dead, and as these two peace officers are here to remind me, it was on my watch. I have to say something.

"I know," I answer, paining to choke down the tears that are so eager to come out. "And I swear to you and to God that I would do anything to make that not be the truth."

Deckard lets out a breath and shakes his head a little. "I've been with the Bureau a lot of years, and I've never seen a case like this. Under ordinary circumstances, it would be pretty cut and dried. Kidnapping, transporting a minor across state lines, reckless endangerment, maybe even manslaughter. I've seen it before. Guys grab teenage girls, take them somewhere, do God knows what. But that's not you. Either of you. Captain Kelsey spoke very highly of you. Almost like she'd known you for years. And then, just when I'm ready to believe you're all right, I find out you were arrested for murder in Atlanta a couple weeks ago."

"The charges were dropped," Rebecca says quickly. "They got the wrong man."

"I know. I talked to the detective in charge of that case. Apparently, Mr. Shays was there trying to warn the victim, to save him. Is that true?"

"It's true," I answer.

"Which makes it easier for me to believe what you're telling me. That you've got this ... ability to warn people. But I needed to see your face, to hear it from you."

"Did you talk to Cassie's grandmother?" I ask them.

"We didn't," Bryson replies, "but Chicago field agents did. She was pretty broken up, you can imagine. But she doesn't want to press charges."

Rebecca and I both let out a sigh of relief. "Thank God," she says.

"Based on everything we've heard," Deckard continues, "we're prepared to close the case and add the murder charge to the case against Consolidated Offshore. According to all eyewitness reports, the man responsible was killed as well. It's not exactly justice served, but it's the best we have. Which means the two of you are free to go whenever you're ready to travel."

"Thank you," I answer.

"But listen to me. Think about what you're doing. These warnings you give—they're an invitation to trouble. For you and for everyone around you. Live your lives, but pick your battles more carefully."

The two agents make their exit, and Rebecca—more gently this time—puts her arms around me. "I think it's really over now," she says.

"Yeah, I think you're right."

"I was scared."

"Me too. When I get out of here, I want to do something for Cassie's grandmother."

"Like what?" she asks.

"I want to bring Cassie back, but I can't do that. What I *can* give is money. I know it doesn't change what happened. But if she'll accept it, I can make her life a little easier."

"To relieve your guilt?" she says.

"Maybe. I don't know."

"It's really not your fault, you know."

"One day I might believe that. Right now, everything I am says it *is* my fault. And that's very hard to live with."

She gets up and walks over to look out the window. Outside, it is a pretty autumn day. The recent horrors feel far away, and that's good. I need them as far away as possible.

"So what happens next?" she asks.

"I'm not sure. I guess that depends on you. You sure you want to stay with me?"

"Yes. I'm sure."

"Something feels different," I tell her. "I'm not convinced that I'll be getting assignments anymore."

"Why do you say that?"

"I don't know. But I feel different inside. I think maybe everything that's happened is everything I was meant to go through. Maybe I'm … done. Would you still want to be around me if I wasn't receiving assignments?"

"So, you're asking me if it's okay if we don't have to deal with exploding cars and falling houses and tornadoes and fires and bombs and serial killers and vengeful psychics and people shooting us?"

"Yeah, I guess I am."

"Gosh, I think I'll learn to muddle through without those things."

I have to laugh a little at this. "We'll tough it out somehow."

"So where to, then?" she asks. "Back to your house in Maryland?"

"We could. But there's another option I'd like to explore."

"Go on."

"Would you consider going back to Key West to live?"

She looks surprised at the suggestion. "Key West? Really?"

"It's a beautiful city, and I didn't get to see much of it when I came to give you the message. I could see us getting a little house by the water, starting a life together."

"I don't think I could go back to exotic dancing."

"The thought never crossed my mind. You could do whatever you wanted to do. Finish college, get your law degree if you want it. I could take up exotic dancing."

This evokes a laugh. "You're lovely, but I don't think you're their type," she says.

"Maybe philanthropic work then. I'd like to do something for people that doesn't involve telling them not to be at a certain place at a certain time."

"I'd like that," she says. "God, it's so crazy. The whole reason we met was because you came to tell me to get out of Key West, and now that's where we're going. How does that make sense, exactly?"

"It doesn't. No more than anything else we've been through. But now, finally, no one's chasing us, nothing's going to go horribly wrong if we don't get somewhere on time, and the one thing I do know for certain is that I love you like I've never loved anyone else in my life. And whether I'm in Key West or Maryland or … Tierra del Fuego, it'll be home if you're there too."

"Can't wait," she says.

I'm driving south on a little strip of road called U.S. 1, down to Key
West, Florida. It's been almost a month since my last trip here, and the
route is familiar to me now. Once again, I'm driving a gold-colored
Chrysler Sebring convertible—the same one I rented in Chicago. The
rental car company wasn't too thrilled about the impromptu paint job
I commissioned for their formerly green vehicle, but they were more
accommodating when I offered to buy the car off of them. What can I
say? I like the way it handles.

Just like my first trip on this highway, I have the top down, so I can
feel the wind blowing through my hair. It's October now, and it's early
evening, so there's a hint of a chill in the air—well, at least as much
of a chill as southern Florida gets in autumn. It feels good. I'm aware
that my body is stronger but still not a hundred percent healed. That'll
take time. A bullet is a very rude guest. It does dreadful things to a
body, and I wish that everyone who wielded a gun with such absence
of consideration could experience its effects just once. Maybe then they
wouldn't be so quick to pull the trigger.

There's one important difference about this trip to Key West: I'm
not alone this time. Rebecca Traeger, my reason for the first visit, is
sound asleep in the passenger seat after a long day's drive. My worldly
goods from Maryland are in a moving truck, on their way to our new
home, a tasteful three-bedroom house overlooking the Atlantic Ocean.
Gotta love the housing market during a troubled economy. The place is
ours, and it's paid for. And soon we'll be home.

We're still about thirty miles north of Key West, and I notice that
the speed limit drops to forty-five. The sign says "Entering U.S. Fish
and Wildlife Service National Key Deer Refuge. Speed limits strictly
enforced. Please do not feed the animals."

No worries. Not a Funyun in sight.

Traffic is very light at this time of evening, so the slower speed
limit doesn't bother me a bit. The scenery is beautiful, and every now
and then, I catch a glimpse of the little deer as they scoot through the
trees skirting the highway. A couple miles into the refuge, I catch sight
of one of them at the side of the road. To my surprise, he steps out into
my lane, about a hundred yards in front of my car.

Not possible.

I slow to a stop just a few feet away from the creature, who stands calmly. He looks at me, then at the car, then back at me. After a month of things too surreal to believe, I don't even flinch when I hear the words, "How's it going?"

"Not too bad," I reply.

"Long time no see," the deer says casually.

"Been busy. You know how it is."

He walks around to the passenger's side, looks intently at Rebecca, and then looks back up at me. "I thought we had an agreement."

I shrug my shoulders. "Guess I changed my mind."

He contemplates this for a moment. "Was it worth it?"

I don't even have to think about my answer. "Absolutely."

Epilogue

"Tristan, honey, we're going to be late."

I'm in our bedroom, trying to make myself look presentable. Rebecca, a stickler for punctuality, is calling to me from the foyer, where she stands waiting for me. "Be right down!" I call to her. I'm putting on a tie, and—for the record—I hate ties. A designer noose is what I consider them. But this is an important meeting, and I don't want to look like a beach bum. So the noose goes on.

I make my way downstairs and present myself to her, seeking a passing inspection. "You look nice," she says. I notice she is dressed a bit more casually than I, but she still looks terrific. She's good at that.

"So do you," I reply. "Are we supposed to bring anything to this meeting?"

"No, we're just supposed to show up."

"Just the two of us?"

"That's what she requested," Rebecca answers.

"Any idea what it's about?"

"All she would say over the phone was that there was an issue, and it would be best if she spoke with us in person."

"Okay. Let's go then."

We lock up the house and get into the convertible (a new one, purchased last year after the last one was put into permanent retirement).

195

I put the top down to let the afternoon sun work its magic on us. I'm not nervous about this meeting, necessarily, but the lack of details has me a bit wary, especially because of who it is.

Life's been good. Rebecca did finish her undergraduate degree and then went on to law school. It meant renting out our house in Key West for a while as she finished her studies, but we knew we'd be coming back here. Now we split our time between two charitable organizations, one that provides clean water to underprivileged nations and another that combats civil rights violations. She's the legal counsel for both. It's rewarding and it lets us make a difference and still have time to do things we enjoy.

After the battle in Pensacola, I never did get another assignment. The strange feeling I had was right: my time as a messenger had ended. Rebecca's abilities were weakened by her ordeal, but that was fine for her. In fact, she worked to suppress them, so that we could live as normal a life as possible.

Katie worked her magic in court, and Daniel Haiduk was acquitted on retrial. He was set free and given the opportunity to go back to Illinois and take care of his mother. They never saw a single legal bill. Never saw another mortgage coupon either. It's what I could do for them.

Stelios has been a good friend these past years. He still lives in Tarpon Springs, but he visits whenever he can. The *Calliope* went to boat heaven, but that was for the best. Too many bad memories from that vessel. His new fishing boat is beautiful. Bigger, shinier, and more powerful. And damn me if that crafty old bastard didn't name it *Persephone*.

Bronwyn's been to visit a few times as well, and we've gone to New Orleans to see her. It makes me believe that we're meant to meet certain people. Some stay in our lives longer than others, but the ones who matter stick around, and we're better for it.

Traffic is light on the streets of Key West as the 4:00 hour draws near. It's only about a ten-minute drive to our destination, Ernest Hemingway Elementary School, and we decide not to engage in speculation on the way there. We'll find out the reason for this meeting soon enough. The students have already left for the day, so when we enter the parking lot, all the school buses are gone, and there are only a few cars picking up children from after-school programs. Many of the faculty are still there, I notice, getting a jump on the evening's tasks, no doubt.

We park in the visitor parking and enter the school, going to room 120 as directed. Alone in the room is a young woman we've met a few times but don't know well. She's pretty but not distractingly so, and has a pleasant air about her—everything a kindergarten teacher should be. My own kindergarten teacher was the exact opposite. Frau Klumpf. Honest to God, she actually went by "Frau." If the Third Reich had kindergarten teachers, I think she would have been employee of the year for most of the 1940s.

I knock on the open door, and the pleasant young woman looks up from her work. "Miss Hedges?" I ask. "Are we in the right place?"

She smiles and stands, motioning for us to enter. "Mr. and Mrs. Shays, please come in. I have a couple of chairs for you."

She directs us to the two adult-size seats in among the sea of miniature desks and chairs. "Thank you for coming in," she continues. "I'm sorry to have been so vague on the phone. I was calling from the school office, and there's a lack of privacy in there. Besides, I wanted to speak with you in person."

"That's fine," Rebecca says. "Is Esther having trouble with her lessons?"

"No, no," she replies. "Far from it. Esther is very bright. She's reading at a third-grade level, and her writing and drawing skills are very strong. If all my students were as ambitious as Esther, I might be out of a job. It's ... well, this isn't easy to tell parents, but it's a behavior issue that has me concerned."

"Behavior?" I ask, surprised at this. Esther is a dream child at home, minding her parents and always polite. To learn that the situation is different at school catches me off guard. "What is it that she's doing to be disruptive?"

"In the past few days, she's been saying unusual things to some of the other children. It's almost as if she's making up stories—little fictions about the students, and then telling these stories to the individuals involved. Mostly it was harmless, but a couple of them crossed the line." She picks up a sheet of paper and consults her notes. "Yesterday, she was talking to a boy named Devin Hudson, and she asked him, 'Why did your daddy steal that other man's money?' Devin's father is an investment banker here in town, and he's quite well respected. Esther's question didn't have a ring of curiosity about it. More a tone of accusation."

"Did you ask her why she said that?" Rebecca inquires.

"I did. I took her aside and asked what she meant by that question. All she would say is, 'Devin's daddy did something bad.' So you see why I wanted to bring you in to talk about it. Was there some conversation at home recently about Arthur Hudson or his financial dealings?"

Rebecca and I look at each other for a moment. "No," I answer. "Honestly, we've never met the man. I've seen his name around town and in the newspaper sometimes, but I wouldn't know the first thing about his financial matters. Rebecca?"

"Same here. We're not exactly plugged in to the social scene."

"Well," Miss Hedges continues, "I gently suggested to Esther that she should be careful about what she says to her classmates, because she wouldn't want to say anything to hurt anyone's feelings. But then she said something to me." She hesitates, and a look comes over her face, one that she has hidden from us thus far. It is a look of unease and maybe even fear.

"What did she say?" I ask.

"I had mentioned to the class that I was going on a scuba diving excursion this weekend, and I would bring back pictures of the fish for the class to look at. After I spoke with Esther about her behavior in class, she looked at me with a very serious expression, and she said, 'Miss Hedges, you shouldn't go on that scuba diving trip this weekend.' Naturally, I was surprised by this, so I asked her why not. And with that same serious expression, she said, 'If you go, you'll get hurt, and I don't want you to get hurt.' I honestly didn't know what to say to that, Mr. and Mrs. Shays. At first, I wanted to attribute it to a spiteful response to the reprimand she'd just received. But there was something in her tone that belied that ... a sense of urgency and a sense of caring as well, as if she genuinely knew this and didn't want anything bad to happen to me. So I have to ask you as her parents and the people who understand her best: what do you think I should do about this?"

A wave of concern passes through me, and from the look I spy on Rebecca's face, an identical wave sweeps over her. With only a moment's hesitation, my wife and I utter the same three words in unison: "Listen to her."

Printed in the United States
by Baker & Taylor Publisher Services